Falling For Fear

A Grim Awakening Novel
BOOK FOUR

Michelle Gross

FALLING FOR FEAR

This is a work of fiction. Names, characters, places, and incidents either are the products of the author's imagination or are used fictitiously. Any resemblance to actual persons, living or dead, businesses, companies, events, or locales is entirely coincidental.

Cover Artwork –© 2016 L.J. Anderson of Mayhem Cover Creations

Table of Contents

For all the dark souls,

With our darkened hearts,

It's okay to like the things we do.

PROLOGUE

The first person I ever saw was a man: a monster. My creator.

I didn't have thoughts at that point in my life; I had bloodlust. Nothing mattered beyond what I needed and craved.

Next to me, two other creatures came to be that day. We didn't call ourselves man or woman, we weren't persons, we weren't meant to be anything other than monsters. The monster I was craved only one thing, an emotion, a feeling. It didn't matter what or where I got it from, as long as I fed on it.

Fear.

Fear… Fear… I remembered that word first because that was who I was and that was all I ever wanted, along with every other darkened emotion.

And I was—no, I am still a monster.

I love what I am. I love the taste of what I invoke on humans and demons alike. When their body fills with dread—horror becomes their expression and with it comes the taste of that emotion. Fucking yummy. Even more so before I hurt them, bleed them out starting with their mind. Always get inside their minds first; fear doesn't taste good unless it's more than their body they're worried about. It's their insanity—the hope to live on after the fear has permanently inflicted its damage on their soul.

I don't feel sorry for what I am. I was made to be this monster. But I did have a downfall and his name was Marcus and how I chose to merge with the incubus demon because I felt the evil radiating off him like a disease. I thought he was like me—but what I didn't know was how different two evils can be.

Our cravings were different. I wanted to keep on living and doing what I've always done, yet… he wanted power and control… more than what I could give him. He wanted something I gave zero shits about, but I was stuck with him. Although he was only an incubus, Marcus had been smart. He trapped me inside my own body with a witch's spell—he could do whatever he wanted with my powers and my body, and I could do nothing— I was stuck on the inside looking out.

But it didn't last forever, I gained back some of my control over time. Not enough to do much; enough to piss him off, though.

And then, we stumbled upon Molly. Childlike, murder-in-her-eyes, Molly. She was a ghost—no, she was a poltergeist. Years spent living without being noticed with the humans turned her into a monster—the things she did to humans fed me the fucking tastiest fear. Marcus kept her by our side and for once, I didn't mind the choice he made. I wanted her to keep feeding me with only the fear she brought with her. It was different than all the rest—different than the taste of my own fear-inducing perception I forced out of humans and demons.

She came with us because she wanted the body of a woman. It made me curious as to what she wanted it for—something other than fear stirred inside me. Lust. I *wanted* to give her what she wanted—then I could do a lot of fear-inducing things to her that not only fueled my monster—but the male in me.

But that was exactly why Marcus kept her at arm's length, but close enough to annoy the fuck out of me—threatening to kill her soul because he knew that wasn't what I wanted her for. I wanted her for a lot of things and don't get me wrong, I wanted to hurt the hell out of her and do a lot of bad to her. But kill her… no. And he wouldn't give her what she wanted because he knew she'd leave the moment she got her body. No, he needed her around, not just because she was fucking good at getting shit done, but because he controlled me with her.

But I lost her the same day I rid myself of Marcus. He dug his own grave the day he crossed paths with Grim and even though I hated Grim—fucking goody-two-shoes—and everything he stood for, he had freed me that day. I'd never tell him that, though.

And the first thing I did the moment I was separated from Marcus and watched him die, I went right back into another merge. Only this time, I chose differently. With Marcus, I chose him for his evil. With Ryan, I chose him because he was everything I wasn't. He was one of the good guys, and I wanted nothing more than to feed on his pain and the agony of becoming me.

Only I never expected his good to be so strong. And once again, I made a stupid fucking mistake when it came to merging. I couldn't handle the flowery shit his heart and mind made me feel, and he couldn't stand the shit I forced him to do, but he had no choice. But I did, and I refused to let his mind change me. I blocked him out of my mind—kept us separated where only one of us controlled the body at a time. It was fun for me. I fed on his fear and hate every time he did what I forced him to do, but I was changing him. He didn't hate it so much anymore. Slowly, I was engraving myself into his mind, but I'd never let him do the same to me.

What I didn't expect was Molly to still be alive and for us to cross paths with her. I didn't expect to see her in the body she had now. I didn't expect to fall right back into the same pattern of wanting to tear her apart and do what I wanted with her.

Worse, I didn't expect the changes she'd force on us all.

CHAPTER ONE

Molly

The thing about untold truths are they are secrets; hidden lies.

They'll crawl out sooner or later...

And when they do, they'll swallow you whole.

His eyes opened. With the knife above my head, I froze. I forgot that he couldn't see me since I was a ghost. And I was the only one that could see him—his brown eyes were wide and frantic as he looked around the hospital room. I hardened my resolve and slammed the knife into his chest.

He died. He never saw me. He never saw me. He never saw me, I kept telling myself.

I took a breath and slid off his body. When I turned, panic gripped me all over again. "He saw nothing, but I did." Red eyes roamed over me and Fear's mouth tipped into a sinister smile. He grabbed my throat just as I woke up screaming.

I took in my surroundings and exhaled when I saw that I was in the Underworld. It was only a dream. Still, I was spooked and the one thing I could never let find me was Fear or the boy I killed that became the monster himself. Even if he didn't know I was ultimately the one that killed him, I still did enough for him to hate me.

I've been paying the prize for the decades spent by Fear's side for centuries. My only goal was to get out of the Underworld. I was hunted by too many demons and with no power or portal chip, it was pure hell down here for me.

I heard movement from the corner of the shop. I stood quickly and darted through the alleyway where I had been sleeping. I couldn't risk anyone seeing my face, so I constantly wore clothes that covered me head to toe. It didn't take demons long to figure out who I was—not everyone knew what I looked like now, but enough did that I needed to get into the human world. The only place I'd be safe from the people I've wronged. There were plenty of bounties on my head.

I've been tortured, beaten, killed, again and again, and was on the run now from the last demon I escaped. She was a real bitch, but I was one of the people that helped make her that way. I kidnapped her two daughters and delivered them to Fear a long time ago. They were dead now. One killed herself before Fear could do anything to her; the other was stronger, but strength alone got you nowhere with Fear. He married her, only to kill her soon after.

The guilt flared to life in my stomach, making me sick. I shouldn't feel guilt, I got what I wanted—screw everyone I ruined, right? Wrong, I was pathetic.

But these demons pissed me off. I didn't see any of them running to Fear and exacting revenge. No, they were scared shitless and the only one they had the pleasure of taking it out on was *mwah.* Who was I to judge them? I'd rather fall into the hands of any other demon than Fear's. I knew exactly what kind of monster he truly was.

Most of all, I made the biggest betrayal when I delivered Melanie to the Devil when Fear wanted her.

… Melanie was the other problem. Along with her husband Grim.

You just had to go and piss off three immortals, didn't you, Molly?

Sure, I hadn't known that Melanie was an upgraded-female version of Grim when I kept trying to kill her… over and over. But I had known how stupid it was to keep going after her when Grim cared for her. And I definitely knew how stupid it was to betray Fear. He lost Marcus that night and merged with the boy, Ryan, right before I gone and grabbed Melanie.

Maybe that was the only thing that saved me that night from him. He was too busy with his merge. But even after all these centuries spent running, the thought of him finally coming for me crossed my mind every single day.

I was paranoid for good reason. I knew the things I did for Fear—and for this body—would come back to haunt me one day, because it had already started centuries ago.

An eye for an eye, a tooth for a tooth.

As I was looking back to make sure no one was following me, I ran smack dab into something… or someone. When I turned, I was smacked in the face. I held my jaw and my eyes widened.

"Think you can escape me so easily?" Lorraine smiled at me and asked.

Shit.

Back to being tortured and killed, I go.

CHAPTER TWO

Ryan

"Fear," she whispered as her blonde curls and luscious curves darted around the corner of her house. I grinned when I heard her giggle. She reminded me of someone. Little did she know that was one of the reasons I chose her to fuck with. That, and she could take the pain.

"You like to be chased?" I called out to her as I followed her around the corner, taking my time. "You know I'm going to enjoy hurting you when I get my hands on you? And you're gonna enjoy it when I do."

"You won't catch me," she yelled from another room. Her words spurred me on, the monster in me roared to life. He liked this game. But he was going to like it, even more, when I got my hands on her.

Before I merged with Fear, I wouldn't have been caught dead saying some of the things I do to women now—or the things I did to them. Yeah, I had loved to fuck women when I was a human, but I was always a respectable guy about it and treated them the way they should be treated. But almost a thousand years spent in the Underworld as something that lived on people's fears and pains, my lines of right and wrong blurred a long time ago.

Now, I wanted to do a lot of horrible things to them. I always made sure to pick the ones that enjoyed it as much as I loved feeding on their emotions. Like this feisty demon I was going after now, Levy, I thought her name was. I've come to her house a few times already, I liked her because she never said no to anything. It took a lot to satisfy me some days.

Her footsteps stopped. I heightened my senses until I heard her excited breaths. From the sound of her breathing, she was two rooms down. I gripped the portal chip inside my jeans pocket and debated porting to where she was. It would surprise her—her heart rate would beat more wildly than it was right now. Or maybe I should run after her, let her hear my footsteps coming for her? Which would give her more fear, I pondered.

I decided on the run. I purposely made my footsteps loud and imposing as I threw open the door. She took off running from the closet, but my hands were already on her—one went to her hair and the other around her waist as I forced her head against the stand next to the bed. Her hands grabbed the nightstand and saved her head from the fall—damn shame, the taste of her pain would have been a good start to the fear.

I felt my skin crawling, changing as I switched into Fear's form. Using his body had its perks. "Look at me," I ordered her. She lifted her gaze and her eyes widened. I inhaled her hatred of me in this form—she didn't like when I took her this way. I wasn't nice to look at in this form—I was fucking scary as hell.

"Not this way," she whimpered. "Please change back."

"No, your repulsion of me in this form tastes too good." I brought my face to her back and breathed it all in, letting my eyes roll back. Every emotion had a different taste, as long as it was one of the bad ones I liked to devour, they tasted amazing. "If you say no, I'll leave right now, but if you want to be fucked, it'll be in this form," I told her. That was the only line I was never willing to cross—I'd never take a woman against her will. No matter how much Fear tried to force me to sometimes. He'd never get inside my head enough to make me go that far. But even so, he'd feed me one of his memories of when he forced himself on someone and make me watch it just for his own sick pleasure. I wasn't stupid, I knew the monster I fed, fed on my own emotions every chance he got. Fucker.

She looked down at the nightstand instead of me. "No, I want you to."

I glanced at her hair, the curve of her back as I ripped her shirt with my tail. She squealed in response. Looking at her this way, I saw Penny. She'd been my fuck buddy for several centuries until she got old, disappeared, and died somewhere. I liked her—grown comfortable around her. She was down with a lot of the shit I did and was fun to hang around with, too. She'd never let me fuck her in this form, though but I was okay with that. Because she'd been Penny. She helped me survive the hell of becoming Fear—kept telling me over and over that I could live with the monster I've become and still be better than him even though I was him. She hadn't been the only person that had been there for me, but I really didn't feel like conjuring up Grim's face at a time like this.

Instead, the blonde in front of me became the blonde of my dreams—the only person I'd ever loved. And you'd think after all these centuries I'd learn to let it go—let her go, but I couldn't. Melanie always appeared inside my head at a time like this. Along with guilt toward Grim and her. Because they were the only two people I had down here left to give a shit about me.

"Fuck," I growled, annoyed with myself. I could feel Fear knocking against the inside of my own mind—laughing and breathing in my self-hatred. I took my aggravation of him out on Levy. My tail wrapped around her neck and her heart picked up speed, and her body radiated fear like she was a fucking heater. It tasted delicious.

"Fear," she half cried, half moaned. I tore at her jeans, my claws catching her flawless skin. When her mouth opened with her cry, I forced my tail in her mouth. She made a gagging noise as I pressed against the wall of her throat. I groaned because my tail was almost like my dick—it felt good.

I waited until her face was beet red before pulling out enough for her to catch her breath and went right back in the same time my dick pressed into her.

I whistled a show tune as I walked around the City of the Dead after leaving Levy's. I didn't really feel like porting back home just yet. Maybe I'd find a head or two to feed the twins—Ruby and River, they were dragons, though Melanie chewed my own head off every time I brought them something back. Something about demons being full of diseases. I didn't want to burst her bubble and remind her that they ate all kinds of carcasses, including demons. I didn't want to ruin whatever vision she had of them inside her head.

"Fear!" I recognized Levy's voice and turned around to see her running toward me. I tilted my head. "Um, I need you to come back to my place." She looked down, around, then back to my face pleading. "I want you again." It was a lie, I could taste her lie before it even left her mouth.

"Are you sure?" I lifted my eyebrow at her. I saw her throat swallow. She was nervous. Extremely nervous. My protective instincts—the human part of me that Fear always tried to snuff out—came to the surface.

"Please," was all she offered.

"Sure."

I followed her back to her place knowing full well that this was most likely some sort of trap set up by some sort of demon that had a vendetta against me. Not only did I piss a lot of people off when I was more Fear than myself—or when he crawled out to play himself and I blacked out, which hadn't happened in decades considering I know to take care of his needs to keep him from doing so, but I also had to deal with all the trouble Fear had caused while he was merged with Marcus.

When I entered her small home again, the emotions in the room hit me full force. Someone was fucking pissed as hell—I tasted vengeance. I smiled, someone was out to get me. Levy turned around to face me quickly, face full of regret. "I'm sorry—"

"You've done enough," a female voice spoke right before I saw her appear behind Levy. Her hands were around her neck within a heartbeat—I heard the snap that I've grown accustomed to over the centuries. Levy dropped to the floor. Dead. My eyes darkened on the woman before me. Fear, on the other hand, was knocking against my insides screaming, "*More, more, more.*" He loved a good killing, more so if I—we were the one doing it, but he also enjoyed when people like this woman before me came for payback.

"Sure, okay," I started, "I feel like murdering someone today."

Her lips tipped upward into a snarl as she studied me, then it became a smirk. "You're Fear now, right?" It was more confirmation than question.

"Yes, ma'am."

My choice of words made her smile wider. "Then you know who I am," she told me, the smile disappearing into a look of pure hatred. "And why I'm here."

Shit no. Fear didn't share memories or anything with me. Our relationship was strictly me trying my damned best to keep him from coming out by feeding him. I tilted my head at her and squinted my eyes with a smile. "Jog my memory?" Inside me, Fear grew quiet. Something told me he remembered her.

"You kidnapped my daughters a very, very long time ago," she told me. "Sibyl was kind and gentle, Tera, strong and independent. They both died soon after you took them from me."

I didn't even know what to say to her. I understood why she was pissed, but her hatred and disgust of me was rolling off her in waves, giving me a high. Tasted exquisite too. Her loathing of Fear had been festering for a very long time, that was probably why. Without thinking, I inhaled sharply, breathing it all in and her eyes pinched together.

"You—" She glared. "You're not even listening, instead—are you?" She realized what I was doing, although I couldn't help it when she was practically giving it to me—her hatred. Even underneath it, I could feel her fear there, whether it was for her deceased daughters or because of me, didn't matter.

"Pardon?" I turned my head, offering my ear, and her face turned red with anger. "It's hard to concentrate when your revenge is giving me a high. I mean, you have no fucking idea how good it tastes." Fear roared with laughter—he was enjoying this.

She blew out of her nose and I spotted something in her hand. Too late. The whip wrapped around my arms. I hissed because whatever magic she had on it was shocking the hell out of me. "You're coming with me. I'll show you exactly how it feels to be taken against your will. I'll kill you over and over like I do her." Inside me, Fear went completely silent, then I felt it—his exhilaration. What was his deal? My skin started rippling as I changed into Fear's form. This whip couldn't hold me.

"No," Fear told me. *"Lethertakeyou, lethertakeyou, lethertakeyou."* What the hell? His excitement was overflowing, so much that I couldn't help but be affected by it. Now I was excited about something that was probably going to be my own pain. But if I refused to let her take me, I'd risk him coming out and me disappearing until he decided to let me back out. My skin rippled with unease, that was the worst feeling. Being nowhere. Yet still existing.

I sucked in a breath and watched the woman that thought she really had me trapped with this measly whip. "Good." She smiled. "It's best not to fight."

———

"Cozy place you have here," I said.

She placed large shackles on my wrists and ankles before porting us to her house. I let her to satisfy Fear. I was a tad curious as to why he wanted her to bring us here. Did he want to bring the fear out of her? I'd admit, that didn't sound like a bad idea considering how good her other emotions tasted. I looked around her home, if this was her home. "Nice chains you got there. And those are some decent swords. I'll admit, though, I'm a gun guy—or was, actually, but I guess I still am considering I blow the brains out of demons a couple times a month."

She turned around and hissed. "Quiet."

I did just that all for one second before looking across the room. “Is that a torture chamber?” I asked. “That’s fucking hot as hell. Can I use it sometime?” She backhanded me and I looked right back at her. “I’d make your pain feel good.” My eyes were heavy, I had no doubt they were going red. Her raw anger was waking the monster in me, bringing it to the surface—not Fear—the monster he created in me, the one I tried to deny until it came to moments like this.

“See that.” She pointed to my face. “I want you on your knees screaming and begging, not that look you’re giving me now. You filthy beast!”

“When I get my hands on you…”

“You’ll what?” She glared. “Kill me like you did my daughters?” Fear was strangely quiet this whole time.

I shrugged. “You can’t even kill me.”

“Finn! Jack!” she yelled. “Go get her out of the dungeon. They’ll suffer the way my daughters did.”

With her words, Fear’s eagerness flew into me.

CHAPTER THREE

Molly

"Get up," one of Lorraine's bitch boys yelled right before opening my cell door. He grabbed me by the arm and yanked me to my feet. I threw a punch and brought his head to my knee in the process. He hissed. I dunked just as the other one tried to grab me. He got my hair instead and pressed me into him. I glared at him right as the other one returned the punch I gave him into my stomach.

Ow, shit.

You'd think after all the times I've been beaten, tortured, killed, and there's just some you refused to let cross your mind, I'd be accustomed to pain, but I wasn't. I still wanted to cry like a little baby every time, although I never did… except on the inside anyway. Where all these pricks could never see.

And he kept on punching me in the stomach until I threw up what tiny bit water I was fed today on him. It was all fun and games for them until that happened. Now he was pissed and started punching me in the face.

"Stop," the one holding me said. "Lorraine's the one that wants to make her hurt." I laughed. Funny words because she had been making me hurt for a very long time now.

"Let me give y'all some advice," I said as they dragged me by the arms up the stairway. I let my legs dangle as they did, already too tired to fight what was about to happen to me. She kept me in the dungeon, so I was filthy and probably stunk but if I did, I had already grown custom to it. "Being someone's little bitch only gets you in trouble in the long run." I nodded my head once. "Take it from someone who knows."

"Shut up," one of them told me.

"When you're dead because of her, I won't even get to say I told you so." Lucky for them, they could die. Unlike me, who kept coming back to life after dying.

One groaned. "She never fucking shuts up."

The other laughed. "Lorraine will silence her soon." He gripped my hair and pulled my head back so he could lean over it. "Maybe we can convince her to clean her up just so we can have a go at her." He licked my face and panic gripped me. *Stop, Molly.* I took a deep breath. What a slap in the face every time this happened. The body I stained my soul to get, became a means to torture me. *You've been raped before and you always come out of it with your mind still intact.* I was a survivor. Nobody in this house could fucking break me.

When we left the dark stairway and opened the door to the room she always tortured me in, I had to close my eyes from the brightness until my eyes adjusted. "Finally," Lorraine said, "we are all together."

We? I opened my eyes and immediately noticed the man next to her in restraints. I squinted my eyes at him as he studied me. Something about him was familiar… very distant in my memory. Sandy colored hair and almond colored eyes. Those eyes… those eyes. My own eyes widened when I recognized him.

The boy. Ryan. *FEAR.*

Oh, no. No. No. No.

I jerked my head to the side, letting my black hair fall over the side of my face. Did he recognize me? Did Lorraine already tell him who I was? There was no way Fear wouldn't know. I started kicking and trying to pull back. I didn't want to go any further. "Still feisty after that beating we gave you?" one of them said to me.

I wasn't even looking at Lorraine, but I could hear the static coming off her whip as she used it. I glanced up to see it around Ryan/Fear's neck. He didn't even flinch, instead, his eyes were on me again. "Mind telling me why you need her?" he asked.

She arched a brow at him. "Are you truly not bothered by the pain?"

He laughed. "I feed on it. Even when it's mine." He looked back to me again. "You didn't answer my question."

My heart plummeted into my stomach. No, she couldn't tell him. Not if he didn't know. Why the fuck was I so terrified? I didn't know. I just didn't want to fall into his hands, but then how could he be any worse than what I've already been through? Easy, Fear knew me. He'd weave his way into my mind and destroy me like he did everything around him. My mind was the only thing I had left. Once that was gone, I wouldn't be able to bear the eons I had left to live.

She circled her wrist and swung the whip across his stomach. It tore his shirt, blood pooled. Still no reaction. He sighed. "Is this really how you expected to hurt me? With a whip? If you want, I can show you how to use it properly." Lorraine's face was blood red. I've never been able to crawl under her skin like that, and believe me, I've tried.

This wasn't good. Lorraine had no idea—yes, she did—who she was dealing with. She must have a death wish. She was going to die by his hands, and I very much didn't want to land in them afterwards.

So, I screamed. And screamed. Like I was possessed, I bit into one of the guy's arms that held me and didn't let go until I was thrown into the floor. "Bitch!" he yelled just as they both came down to reach me. Good, good. I needed one of them to kill me, so I'd be dead until Fear was gone. I just needed to provoke them to.

I laughed and spit in their direction. "You can't kill me. Only Boss Lady's allowed and you both follow her every word like good little doggies."

"You little—" His boot landed on my throat, adding pressure.

"Finn!" Lorraine yelled. "She's trying to ruin my plans for them. I won't allow it. They'll suffer together like my daughters did." I would have rolled my eyes at her if I could. Her daughters didn't die together. One chose death and the other died by Fear's hand.

"Told you." I grinned up at him and I saw the wheels turning in his head. He didn't like the truth about himself.

"Let us kill her," the other one spoke up next to me.

"Shit!" I couldn't tilt my head to see what was happening, but something about Ryan's voice hadn't sounded right. "No, no, fuck no!" he yelled. What. The. Hell. "I'll do it, shut the hell up!" Even the two bozos next to me went still.

Lorraine snapped, “Don’t you dare play games!” This woman was killing me. Did she honestly expect she could hold her own against him? Those shackles were still on him because he hadn’t decided to take them off yet. Losing her daughters had truly messed her up in the worst way. I would feel guilty about it if she hadn’t been torturing me for months! I thought my part of delivering them to Fear had been paid in full with the many times she had killed me already.

“You!” he hissed at Lorraine, maybe, I couldn’t see with a boot pressed into my throat. “This ends, because of you, I—” his words cut off and I heard his shackles fall to the ground.

“Get him!” Lorraine yelled. I heard her shuffling backwards or maybe she was running toward him—I extremely doubted that. One took off running and a second later he was thrown against the wall. Mr. Boot-In-My-Throat finally moved next.

Oh, no.

I didn’t even look back in that direction. Everyone over there was already goners. Not me. I was crawling on all fours to get to the guy he slung across the room. When I did, I searched his pockets until I found a knife. He couldn’t know that I was immortal, could he?

“Told you so,” I couldn’t help but say to the dead man that couldn’t even hear me now.

“Molly.”

Fear’s words sent a shiver up my spine.

No way in hell.

I closed my eyes and slit my own throat.

CHAPTER FOUR

Molly

I startled myself awake with a jolt and immediately knew I was no longer at Lorraine's. I was on a couch. I looked around. This place was… warm. I couldn't help but notice. And cozy, I also couldn't help but notice. I perked up for a moment, this couldn't be Fear's home. It was too homey and less monster-cave. Then I glanced down at myself.

"No." I whispered. "No, no, no, no, no!"

Fear's mark. I was covered in them. One on my chest. One on each of my wrists. Two ripped through the pants I wore. Even my back felt tender, there too? My heart plummeted. I was covered in red X's.

The front door opened and I jerked back in the cushion. Ryan entered and I brought my hands out in front of me. He studied me a second. "You're finally awake," he said nonchalantly. He wore a pair of jeans and a white t-shirt, tattoos covered both arms. He had clearly changed since being Fear.

"Why?" I whispered first. "Why!" Then I screamed.

He grabbed his chin and studied me some more. "I'm just as surprised as you."

I gave him a dubious look. "Don't play games with me, what are you going to do with me?"

"I don't know what he—I plan to do to you." I visibly watched him shudder as he closed his eyes. When he looked at me again, they were red. "Okay, maybe I do know what I want to do to you, but I don't know why I marked you. Or what's so appealing about you to hi—me. Me."

This time I studied him. He clearly said my name at Lorraine's, yet looking at him right now, it was almost like he didn't recognize me. Something was strange about the merge… it was almost like he was two different people. He walked over to the table—the kitchen and living room were one giant room. A fireplace rested to my right and… animals? He had animals hung up on the wall? I squirmed uncomfortably. No doubt, he was Fear.

"Do you know my name?" I tested.

He pulled out a chair and sat down before looking back over at me. "Not until you tell me." See that there? Something was fishy about him. Could two people merge without becoming one? The wheels inside my head were turning.

"Like I'm telling my kidnapper my name," I replied.

He exhaled and got right back up from the chair. "Don't make this hard on yourself. Those marks." He pointed *all* over me and smiled. See, now that looked like a Fear smile! "Mean you're mine. It's safe to say I didn't fucking bring you here, but now that you're here, I might as well make use out of you."

I hope he felt the murder coming from my eyes. "I'll die before I let you touch me." I got up and ran for the door. He was there before I was, slapping his palm against the door. When I met his eyes, they were burning red and a bit of fear crept up my back.

"Let me give you some advice. Don't challenge me because it only makes me want to accept." Then he brought his face next to mine, he inhaled, and I pushed him, but he didn't budge. I stepped back, flushed with embarrassment. What the hell? "Damn, that's good," he muttered.

"Don't sniff me!" I smoothed my palm down over my hair as I glared at him.

He smirked and it wasn't something I was used to. Fear had always been Marcus to me—an angelic pretty boy that had an attitude that was no different than the Devil. He'd been beautiful, skinny, and terrifying despite his feminine looks. Ryan… he… he was a man. The ones that were grown right. Wide shoulders, muscular arms, and the tightness of his t-shirt only proved how right I was with how perfect he'd grown down here in the Underworld. He was so much bigger than the boy I killed forever ago. This Fear, I didn't know how to look at him. I didn't want to look at him as anything other than the monster he was. Even if I had a soft spot for Ryan's life I stole—the guilt just never went away.

Only the terrifying truth was—guys like him were the reason I craved this body. I all but shut down those thoughts.

"Then you better hope your fear doesn't taste this good the next time it seeps out of you for a second, or else, I'll keep raping your emotions just so I can taste it again." His eyes held mine. He wasn't kidding. It made my blood boil. "What's your name?" he asked again.

I turned and headed back to the couch. "Whatever you want it to be."

"Okay," he answered right away. "Blue it is."

I couldn't help but look back. "Blue? Why Blue?"

He walked toward me and the hairs stood up on my arms as I waited for him to finally admit that he knew who I was. Instead, that moment never came and he grabbed a few strands of my matted, dirty hair. "Because of your hair. It's so black that the underneath lighting it looks like the midnight sky. Although, I'd imagine it's much more noticeable when washed."

I pulled away from him. "Why not Midnight then?" Why did I care? I didn't know the answer to that. Hell, I didn't even know why I was going along with this. Yes, I did. I would go along with anything until I could get the hell out of here. I laughed at myself on the inside, and go where? He could find me anywhere now that I was marked. I would never be free from him.

"Because midnight sounds appealing, I wanted something plainer, like blue, Blue." He smiled and somehow, I was pissed as hell.

"Plain?" I asked. "Plain," I said again, angrier this time.

He smirked. "See, that? Yes, that's exactly why I chose some ordinary color as a name. You can't stand feeling less than, or being talked down to."

I scoffed. "Right." I rolled my eyes. "My entire existence has revolved around me being ignored, talked down to, and being less than everyone else."

"That doesn't mean you want it to be that way." Fear was amazing at fucking with people's minds and he was already doing it right now with me. He was just messing with me, he knew exactly who I was. "Remember, I sense every emotion you're feeling, so there's nothing you can hide."

Still, there was no way I was calling quits to this charade if it meant I was safe for the time being. "Go crawl in a hole somewhere." He laughed, so I added, "And don't ever come back out."

"Bathroom's that way, first door on the right." He pointed toward the hallway.

I raised an eyebrow. "Why do I need to know that?"

"Because you're staying here now, like it or love it, your choice, and two, you stink and look like roadkill. Clean up, I want to see what you look like."

“Or you can just take away these marks and let me go, and I can merrily go somewhere else.”

“Christmas has already passed, so this is no time to be merry, go,” he shooed me away, and I glared.

“Fine, I can *happily* go somewhere else.” I blinked my eyes several times and gave a fake, sweet smile.

“Never know, that might have worked on me if you didn’t look like the fucking exorcist standing there. Go bathe and you can try batting your eyes at me again when you get out.” I flinched at the unexpected comment. Even now, I guessed I looked no different than the ghost-me I left behind. Only now, I was in an adult body and graduated to a woman that looked possessed.

I backed up and turned, walking in the direction of the hallway. I would go bathe, not because he wanted me to, but because I couldn’t remember the last time I had.

CHAPTER FIVE

Ryan

Fuck.

Fear really went and done it this time, marking and bringing home some random woman. After all these years I've managed to keep Fear satisfied and safely tucked away, he crawled right back out just like that. Which only proved how little control I did have. Something happened, he went ballistic, ripping at me from the inside as soon as he saw Blue—didn't know her real name, but that didn't matter because she was stuck here now and there was no way I could let her go. Not if I wanted to keep Fear happy. I'd only risk him coming out again if I let her go. When he came out, I blacked out—I might as well not exist when that happened. And I liked existing despite how fucked up I was now.

He was on cloud nine right now. His eagerness was spilling into me. I'd never felt him so excited and that was saying something. He could see a dying bird and get a hard-on off its pain. He found enjoyment in the most fucked up things but given what he fed off…

Hot-headed Blue had no clue what danger she was in with me. He was probably plotting all the ways he wanted to fuck her up as I walked back outside, and given my own reaction to her anger—and the bit of fear that seeped out of her for a second there—I might even find some enjoyment in this arrangement myself. I couldn't tell what she looked like with all the filth she was caked under but her emotions were very appealing at least.

I grabbed the muzzleloader off the porch and slung it across my shoulder as I made my way back into the woods. I made this choice—a protection, actually—from the monster I've become by still remembering who I once was. When I was human, I loved to hunt. That part of me never changed, only the animals I hunted. There was animal like deer and elk in these woods, just not the ones from the human world. Down here, they were much bigger and a lot more vicious if given the chance. But that was no surprise, nothing in Grim's woods was ordinary. The trees, grass, mountains, and lakes all glowed. It wasn't just that; this place was like a pack of skittles. Everything was colorful.

And it was home.

Or, as close to home as Fear would let me feel. To him, this place was a torture. One: it was beautiful, he needed darkness. Two: this was Grim's territory, he loathed the sight of Killian. So, his emotions were always wrapping around mine, trying to make me think and feel how he felt about this place. It was a miracle itself that Fear allowed me to live here.

I had planned to go to my usual spot in my tree and wait out the Devil deer—what I called them—to make their appearance, but when I saw Killian tied to a tree I knew lunch would have to wait. I arched my eyebrow and made my way toward the tree he was stuck against. He was wrapped in golden chains so I knew whatever was going on was Melanie's doing. He saw me coming and groaned, looking the other way. I smirked as I stopped in front of him, whistling. "Do I want to know?" I asked, not hiding my amusement.

"Be a good neighbor and get me out of this chain," he told me.

I shook my head and laughed. "Are you crazy? I ain't touching that chain, who knows what might happen to me if I do. That's Melanie's doing, I don't want to have to wait for my hand to grow back or something if I risk touching it. Nor do I want to deal with her, if this is some sort of punishment." I crossed my arms over my chest and couldn't help grinning again. "Is this a type of foreplay or something?"

He groaned. "Go away, you little shit."

"That only makes me want to stay." I walked to a decent size rock and parked my ass there so I could sit and enjoy this more. "Does Melanie let you kiss her with that mouth?"

"She lets me do a lot more than that with my mouth." I shook my head, ignoring the tug in my chest. I didn't know why I put myself in these situations where I heard more than I wanted, but I just kept digging my own hole. "Besides, my mouth is a lot tamer around her. *Mostly.*" He smiled and this was the part where I pretend it didn't faze me.

"What'd you do?" I asked him.

"River chewed up her favorite boots," he answered.

I scratched my chin. "And she took it out of you? You two are the reason I'm glad I'll never get a chance to marry," I added.

He laughed. "No, it just happened. We just got back from the human world, and I don't know, she was giving me that look so I gave her what she wanted right here." He glanced down at the ground. "How was I supposed to know River would swoop down and see them as a chew toy." River was a dragon and a big baby.

I couldn't fight back my smile. "I still feel like you're not giving me the full story."

He shrugged his shoulders the best he could wrapped to a tree. "Said I shouldn't have stripped her here and believe me, it was mostly her fault, she was the one stealing glances my way and—"

I held up my hand to shut him up. "I get it, stop already."

"Killian." Melanie faded in front of the tree with her hands on her hips as she glared up at him. "I came to see if you were ready to get down, but you're busy chatting with Ryan, so guess I'll leave—"

"Come on, Love, let me down," he said, voice morphing into that lovey-dovey one that made Fear want to hurl. "You know I can get you any pair of boots you want."

She squinted her eyes at him. I could already see her wanting to cave and not to mention their lovesickness was seeping out of them, spreading all over the place. Fear didn't feed on love or any other flowery emotions that involved "warm" feelings. My insides were screaming for me to get the hell away from them but if I listened to that instinct all the time, I'd never get to stay around them. "Maybe I was being a little over-the-top," she admitted with a smile. The gold chains fell from Killian and disappeared. The moment it did, Killian grabbed Melanie. She squeaked, "What are you doing?"

Something devious played out on Killian's face as he gazed down at her. "You didn't think I'd let you get away with leaving me tied to a tree, did you?" Her face reddened right before he slung her over his shoulder.

"Killian!" she screamed. He couldn't see the smile on her face, but I could.

"I'll chain you somewhere a lot better than a tree," he told her then glanced back at me. "Later, Ryan." They faded.

I sat there for a second before sighing and standing up. After that much exposure to love, I'd need a good night of killing or fucking.

A couple hours later, I had my kill hung up and skinned. I bagged up the meat from the deer and walked inside to clean it. What I didn't expect was the scent of Blue about knock me down the moment I opened the front door. I didn't even see her anywhere, yet I knew it had to be her. Nothing in my house ever smelled that amazing before. The filth she'd been wearing must have been masking her scent, but now it was all out in the open, invading my entire fucking house.

Jesus.

Everyone seemed to love caramel, you mostly heard people talk about it more than butterscotch. But not me, I loved butterscotch. And that was what her scent reminded me of, sinful and sweet, *addictive*. Even Fear reacted to her, and by react, I mean a wave of lust crashed over me so powerful I grabbed the door and stopped myself from entering the house any further.

Fuck.

I heard the shifting of plates in the cabinet; she was raiding the kitchen. I took a deep breath and gripped the bags of meat in my hands before entering. I caught sight of her back as she tiptoed trying to grab something from the cabinet. I swallowed. Her scent had already sent signals straight to my dick, but the sight of her in my t-shirt and rolled up jogging pants were overkill. Her black hair was almost dry now and it hung all the way down to her ass. I knew she was small but in my clothes, it swallowed her thin frame.

I hurried to the sink to clean and cut the meat, and to hide the hard-on I had since opening my front door. I dropped the meat down into the sink next to where she stood and she jumped a mile, grabbing the closest thing next to her—which was a plate—as a weapon. When she saw it was me, she relaxed. Which was stupid on her part, she had no idea what I planned to do with her yet. And the sad truth was, neither did I until Fear filled me in.

She was beautiful. Petite, not usually the type I went for, yet she was tall. I was right about her hair. The black had a ghostly blue look to it underneath the kitchen lights and it only added to the beauty to her dark, marble-like eyes. Doe-eyes.

The perfect prey, Fear's words slipped through me.

"You forgot to mention you live in Grim's territory," she said the moment she lowered the weapon of please-don't-fucking-break-my-favorite-plate. Yes, I had a favorite plate, a favorite cup, and a favorite recliner. All kinds of things I didn't want to share with some random she-devil Fear marked.

"Considering we've only spoken for a total of three minutes today, I wonder why that is?" I rubbed my nose across my wrist to ease the sudden itch, not wanting to get blood on my face since my hands were still covered. "Why? Do you have a problem with Grim?" I asked.

She made a sound in her throat before rubbing her tongue across the inside of her jaw. I watched the imprint disappear as she glared at me. "Such a smartass," she huffed. "I just find it funny is all," she stated quietly as if to let the subject drop or make me talk; I wasn't sure with her.

"How is it funny?"

She was about to say something until her eyes traveled to the meat in the sink. I turned on the water. "What is that?" she asked warily.

"Our food," I replied.

I could already see her gag reflexes working on her at just the thought. "I'm not eating whatever that is," she said, matter-of-factly.

"Relax, it's just Devil deer," I told her.

"Devil deer?" She gave me a snooty look.

"Yeah, that's what I call them since they're from the Underworld."

She looked at me for several seconds like she was studying me. "Fear," she finally said.

I started on the meat and said, "Ryan, my name's Ryan."

There it was, I could feel her intense gaze heating me up as I cleaned up the meat. "What is the deal with you?" The question caught me by surprise because I had no idea what she meant.

"You never did say why it's funny that I stay here."

"Because you're Fear and he's Grim. What other explanation is there?" She kept a safe distance from me but stayed where she was and watched me clean the meat with a hint of confusion and… curiosity? "Everyone in the Underworld knows of your hatred for one another as well as your past, unless you were born yesterday and I was not, so I know the stories and I know the things you've done." She went on, "You even opened a portal in the human world and granted access to demons trying to spill blood and avenge your hatred and loss to Grim and his wife, Melanie, I think they call her, many centuries ago…"

I nodded. It was all true. Blue knew that much, at least, but not enough. "Then you must have also known that a merge ended that night and a new one began. I'm not the Fear from the past, I'm only the future."

"I've heard the stories… Marcus, right?" she asked. I wouldn't have noticed her inch closer if I hadn't been watching her from the corner of my eye as I cut up the meat. "I've heard the stories of Fear during his time with Marcus. He was horrible, from the sound of the stories anyway. So, you're saying you're a newly made monster?"

I tilted my head and smirked at her. "That's exactly right. I'm a monster, that's true, but things like power and control, the things Marcus aimed for mean nothing to me. I'm doing great as is." That wasn't entirely true, but I wasn't about to tell someone that seemed to be asking questions like she was trying to get information to later use on me, that I wasn't truly merged with Fear. I was, but not in the way that Grim was. He always told me he was one person, he never felt he was Killian or Grim—he was both. Everyone called me Fear—I even called myself that—but the only thing I did was keep my urges under control so the real monster didn't come out and cause more harm than what I was willing to do to feed his needs—my needs.

"Hard to believe," she said, tilting her head to the meat I was cutting in the sink. "You mean you're perfectly content living here alone, no control—nothing. Just you and your Devil deer?"

I studied her for a second. Why was she so insistent on this? It was almost like she needed to hear me say I was the big bad monster she conjured up in her head of what I was supposed to be. Which was partially true but when it came to Marcus, I was nothing like him. He changed my life the day he decided to kill me. He was also Fear at the time, but there was no point in dwelling over the fact that I became the monster that was responsible for my twist of fate—which also cost me a lifetime I could have had with Melanie.

Don't go there.

"Do you know anything about me?" she asked.

I dropped the piece of meat and turned toward her with the knife still in my hand. Her eyes widened on the blade and she retreated a few steps. That tiny bit of fear she kept so well hidden seeped out, and I inhaled it as quickly as it came and departed.

Concentrate, I told myself.

"The answer to that question is no," I told her as I leaned myself against the counter and gave her all my focus. Fuck, she was nice to look at even with that uncertain scowl on her face. "You probably don't know that I was a human once, before Fear killed me, and later merged with me while I was a ghost." I crossed my arms. "So, yes, Blue, I'm perfectly at ease with my life here. Besides, I'm not alone here and I'm fucking powerful as is already. I don't need anything more, and I don't need to sit on a throne and look down on everything because I'm Ryan, not Marcus. I feed, I fuck, I hunt, I sleep, I eat, what else can I ask for?"

Her dark doe-like eyes blinked at me several times as she swallowed once, twice, and looked away. Her state lasted several more seconds before she finally snapped out of it and glared at me. "Then why mark someone the same as he would do?" Her words angered me. "Why am I here, RYAN," she said my name loud and clear to get the point across.

At this point, I felt more anger than control and when I was like that, I only focused on one thing—toying with people's emotions. "Whatever reason I want you to be," I said with an irritated smile as I turned back around to the sink. "I haven't decided yet."

"Not with me," she said right before I heard the rattle of her opening a drawer and the clinking of silverware touching. I turned my head just as she shoved a knife into the side of my neck.

"Jesus!" I hissed as I grabbed my neck. Why did I think it was a good idea to let someone Fear had chosen as a mark to roam around free in the house? Her hand slipped in my pocket, and I went to grab her but she punched me in the face, followed by a swift kick in my groins. I doubled over and watched as her little ass ported with my portal chip.

Fear came to life inside me, roaring with amusement mixed with his hunger and lust for Blue.

Me, on the other hand, I was pissed as hell. When I got my hands on her, she was as good as dead. Like she had just reminded me, I was indeed a monster so why try so hard not to be one?

At least for the day, I'd let loose more than I normally did. For myself, and the fact that Fear obviously wanted to keep her around, and that right there was reason enough to make sure she died by my hands.

CHAPTER SIX

Molly

I pleaded temporary insanity. I had no idea what I was thinking when I stabbed Ryan in the neck with a kitchen knife and stole his portal chip. Okay, I knew exactly what I was thinking, but now I wished I would have rendered him incapable of following me a little longer than a jab in the neck would do to him. I was hoping he had no other portal chips hidden somewhere. There were none in his house because I had checked after the shower while I raided his room for clean clothes—his clothes swallowed me up whole but I wasn't complaining since it was the first time I've changed clothes in months. That was also when I noticed he lived in GRIM's woods.

No, just no. I couldn't risk staying there. Melanie saw me the day I changed. Grim might be able to know just like Fear had… Ryan, well, I didn't understand what game he was playing. He genuinely didn't seem to know me, but how was that? Was it truly possible that two different beings still existed inside one body?

I took a greater risk at running away. I knew I couldn't hide from him because of all these damn marks all over my body, but maybe there was another way. I ported to the edge of the Underworld. This place was hours away from the City of the Dead and was less populated. More like abandoned. The only things that resided here were witches. They pushed all other demons out long ago, claiming it for their own.

I ran up the steps to Marybeth, the witch I was looking for. I didn't even knock. I slammed the door open and stepped in. "I sensed you coming, Molly," Marybeth said as she sat next to a fireplace with her feet propped up on a wooden stool. The chair she sat in was worn and dingy looking, as was the house, but witches didn't care much for luxuries despite having the abilities to get whatever they wanted, whether it was wealth or beauty. Or at least, most were simple such as Marybeth.

"I came to cash in what you owe me." I stopped and stood in front of her chair. Her eyes never left the fire. It was there that I saw how much she had aged over the centuries. Witches could live forever if they stole the life of others. I wondered if that was what she has been doing… because I knew she was well past her time. "I saved you and your daughters all those centuries ago from Fear when he was using you all up like hairspray, draining their power."

"I know what you came for," she answered, her voice neutral, void of any emotion. It was unsettling, but I had nothing to worry about with her because for once, I had protected others. Although it was for my own gain. I needed an I-owe-you when it came to a witch so I could've cashed it in getting a body. Of course, I made the deal with the Devil soon after my encounter with her and he gave me what I wanted and more than I agreed to. "I can't help you with the marks. You know the rules down here. You belong to him now."

I dug my nails into my palms and glared. "No, you owe me. Besides, I already know that."

"You really think I can hide you from him?" She finally decided to meet my eyes. She smiled, and it was nothing but rotted teeth and wrinkles.

"You can mask the marks. Keep them hidden so that he can't find me with them." I couldn't waste time. He could already be on his way here. I looked around the small, dusty house. With this portal chip, I was well on my way into the human world as soon as I took care of these marks. "Hurry, he will come for me at any moment."

She moved her thin hands from her lap and used them to raise from the chair. "I can't." I sighed and was about to start yelling when she said, "But I have something you can use against him."

She pulled something out of the apron she wore around her dress and handed it to me. It was a small vial with clear liquid inside it. "What will this do?"

"Trap Fear."

I raised an eyebrow and studied her. "How?" It sounded like a lie. How could a sip of liquid do that?

"You must have noticed Fear's merge isn't without its issues. Considering how different the two souls are, it is no wonder…" How did she know that? I only just now came to understand something wasn't right about the merge. No one spoke about it in the Underworld. He was still treated as the same monster.

"Hurry," I urged her. "I don't have time for you to explain. He's not going to be nice when he finds me. How do I use it against him?"

"When the one he merged with is completely in control, have him drink the liquid. It will give him absolute control over his body but will render Fear and his powers useless. He'll be trapped inside the man, but if you give it to Fear, it will trap him instead. If both are present in the mind when you give it to him, then it could very well break the merge and they'll be separated, and for you, that's just as bad."

"How can this work?" I asked. "You're setting me up to fail!"

"No, I'm giving you a chance that can go three different ways."

When I brought my hand into my hair, I realized I was shaking. I hated this feeling. I was terrified, and no way was I allowing that monster to feed off my fear. But I knew he was coming and I couldn't stop the shudders taking over my body.

"Shit!" I yelled, running my fingers over my face and trying to calm down. "Please, Marybeth. If this fails, I'm stuck as his forever. I can't ever die!"

"Did you just beg, Molly?" When I glanced at her, her wrinkled face was fixed into a glare. "You know, I've heard and sensed the things you've been through and you don't give in. You keep your hands stretched out, clawing to get out of the hell you're in. Why are you so desperate now? You've known nothing but pain for centuries now." Her eyes were devouring me, waiting on my answer. I shook my head silently because I had no idea.

"Because … it's Fear," I whispered like it made all the sense in the world.

"No." She shook her head. "It's not, and you don't get to blame it on that monster. He's responsible for his own deeds. You are responsible for yours." My stomach twisted worse than anytime a knife had been stuck into it. "You don't get to act this way now. You're stained from the blood you've spilled. The man," she started and I looked down quickly. "He was human once, you know that, right? Because you stole his fate from him and now, because of that he's a nightmare. Yours."

"How do you—"

"Everything around us will speak to those that listen." I didn't get it, but witches were full of magic and spells so they could find out anything if they wanted. "If you want to run, drink it yourself and end your immortality. That way he can only hurt you once and your suffering ends. Or trap Fear inside the man. The choice is yours."

My throat was lumpy and full of a feeling I wouldn't dare admit. I tried to swallow and couldn't. I could finally end this suffering… or I could trap Fear and finally be free to get the life I wanted in the human world.

"Hide the vial," Marybeth spoke quickly. "He's coming."

Her words sent my heart racing. I tucked my hand underneath my shirt and put the vial inside my bra that I thankfully had decided to put back on after the shower despite how filthy it was. I couldn't say the same about my underwear, but there was no way I was putting those back on...

My eyes darted around the room looking for some sort of protection, but when the room brightened behind me before going back dark, I knew he was already here. Not just that, the tiny one-room house seemed to lose its air with his arrival. I stiffened before setting my body into motion all at once. I ran forward and bent down to grab the wooden stool a few feet in front of me. Once it was in my hands, I turned to face him and used all my weight to hit him with it.

He blocked my attempt easily. "I'm still trying to figure out how I deserved a fucking knife in my neck," he muttered, darkly.

I was breathing hard, pouring out every bit of my fear into my stamina so that it was nonexistent—so he couldn't feed off it. It was working because right now, all I could feel was hatred as I glanced into his eyes that were no longer brown but red. Murderous, blood red. "You're dead." He made it sound like a promise.

I only smiled because I could never stay dead. This idiot still didn't know it yet. Fear was keeping all my secrets from him. "I don't belong to anybody," I hissed.

"You belong to me now, and your soul will belong to me even after I kill you. You're shit out of luck either way," he said right before he crumbled the stool in his hands. What was left of the wood fell between us as his hands came out for me. One arm wrapped around my neck as he pulled me into him, and my ass came into contact with the tent in his jeans in the process. I couldn't stop the fear escaping into my veins this time because the thought of Fear touching me made me want to hurl. "Get your dick off my ass. You sick fuck! I stabbed you in the neck and you're turned on right now?" I asked him. I started giving him a hard time, trying to get away from his body and heat. He tightened his arm around my neck and held me still.

He inhaled against my neck and ear. “There it is. Do you know how good your fear tastes? I only get bits here and there because you’re good at keeping it from me… but when I do, you have no idea…” I was furious, but his voice in my ear had my entire body flushing with heat. I blamed it entirely on my ear being one of those spots of my body that seemed connected to my vagina. And the fact that Ryan was attractive, and so was his stupid voice, and the heat of his breath blowing into my ear only topped the cake.

What the hell was going on with me?

“You…” The sound of his voice changed… the one word sounded darker, laced with something that made me want to scream never-even-in-your-dreams in his ear. “I taste that too, Blue.”

I was mortified that I momentarily reacted to him in a way I never wanted to. “Both of you get out.” I glanced to where Marybeth was. She was back in her chair, gazing into the fire. I felt sick all over again. How could I let him crawl under my skin so much that I allowed him to ridicule me in front of her like this?

“You heard the witch,” he said then ported us outside of his home in Grim’s woods. He slung me into the glowing grass—this place was so unreal and colorful it made my eyes bleed. I kept my gaze on the grass until I heard some sort of strange sound I wasn’t accustomed to. When I looked back at him on his porch, he had a huge rifle, or shotgun—I had no fucking clue what type of gun it was exactly! But from the looks of it, he was loading it. I got to my feet and studied him cautiously.

“What are you doing?” I asked him through clenched teeth.

“I need to blow off some steam, thanks to you,” he said casually. It almost had me believing I was in the clear. “And now that I have a mark, my aim is to kill.” My eyes widened as he brought it up to his shoulder and aimed it at me.

“Let’s make this interesting, Blue.” He looked me dead in the eyes. “I’m sporting a woody thanks to you, but I feel like this right here will be much more relieving than fucking you.”

“Go ahead and shoot me then,” I baited him. I’d die and come back. Pain was pain, no matter what form it came in.

“Run,” he ordered me.

I stood there for several seconds and just glared at him before shaking my head and laughing. "Just kill me, I won't play your games."

"See, I knew you'd say that. You're not afraid of death, but you showed me earlier exactly what you don't want to happen." He wasn't going to— "Run, Blue. Give me a good hunt or your mouth will be wrapped around my dick instead."

I stumbled back a step before turning on my bare feet and running into the woods. "I'll give you a little head start," he yelled, but the pounding in my ears soon became the only thing I was hearing. I'd become the hunted any day before placing my body beneath his.

I came upon a steep hill before I realized it and started toppling down it. Something sharp hit my leg on the way down, but I ignored it and got the hell up the moment the ride was over. I didn't even know which way to go. I didn't even want to go even further, but if I stopped now… I ran for a good five minutes until I knew I had to stop. My lungs were on fire and more than anything, I should hide. Not a good hunt if I was right out in the open for him. I had to be good prey, instead of good pleasure.

All these trees were huge and tall. I couldn't climb any of them. Then I remembered the portal chip… I searched the jogging pants I wore. I still had it. I pressed the button and ported to the highest branch of the tree I stood in front of. I wouldn't even try to run when I knew I couldn't escape the mark. Besides, I still had my own secret weapon hidden in my bra… I just had to find the right moment to use it.

I took a deep breath and slowly walked across the thick branch until my back was pressed firmly against the tree, and I slid down on my ass and waited. My breathing seemed loud in my ear, and the woods were strangely quiet. Where were the animals? Ryan had no problem finding his last hunt earlier. Which meant he was good at this. A strange feeling hit my stomach. A slight thrill, but that couldn't be right. Nothing was exciting about this.

Something snapped below me, and I would have gone silent if I hadn't already been. I leaned over and looked down. It was him. That excitement hit my stomach again at the sight of him—or maybe it was the feeling you get when you knew you were about to get caught. I knew the thrill of being the one to control and hunt others—I did a lot of that by Fear's side, but I never realized until now how it felt to be the hunted. Don't get me wrong, I've been hunted by all sorts of demons over the centuries and I've been caught… but I couldn't even explain how different this moment felt.

His gaze snapped upward and a split second later a bullet blazed past me, barely missing my head. I jerked back and took a deep breath. That right there dulled this new feeling but only for a second. "Blue," he sang and every time he called me that, he made the word seem special. As fucked up as that sounded even to me. "Are you enjoying this?" he asked slowly.

My eyes widened. Of course. He wasn't hunting me by sound or tracks. He was following my emotions. He could sense my mood even from this distance. I couldn't stay here. I pressed the button with a grin. He said he wanted a good hunt…

I ported a distance away just to grab a huge rock and ported again behind him. "You think I wouldn't have noticed—"

I smacked him in the back of the head with the rock. He started turning around, and I punched him in the face. He wasn't even trying hard to fight me off. In fact, he was smiling. He thought this was a futile effort on my part… but he was never my target, to begin with. I yanked the rifle/or whatever type of gun it was out of his grip. His eyebrows shot up with surprise and challenge.

"You still have the portal chip." He only just now seemed to realize. I smiled and ported again right as he moved to grab me. When I reached my new destination, I was fighting off a laugh. I saw this hollow tree while I was running earlier. It made the perfect spot to hide his weapon. I got on my knees and shoved his toy as far as it would go inside the tree and hurried to leave the spot before I gave it away.

I hid in the trees again trying my hardest to mask my emotions, but that was impossible. I was excited as well as anxious and worried. I had no idea if he'd keep his words from earlier.

Boom.

Something tore into my shoulder and it caught me by surprise. I fell through the branches until I landed on my back. Mother—I groaned and grabbed my shoulder. I heard footsteps followed by his boots. I looked up and he didn't even hide his cocky grin. Leaning against his shoulder in his hand was the very toy I took from him. "How'd you find it so quickly?" I said through moans and groans. I felt like I was hit by a truck. Did I still have a shoulder? I moved my head lazily to look.

"Your scent's all over the damn place. It wasn't hard to track those emotions to where you hid it," he answered before squatting down beside me.

I looked into his eyes—they were no longer red but back to his charming dark ones. He seemed calmer now. "Isn't it a hunter's way to put their prey out of misery instead of letting them suffer?" I asked.

He smirked. "You really want to die, Blue?" He shook his head and sighed. "The knife incident, it's forgotten. You gave me plenty of emotions to devour and because of that, I'm levelheaded. I don't have to kill you, but don't test me again."

I sucked it up, ignoring the pain and leaned forward, so that I was closer to him. "No, end this. The hunt isn't over until you kill me and I know I made a damn good prey, so that means your dick isn't going anywhere near my mouth."

At my words, his eyes landed on my lips. What was on his mind was so clear to see in his expression and thankfully, I was in a ton of pain so I didn't have to face whatever way I might have responded with his eyes on me like that. He pulled himself out of his trance and looked away from my lips to gaze into my eyes with sincerity I wasn't used to. "Despite what you think, I'd never do anybody that way. I only said that to get your ass a-movin'." When he went to stand, I grabbed his boot. His eyes seemed darker. "Death is death. I'm not going to kill you just because you think I'm going to—" He stood up and walked away for a second and came back. "I'm not interested in you that way." He didn't sound sure and I sure as hell didn't believe that since his attraction was very apparent back at Marybeth's.

I glared and made a sound in my throat. At least he had it in him to look away. Guilty. "Then why'd you mark me, huh?" I tested him.

"I don't know," he yelled. "I don't know," he said again. "I honestly don't know what I want with you."

That I believed. That also proved Marybeth was right about the merge. Something was odd about it. He bent down next to me. "We're gonna have to stop the bleeding," he told me.

I shook my head. "No, just kill me."

"Again," he blew out a frustrated sigh.

"If you'd just get it over with already you'd see why that's the easiest solution."

"The answer is no." When his hands moved to grab me, I shoved him back and grabbed his gun. "BLUE!" he yelled my name as he stumbled to grab it from me. But the only thing I did was point the end into my chest and pulled the trigger.

CHAPTER SEVEN

Ryan

I wanted to fucking kill her. She tapped into all that rage I tried to keep controlled when she stabbed me in the neck when I had done nothing to deserve that kind of behavior. Then that rage blended in with Fear's lust for her—I swear he was so hot for her I couldn't decide if my body was responding to her because she was sexy as hell or Fear's obsession with her.

Then the strangest thing happened at the witch's house. When Blue emitted repulsion at the thought of my dick touching her—or after that when I threatened her with it to get her running, Fear seemed almost down about it. Which was crazy since I've been him for so long that I knew he got off on chicks screaming and protesting at the thought of fucking him, but this was not just him, but me as well that Blue harbored those feelings toward. For a moment, I thought I might have caught a whiff of desire coming from her, but it was there and gone so quickly that I had to be wrong.

That only pissed me off that she was so repulsed by the idea of me touching her. So, there I was full of rage, lust, and piss as she took off running in the woods as prey. I had every intention of killing her the moment she started this between us, but that idea also died the moment I got to her at the witch's house where I met her with the same defiance she kept showing me. I kept telling her I'd kill her just to make my own damn self happy.

Oh, and happy did this game with her make me.

I tracked her emotions all over the place. From repulsion, to worry, then the longer it lasted, her emotions became anticipation, excitement, and eagerness. The fact that she was enjoying this chase only made my dick strain against my jeans. She wanted nothing to do with me but she kept speaking my language when she kept proving to be such eager prey.

When I found her hidden in a tree, hiding and waiting on a large branch, Fear said, *Shoot her!*

I missed her on purpose and Fear knew. He wasn't happy about it until she made a move against us and stole my gun, which wasn't hard to find after she hid it. Or her for that matter. She hid in a tree *again.*

Blue, Blue, Blue, I said with a tsk to myself.

Only this time I did shoot her out of the tree, and Fear felt out of control inside my body. Only he wasn't. He was just that into the game I was playing with Blue, even more so that we caused her pain and devoured it like it was chocolate.

Only I freaked the fuck out when she shot herself. "Blue," I yelled and moved a little too late. She tore a hole in her neck with the muzzleloader. I dropped to the grass again and just looked at her wide-eyed.

I couldn't believe she did that to herself. I couldn't believe she'd choose death over the risk of me touching her in some way. And I really couldn't fucking believe how hurt, disappointed, and upset that made me, knowing she wasn't around to prey on. Or the fact that for a moment in the woods chasing her, I enjoyed the idea of keeping someone around to aggravate and annoy—shit, maybe even talk with other than Grim and Melanie.

And why wasn't Fear upset about it? He was the one that brought her here and now, he felt like a purr against the inside of my ribcages—it had to be laughter. I was feeling his laughter. What the hell, Fear? This was all he wanted her for?

See, perfect prey, Fear said just as I looked down at Blue and saw her wounds stitching themselves together until her skin was smooth and flawless again.

She was alive?

I touched her neck and felt a pulse. I sighed in relief. Just what was Blue? I wasn't curious about who she was before but now…

I scooped her up in my arms and carried her back to my place. She slept on the couch for a couple of hours while I finished cutting up the meat in the sink I left earlier and bagged it up in Ziploc bags for the freezer while leaving some out to make. I was setting the food on the table when she stirred on the couch. I heard her suck in a breath, followed by a thud. She fell on the floor. She got to her feet quickly, her eyes landing on me in the kitchen then the table of food. I made deer meat, fried taters, and cornbread. I'd never abandon my Kentucky roots. I even took pride in the fact that I could cook up just about any meal if it was southern. My parents hadn't been around much, but my dad had always made sure to be during hunting season. As a kid, that was one of the only times I spent with him but I had loved it. He was also the one that taught me how to make certain foods and the rest was learned from my grandpa.

And to think, nearly a thousand years later, I was still cooking up some of the same meals I ate with them.

"It would have been nice to know you were immortal before you shot yourself." She shrugged her shoulder but otherwise stood where she was. "Are you hungry?" I asked, and it was cute the way her stomach decided to answer for her and grumbled.

"I am, but I'm not sure if it's enough to try your devil deer," she said, stepping into the kitchen.

I tilted my head and arched a brow at her. "And just how long did that woman have you locked away, feeding you who knows what for you to even complain?"

"Asshole," she muttered as she studied the food on the table. "That's probably why I can't recognize a decent meal when I see one."

I watched her for several seconds. Her dark strands fell off her shoulders occasionally as she walked around the kitchen. Her shirt and neck were covered in dried blood, but she wasn't bothered by it. She kept glancing back toward the food. I could also feel her hunger filling the room, yet she didn't seem to want to take the meal I offered. I was only getting more curious about Blue. What was her deal? Who was she? At least one of my enemies had also been hers and given her delightful personality, I was sure she had a lot more.

"How long were you stuck there before I showed up and saved your ass."

She snorted. "I could be wrong, but I don't think it's called saving when you steal me from one prison and trap me in another." Okay, I kind of walked straight into that one.

"You belong to me now, time to get over it, Blue." I sat down and scooted a plate toward her on the table. "And I've been nothing but a ray of sunshine until you stabbed me in the neck with a knife. It was only fair I shot you earlier, but let's talk about you for a minute, and the fact that you died earlier, yet here you are perfectly okay with your cute, angry glare. What are you? More like, who are you, Blue?"

"Immortal," she answered. "And Blue's my name as long as I'm here with you. If you're curious about who I am, find out by someone else because I sure as hell ain't telling you." She eyed me with complete defiance and hell if my dick wasn't already responding.

"Sit down and eat," I told her, making it sound like an order because it was. "You're already thin. Do you even have tits under that baggy shirt?" I asked, and her face turned every shade of red. Embarrassment, shame, fury left her body, and I gobbled it up as I filled my plate with food.

She sighed deeply before grabbing the plate and flopping down in the chair across from me. "So, what's next now?"

"Let's eat," I replied, tearing into the meat. It tore apart easily, and even I was impressed myself with how tender the meat was.

She gave me another one of her snotty looks and said, "No, I mean what now? As in what the hell are you going to do to me?"

"I don't know," I said with a mouthful of food and no table manners that I was taught so long ago. "What do you want me to do?"

"Remove these marks from my body?" She batted her eyes sweetly, only she didn't hide the venom that came along with it.

"Nope."

She smacked her hands down on the table in frustration. After a few silent seconds, she finally made herself a plate of food. I watched for her reaction when she tried the first bite of meat. Her eyes lit up and I knew it didn't have anything to do with my cooking and everything to do with the last time she had a decent meal. All it took was the first bite and she stopped holding back. She inhaled the food without breathing, so fast and quick that more than once she choked.

"Slow down," I told her. "Drinks are in the fridge." She hurried out of her chair and went to the fridge. She grabbed the first thing she came across and chugged it down then back to the food she went.

We ate everything. No, she did. I even held myself back from grabbing seconds because she was completely exposed. She wasn't angry or glaring. She wasn't full of remarks. She was someone who looked as if she'd never had a decent meal her entire life.

Fear had been silent since Blue shot herself in the woods. These were normally the moments I enjoyed to myself when I had myself completely to *myself*. But watching her eat made me fucking depressed. I mean, she was a gorgeous—a little too thin—woman. She was also bitchy and full of backbone, yet all that was gone as she ate. In her eyes, none of what she'd been through was hidden, I could see it all. Blue's been through a lot. The scars weren't visible most of the time until she left herself wide open. Like now, she wasn't even trying to hold back on eating to save face.

But the moment she was finished, her eyes looked up at me. "Don't ask if it was good. There's no way I'd know." She basically just admitted to what I already knew.

"How long have you been her prisoner?" I asked again.

"I've been a prisoner for the last thousand years." She sat her fork down and stood. "I didn't wind up in her hands until six months ago, though."

"Sounds like you've made a lot of enemies," I said because I wasn't going to pretend I cared when I was only curious.

Her eyes darkened at me for a moment before she said, "No kidding."

"Where do you think you're going?"

"To the couch, or is there a cell I'm supposed to go to?" she replied sarcastically, and I couldn't help but grin as I watched her flop down on the couch.

"There's an extra room across from mine. You can claim it," *while you're here,* I added to myself. Fear was interested in her for now, but who knew how long that'd last. And if anything, that was a horrible thing itself. Having Fear's *interest.* As for me, of course, I wanted to fuck her. She was hot in a wild, abandoned sort of way. She looked dangerous despite her weight, yet lost and broken in a way that made me want to break her some more.

I wasn't a good guy, at least not the one I used to be. Even I had a monster residing in my soul that wasn't Fear's. And it screamed to get underneath her skin and break her in a way she had never been broken before.

I left her to do whatever while I took a shower. When I came back out, she was curled up on the couch asleep. Completely defenseless.

Touch her. Make it hurt, Fear told me, and I shook my head. I didn't think so. I wanted her kicking and screaming at me when I sunk inside her the first time but not out of repulsion or fear—I wanted to bury myself in her rage. She was full of it. *You know you want her now. Doitdoitdoit!* Fear chanted with anger and lust as I forced myself to turn around and walk back toward my room. I couldn't even chance picking her up and carrying her to a bed. Fear already had my skin tingling, he was so pumped up.

Fear hadn't realized we were on the same level when it came to Blue. I'd get us there. One fight at a time with her. Because I had a feeling that was all broken Blue knew how to do.

CHAPTER EIGHT

Molly

I jumped from where I slept when I heard gunfire, followed by all kinds of other noises. What in the world was going on outside? I wiped the drool off my face and looked around. I must have fallen asleep right after I ate everything Ryan made to eat. Every bite. I didn't tell the actual truth about what I thought about the taste. It had been delicious, and I didn't think it had anything to do with me not eating a meal in close to a year despite a crumble of hard bread here and there.

I also noticed the sudden urge to go to the bathroom. Well, what did you know? I haven't had the urge to go other than peeing here and there in a long time. One meal and my body was showing signs of life. My body was weird like that. I didn't have to eat or drink to survive but believe me when I said I feel every bit of the starvation and weakness of never eating. It was torture of the worst kind. The constant hunger.

I got up and hurried to the bathroom as I listened in on what was happening outside. I could hear flapping above the house—dragons flying over the house? And more gunshots and screaming. Lots and lots of screaming. It had the hair on my arms standing up. My body had to go at a time like this… I moaned and hoped whatever was going on stayed outside. Which it seemed very unlikely for Grim to let his woods be attacked… maybe Ryan was doing something ridiculous. He was Fear now, after all.

But not exactly. I cupped my breasts with my hands to make sure I still had the vial in my bra. Good, it was still there. I needed to hide it somewhere. I couldn't risk it getting shot the next time I pissed Ryan off and became the hunted. I shook my head when I remembered the feeling of excitement yesterday. I cleaned up in the bathroom and still, my stomach was determined to make me remember the events that took place yesterday. I was getting a weird feeling of excitement all over again… not that exactly. More like a feeling of dread and wonder of what he planned to do to me next.

I found the extra room and started looking for a place to hide it. But wait, what if I could get it over with right now and place it in a drink? I just couldn't risk Fear being the one that drank it. I muttered under my breath and decided it was best to give myself time to study him more.

If I were honest, I didn't think I was in any trouble right now. At least for now. I had no idea what Fear planned with me, given he knew who I was and Ryan didn't. A feeling of trepidation hit me, I didn't want that to happen. I didn't want him to know who I was. But how long would Fear keep it in the dark from him?

I placed the vial in between the mattresses and smoothed the covers back over the bed when the front door slammed open. I hurried out of the room quickly, trying not to look suspicious. Which I shouldn't anyway. He had no clue I had anything.

Only who I saw wasn't Ryan or Fear. I didn't recognize the demon, but the moment his eyes found me, he smiled and came after me. I made a run for the kitchen, looking for the same knife I used on Ryan yesterday. "What do we have here?" he said, right before his arms snaked around my waist and pulled me into him. His hands were roaming up my stomach, onto my breasts. I took a deep breath as he blew into my ear. It sent a wave of nausea through me—nothing like the way it had felt when Ryan had me in this same position. I didn't know why I even thought of that. "You look important," he told me. He couldn't have been more wrong.

"Let go of me!" I hissed. When I was able to get ahold of a weapon, his ass was dead. I couldn't budge from his arms no matter what I did, so I threw myself back against him. Something pierced my neck and I screamed in frustration. He bit me. *Vampire.*

He sucked hard as his fangs dug deeper before pulling back up. My blood dripped from his mouth. "You taste good. I think I'll piss him off and fuck his girl before he kills me," he snarled as he pushed me forward. My stomach and arms smacked onto the table and it skidded forward until it hit the counter and stopped.

Okay, what the hell was going on? How was a vampire here? I tried to raise up but he pinned me down, so I started crawling against the table. He trapped my legs from doing so. I looked back and a wave of panic washed over me. I was already mentally preparing myself to shut down—shut it all out like I always did. "Not so fast, don't worry, I'll make it quick." He pulled my—Ryan's—jogging pants down, leaving nothing else between me and him.

I closed my eyes. These were the moments I missed having power the most. The door slammed opened and Ryan stepped in. His eyes scanned the room for a split second before locking his gaze on us. His jaw tightened and he looked livid—his eyes changed to the red color of Fear's as he stalked toward us with an angry urgency. The vampire jerked me up and used me as a barrier to protect himself from him. "Come any closer and I kill her," the vampire told Ryan not having a clue I was immortal. He held my neck like he would twist it at any moment. One second I was being held by the neck, and the next I was shoved aside. Ryan's hand covered the demons face, and he kept walking forward with him as the vampire struggled and screamed until his skull crushed under the pressure of his palm. I bent down and pulled the jogging pants back up only to have Ryan pressing me back into the table the moment I lifted back up.

I made a surprised sound in my throat just as his hands found their way to my neck. His bloody hand at that. He forced my neck to the side and studied the place where I was bitten. I couldn't tell if I was still bleeding but the longer he looked at it, the angrier he seemed to get. His hand was shaking and it traveled to my shoulder while the other did the same. His gaze lowered. "What else did he do?" his voice was on edge and darker than it had been when I stabbed him.

"Nothing," I managed to get the words out. I was completely off guard by his reaction. Even my pulse was roaring in my ears. "You got here before he could."

"Ryan—" My eyes widened with panic when I saw Grim enter the house. He took one look at us and hesitated at the door. "Is everything okay? I came for the vampire's soul, I didn't realize you had someone here…"

"Get out!" Ryan roared and Grim's essence pooled around him.

"Is Fear—" Grim never got to finish. Ryan's hands left me as he gripped his head and fell to the ground. I was confused, but strangely even worried for him as he tried to stand back up. Ryan's eyes zeroed in on me as he gripped his head like he was in pain—or fighting a hard battle, and suddenly I knew what this was about. Fear wanted out.

Ryan grabbed my ankle, and I jumped because I wasn't expecting it and two, so much kept happening that I couldn't focus on shutting out my fear. He pulled me into the floor and dragged my legs toward him, wanting me closer. What was happening? I didn't know—I didn't know. "Blue," he growled the name he called me. "Don't let him have you first."

I shook my head and tried to get a better look at his eyes. I needed to understand what was happening, but when a tail moved out of the back of his pants and horns began to grow from his head—I knew. Ryan's sandy-brown colored hair darkened and his skin paled. When he lifted his head up, it was Fear that held me on the floor.

"Fear," Grim's essence darkened.

"Leave, Grim," Fear spoke calmly, yet he never took his eyes off me. The only thing I focused on was breathing. In and out. In and out.

"You're not killing her," Grim paused, his eyeless expression moving over me. "What are you?" he asked me. "I don't sense any death coming from you." He didn't seem to recognize me. A little bit of relief hit me, but not enough.

"She's mine," Fear still never took his eyes off me as he spoke. "My mark."

"You," Grim hissed.

"It's fine," I spoke up. "Just go." My eyes fell on Fear and hardened.

"Ryan better be the one I greet tomorrow instead of you," Grim said right before fading away.

"Molly," he called me. He looked different now that he was merged with Ryan. His features were mixed in there as well. This Fear—did I know him? He was the one that put the mark on me.

"Tell me what you want? Is this some sort of payback?" I asked, gritting my teeth together. Playing tough when I was nothing but confused on the inside. And worried. Nervous.

He laughed. His hands moved back over my legs and I jumped. It made him laugh more. He pulled me closer until his weight was against me, and I had to lean back to keep distance from him but it didn't matter. I felt him everywhere. This was what Fear was good at. Exposing people. "Why would I want payback?"

"Because I took Melanie to the Devil, betraying you," I snapped because I couldn't stand the game he was playing.

"I never cared about Melanie or her power. Or fucking Grim—self-righteous bag of bones," he spat. "Why do I need any more power, Molly? I'm fucking fantastic as I am." Now I truly had no idea what this was about. He could be lying… yet this sounded nothing like the monster I remembered.

"Then why did you mark me—more than once I might add! I don't want anything to do with you anymore! Do you know what hell I've been through because of the things I did for you!"

"*Marcus,*" he corrected. "I had nothing to do with any of that. He had me trapped inside my own skin." He laughed. "Kind of like the way I have Ryan." I glared at him. "Besides, you didn't do the things he asked you to for him. You did it for yourself." His eyes fell over me with a smile. "For this body."

I shoved him and moved to stand. He came down over me completely and prevented me from going anywhere. "Get away from me, Fear," I hissed.

"You said you wanted to know why I marked you." I glanced up at him. His red eyes glowed and matched the evil in his smirk. Then his hand went to my jaw and shoved my face to the side. My whole body shivered when his mouth came down over the vampire's fang marks. He sucked, and I gasped.

"What are you doing?" I pushed him up. He lifted his eyes and grinned.

"You're mine, Molly." His smile vanished. "I don't want to fucking see another mark on your skin from anyone else unless it's from me." His claws moved back to my face as he held it down and began to sear my skin with another one of his marks, using his clawed finger. I yelled at him through the pain and the burning as he carved the X over the spot the vampire had bitten. "Much better," he said, releasing my face. The moment I faced him again, I spat in his face.

"You don't own me," I told him. "I don't care what this mark means."

He moved off me but still loomed over me. My stomach churned with dread. Then he ripped my shirt open. "Let's see what you darkened your soul for," he said and I tried to fight him, but he pulled both my wrists back with one hand and used the other to slide over my stomach and chest. Goosebumps broke out on my skin.

"Stop," I screamed.

Then he ripped the bra with his claws and moved them from my breasts. I closed my eyes and felt the heat spread over my face. I was ashamed that instead of disgust, I felt more self-conscious about my tiny breasts. Especially when it came to Fear's gaze. He knew just how much I wanted a woman's body, only to end up with these. He was going to laugh in my face.

"You ain't got no tits, Molly," he told me, and I fought back my embarrassment in the form of tears. How did he get to me so easily? He brought his mouth down below my eye and caught the tear as it fell, then he inhaled and I shivered. "You're tiny, Molly. That's exactly the way I like it. Easy prey. Head to toe, you were made the way I imagined you'd be." My skin felt blistering and my heart pounded. Why was he imagining what I'd look like to begin with?

"Stop," it came out more like a whisper than a yell. I should be disgusted, I hated Fear and everything he was but it was Ryan's voice falling from his lips. Ryan's facial features hidden amongst his. I never expected to feel conflicted like I did now. The only thing that made sense was my fear for him, and it was clawing at my chest as he watched me.

A sword went through Fear's head. Blood splattered across my bare chest and face. I sucked in a fearful breath and touched his head that lay on my naked chest. "That should bring him back," Grim said standing above us with the sword. I didn't say anything back, not sure if he was talking to me or himself. "Are you okay?" Now I couldn't pretend he wasn't talking to me when his eyeless gaze landed on me.

I looked away quickly, not wanting him to stare too hard at my face and see the resemblance of the ghost-girl that gave him a shit load of trouble in the past. "Yeah," I said, looking at Fear only to see it was Ryan that lay against me. I picked his head up—the hole was still open in his head—and scooted out from underneath his body.

"You really are marked." Grim turned around and I realized why, I had nothing left of my shirt after Fear ripped it. I covered myself with my arms.

"Are you sure you should have done that? Won't he be pissed?" I asked to his back.

He snorted. "Maybe, but not for long. He lives off fear and pain, even his own."

"He doesn't like you," I stated because I found it so odd that he could let the monster that did so much to him and Melanie stay and live so close to them.

"I don't like him, either," he answered straight away. "Mind telling me why Fear marked you?" He didn't turn around, but his words had me on edge. He sounded suspicious. "It's weird that Fear marked someone, he hasn't since—" He cut off.

"I don't know," I lied.

"I can't stop him from doing anything to you the next time. You belong to him." I knew that already, and I hated that Grim was trying to look out for me without a clue who I was. He'd throw me out the door if he knew.

"I can take care of myself," I said sharply.

He nodded and walked toward the door but not without saying, "Not from where I was standing. Lucky for you, Ryan's good at keeping him happy and he doesn't come out much."

"It doesn't seem that way to me," I muttered. He had already been out twice since I encountered him. "Besides, am I really safe with either of them?"

He stopped at the door, still not looking back. "Probably not. By the looks of it, Fear wants something from you. Sooner or later, Ryan's going to act on them." He left me alone with an unconscious Ryan or Fear on the floor, lying in a pool of blood. I didn't know which one I'd encounter when he woke.

CHAPTER NINE

Ryan

Ow.

I winced and coughed, feeling something wet all around me. I was already thinking, *What has Fear done this time?* before I even opened my eyes and saw that I was lying in blood. I had a feeling it was my own, considering the massive headache I had. "Ryan?" My head snapped around to the sound of Blue's cautious voice. She sat on a kitchen chair with her knees pressed to her chest as she watched me. She looked like she had been waiting for me to wake.

My hand slid in the blood as I tried to use it as leverage to stand. After another attempt, I was on my feet. Fear had managed to get out despite me dragging Grim away from Melanie at the crack of dawn and asking him to gather demons for me to hunt. That was something that he always did for me at least once a month. He'd bring the ones he was supposed to kill. They weren't good demons, they were evil—filth that needed to leave this world. It helped keep Fear satisfied.

He'd been furious with me the night before for not having my way with Blue. As the night went on, he only got worse, so I had no choice but to ask for Grim's help. For some reason, it wasn't making him happy, and it only got worse when I walked in on one of the demons holding down Blue with her pants pulled down against my fucking table. Even now, I wanted to rip a dead demon's head off at the thought of what he had planned to do to her. I was furious but Fear was too, and I couldn't keep him from coming out.

I made my way to Blue and dropped in front of the chair. Her big brown eyes studied me cautiously, hugging her legs. I breathed in her nervousness and uncertainty. Since when was Blue nervous with me? "Hey, did I—" Even I was afraid of what she might say. I touched her knee softly, and I could taste the relief wash over her.

"You're getting blood on me," she whispered. "I already showered it off me once."

Now that she mentioned it, her hair was wet. Was that why she looked so vulnerable and innocent? I wish she didn't look that way, it made my monster want to come out and play. "What happened?" There was no way she could have won in a fight against Fear.

"Grim put a sword through your head." I shook my head at her words. That sounded like something he would do.

"What was I doing?" I closed my eyes, then reopened them. Her tongue darted over her lips and she looked down. Stop, *stop*, she needed to stop acting so docile, even Fear stirred inside already.

So easy, I can break her, Fear's words inside my head sent a shot of anger into my stomach. He better not have—I wanted to be the one—then I caught my thoughts red-handed. I wasn't worried about Blue, I was worried that he got to her before me.

"What did he do?" I flipped like a switch, leaning onto her knees and grabbing her cheek, then my hands were sliding down her arms, looking for some clue. My eyes went to her neck and found it.

"He?" she asked, wide-eyed. Her heart rate increased, pumping renewed fear into her veins. Not just that, she was confused, uncertain, excited, and anxious all at once. My little Blue didn't know what she wanted to feel.

"I meant me," I told her, standing and forcing her to with me. She tried to slip her arms out of my hand but I gripped them tighter. "Since you're gonna be around, Blue, you should know that I black out occasionally and when that happens, a monster worse than me comes out." I liked that about her, despite all the emotions whirling inside her as I kept her standing in front of me, she kept her eyes on me. She never dared to break our stare. My dick was reacting, of course.

"Fear?" She figured it out, did she? Or had he told her something?

I nodded. "Now, what did he do?" I asked, and Fear was quiet. I was surprised he wasn't laughing against my innards because he knew how furious I was.

She shook her head and that was when I spotted the X on her neck that wasn't there before. Underneath lay two puncture marks from where the vampire had bit her. I bit my own lip with anger. "He put another mark on me… that's it. Chill out." What time I seemed to be losing it, Blue gained back some of herself that Fear stole—maybe even the vampire, too. The lower half of her body jerked away from me. I had been pressing into her, trying to give my dick what it wanted without really knowing. "What is it with you? Does it always make an appearance in the worst situations?" Yeah, my dick knew what she was referring to and reacted again, sending another wave of want and need through me.

Jesus.

I no longer knew if I was reacting to my feelings when it came to her. Maybe this was me reacting to what Fear wanted. It never mattered to me before, but when it came to Blue and the possessiveness I felt… it didn't feel like me. No woman got underneath my skin, the only one that I've ever wanted to, belonged to someone else.

And I've only spoken a few words to her at most. I didn't even know her real name. I let go of her hands and walked away from her almost desperately. I didn't want to be caught up in a feud with Fear over her. But, at the same time, how could I stay away from her when he/I/we clearly wanted to pounce her?

"Are you going to shower?" I heard her sliding her feet across the floor behind me. Even that was putting me on edge.

"Why?" my words came out harsh.

"Because you're covered in blood," she reminded me. I clenched and unclenched my fists and turned toward the hallway. My face felt tight, so the blood must be drying. I slammed the door shut once I was in the bathroom and started tearing out of my clothes. When I looked in the mirror at myself, I would have laughed, but my thoughts were so far from smiling that I couldn't muster anything other than a glare.

Go back to her, Fear tried to order me but I wasn't having it. Instead, I went to the cubby hole in the bathroom and yanked out the old CD player. I plugged it into the wall, let the CD load before I turned the music all the way up. AC/DC filtered through the speakers. Music that was a part of history now. Music I clung on to, to remember I was still, who I used to be.

Go to her.

Ignoring him, I twisted the knob until the water was scalding and stepped into the shower. I was pissed, agitated, and horny. On top of that, Fear was clawing at me from the inside. I was all fine, or at least I thought I was until I no longer felt like *Ryan Jones.* I guess I wasn't. My name was Fear down here. Everyone called me that and I responded.

You want her too. Stop fucking pretending.

I yelled to drown out his voice in my head. My fist slammed into the wall. I let the water fall over me. I grabbed my dick, then let go because I couldn't get off on my own. Not when there was someone in the other room that could do it for me.

Fuck. Then I realized I had screamed the word.

She's mine, he told me.

Fear was laughing. I was breaking. I knew he was right. I wanted to hurt her just like he wanted. Not because I was him, but because of the monster he created inside me. I was perfectly okay with that before… only now it ate at me like a disease because with Blue around, he was going to keep forcing himself out. Not because I wouldn't give him what he wanted because we both knew I would. You didn't have to know someone to crave them like a junkie to a fix. That was how I felt toward Blue, she was irresistible with her giant eyes and piercing glares, and I knew the taste of her fear that waited to be coaxed out was sure to be addictive.

No, he'd keep coming out because I've never sensed him like this before. So restless and obsessed. He'd always stayed inside as long as I fed him, but now… he didn't want to stay tucked away.

He wanted Blue all to himself.

I wish Blue would try escaping again, so I'd have a reason to hurt her again.

CHAPTER TEN

Molly

I paced back and forth, feeling anxious and if I admitted, still afraid. And that itself was messed up because I knew who I was. Yes, I had plenty of things to be afraid of, but I was good at hiding it—masking it with stupid words that tumbled from my lips. I was good at *pretending* I couldn't be exposed when right now, that was what I felt was beginning to happen.

Which only made me more desperate to escape.

I didn't know what was going on, but Ryan had been in the bathroom for a while with the music blaring and screaming, punching the wall by the sound of it. Words like "fuck", "dammit", and "shut the hell up" tumbled through the walls. I clutched the vial in my hand. I had grabbed it from the room, but I was beginning to think I wouldn't get to use it on him. Not with him like this. He sounded like a madman in there.

Clearly, I was screwed.

Clearly, I was confused.

But when his yelling went quiet, I darted back into the empty room and hid the vial. The music cut off, and I hurried out of the room and walked by the bathroom door just as it opened. I stopped, feeling a tad caught when I knew I wasn't. The steam and heat rolled over me and when I saw him standing in the doorway, holding the door with one hand and his towel in the other... I might've let my mouth fall open and maybe even stood there and stared. Did I forget he was my worst enemy in that moment? Yes. My ovaries sang, for crying out loud, by quivering and panting over him. He was in shape—of course, he was in shape. I let my eyes trace every ridge in his abs. I hadn't expected all the hair on his chest or the trail leading down to the huge bulge in his towel. Maybe it was because of Fear. When he was Marcus, he had been pale, flawless, and thin. Ryan was none of those things. He was male. To me, men were supposed to be big, male, and hairy. Exactly like the one I was looking at. Maybe that was why he was so fucking intimidating.

This wasn't the boy I killed. This was the man he became because of me. Those thoughts sent a wave of heat through my entire body. I knew it couldn't be hidden from him. His eyes were on me like a predator watching his prey.

"I smell you, Blue," he told me casually. He didn't sound bent out of shape like I felt. The only thing that said otherwise was his dick.

"Your tattoos," I blurted a little breathlessly. I traced the ink on him with my gaze. The right side of his chest was a deck of cards surrounded by dark smoke with some dice. Both arms were covered with different words, animals, and the upper part of his arms were each inked with a demon that looked scarier than Fear. None of it was in color, but it wasn't hard to guess that it was blood dripping from their mouths.

I just knew he was going to call me out over lusting over him but instead he said, "You keep stealing my clothes to wear and soon I'll have none." Him walking around like he was now was totally fine with me. It didn't even seem to matter that he had Fear inside him right now, but I was sure that would change again with my mood.

He stepped out of the doorway, and I moved out of his way but not without breathing in his body's scent as he did so. "What to do with you tonight?" I didn't know if he was asking me or himself but my lady parts trembled the same time my heart pounded with fear.

He went into his bedroom. I didn't follow, but I stood in the hallway wondering why I wasn't running into the empty room and pretending to sleep. But all I could think about was how wrong his life was.

Ryan was different than all the others that held me captive. And the fact that I knew he used to be a good guy only complicated my feelings. It hit me right there. *I want to free him from Fear.* Not just to save myself, but because he was good once and he could be good again. I'd make things right.

I wanted to redeem myself because if I were honest, Fear wasn't the one that haunted me all these centuries. It was Ryan. I took his life and it changed his entire fate. Of course, it was an order given by Fear who claimed it was all Marcus earlier as he held me down and shamed me, but I had ultimately been the one to do it.

"Shut up!" I jumped at Ryan's voice in the other room. I knew he wasn't talking to me, I hadn't said a word. I believed it was Fear he was talking to. I couldn't imagine how it would feel to share a body and mind with Fear.

"I didn't say anything," I spoke up so that he would hear me. I couldn't stop myself from interrupting his madman antics with himself, not when I wanted a reason to continue talking to him.

"Are you still standing in the hallway?" he asked. I watched his shadow peeking out of the room. He looked like he was putting on a shirt.

"Yeah, there's nothing to do," I said lamely. His shadow shook his head right before he laughed.

"I figured you'd be fighting me about freeing you from the mark… not telling me you're bored like I should fix it."

I rolled my eyes. "Asshole," I muttered.

"I heard that." *Naw, shit. I meant for you to hear it.* Why I decided I wanted to save him beats me. His words always rubbed me the wrong way. My emotions were very unstable around him, that was for sure. Lucky for him, I felt guilty and he happened to look like my perfect fantasy, or else… who was I kidding, I'd probably still want to help him.

"Give yourself a cookie," I couldn't help but say.

He was quiet for a second before he said, "Want to fuck?" My heart stopped. No, more like it halted, stumbled a few pathetic times into Ryan's hands until it started again at an insane rate. My whole body might as well have been dipped in lava I was so heated and turned on. I hadn't expected him to ask that. I wasn't surprised to find out how easily I realized I wanted him to fuck me, though. Still, my reluctance to admit anything out loud led to him stepping back into the hall, dressed. "You don't have to answer. Your emotions are broadcasting the truth enough." It was damn infuriating that he could sense my every emotion. The prick fucking *ate* on them. Literally. His eyes fell over me, reddening. "Jesus, Blue, really turn that shit down. I can't think with you not even bothering to hide it."

I just stood there glaring because how could I turn it off? I was pissed at him, but lust was a powerful thing and mine was still begging for him. "Get dressed. We're going out," he said, walking past me.

So, we aren't fucking? I wanted to ask him, but instead, I gave his back a funny look and asked, "Where are we going?" Then I looked down at his clothes I wore. "I don't even have clothes to wear." Not that I cared, but it felt like when he said, "We're going out," he literally meant we're going out and probably getting into trouble. My stomach fluttered with excitement.

"Oh right." He turned around, his gaze on me sliding up and down. I curled my toes into the carpet. "I forgot you were taking mine without asking." He sighed. "I'll be right back." I watched him slide his hand across his pocket where his portal chip must have been and ported. I went to the couch and waited. He came back a few minutes later tossing some skimpy looking dress at me with a pair of black heels. I held up the pink material and glared.

"You really expect me to wear this?" I wasn't a pink kinda girl. Sure, I've never gotten an actual chance to figure out just what kind of girl I was, but some things you just knew, and I knew I definitely wasn't a pinky. "It's pink," I finally said, wrinkling my nose up at it.

His grin was an I-knew-it one. "It's funny how easily I predicted that kind of reaction from you and that's exactly why I chose it, and that's pretty much the only color she had that would fit you around the tits." I curled my lips at him and looked down to hide my embarrassment. All the women he slept with probably had giant boobs, and no doubt this was taken from one of their houses. I felt strange, not in a good way at the thought of him and other women. "Hurry, I got big plans for you."

I groaned, stepping toward the hallway when he laughed. "No, Blue. Change right here. I wanna watch you." Those last four words really did it for me and desire crashed over me all over again. *I really want to fuck him.*

I turned back around to face him and his eyes darkened. "No, turn your back toward me and strip off your clothes. I'll put your dress on." His voice was dark and commanding. I hated being ordered around until that moment. My stomach coiled with heat as I turned around and did as he said, tossing the pink dress onto the floor, lifting the giant shirt over my head, then sliding down the jogging pants. When I straightened my back, his hands found the curve of my back and I yelped softly out of surprise and expectation. Then they traced around my flat stomach as his breath caressed my neck. My nipples were pebbles and my body was so tuned in on what he might do next that I felt lightheaded.

He started lowering himself. I felt every bit of his breath against my back as he slowly squatted. Oh, fuck. His face was right against my ass cheeks. He grabbed the pink material next to my feet and said in a voice laced with something I recognized in me, "Lift your legs." I did as he asked, lifting one leg up at a time as he slowly started sliding the dress up, and as he did, I couldn't think of a time I was more turned on than I was right now as he dressed me. Every cell in my body was lit up, drumming along as the material moved its way over my ass, oh so slowly, because he wanted me to burn, and I was without him even touching me. His hands come to the front of the dress as he stood up to continue covering my body in pink. This time, he did let his fingers catch my nipples as he slid it up over my breasts. I hissed from the contact, instinctively leaning into his hands, but he pulled away just as I did.

"Think you can get the straps on?" he asked. Those words should have been sweet but they weren't. They were dark. They were evil, condescending. Then I realized very cruelly, this was the torture he was giving me. I always expected pain to come in beatings and the killing of my body, but what I never realized before was the way someone can tease you with something you suddenly wanted out of nowhere. And that out of nowhere feeling would be the one thing I could be controlled with.

Lust was a powerful thing. Right then, my legs were shaking so hard, I let myself get built up when he'd never planned to take me down into the high. But he'd never once made it out to be something else, that was all me. The moment he invaded my space, it was all I could think about.

I sucked in a hard breath and stepped away, sliding into the tiny straps. My nipples were sharps points against the thin material as I knew they would be for many hours to come. Because even with his obvious plans to torture me, I was still wound up. "Easy," I said, turning and running my hands down the front of the dress. His eyes drank me in and lit up over my breasts. That's when I noticed what was going on in his jeans, and smiled.

The thing about lust. It was a dangerous thing to play with. Physical and *sexual* attractions could come in twos and right now, he was torturing himself just as much as he was me.

"Is this the moment you tell me where we're going?" I asked, coolly.

His eyes danced with mayhem. "Ever heard of The Den?"

I might have thought I'd lust after him the rest of the night, but those thoughts died the moment he mentioned The Den.

We weren't doing anything remotely close to screwing. No, I had a sick suspicion that I hoped was wrong.

But, I already knew it wasn't.

The fucker was sticking me in a cage fight.

***

I was no stranger to paid fights. I've been forced into a lot, I've won a lot, lost a lot, and always bled a lot more. But The Den was notorious for always giving one of the fighters an advantage over the other, hence why it was so famous in the Underworld. Everyone were crooks and this place was crawling with Underworld's biggest villains.

I've never been here before, but that didn't mean I wouldn't run into someone that recognized me. In my fear and guilt, I wondered if maybe I should tell him who I was before Fear or someone told him first, but I was too afraid to utter the words. So, I waited for a better chance. Just like I was waiting for the right opportunity to slip the liquid into Ryan's drink.

The Den was one of the better, more put together places for these sorts of things. It kind of looked like a human warehouse only built with bones. Even the cage that the fights happened in were made of them, blackened over time and colored in the blood of its fallen victims in the ring. There was also a spot in the large room where women were available, and all around demons were fucking and screaming, placing bids on the current fight. It was loud and insane.

When we ported there, I tensed up next to Ryan as he took my portal chip from my hand and stuck it into his pocket. I glared, but I figured it was because I had no pockets. All eyes fell on us when we arrived, or more like Ryan. It was obvious that every demon here knew who he was, so this wasn't the first time he'd been here. Eyes were on me too but not on my eyes like they were Ryan's. No, their focus was on the thin dress I wore. It clung to my body, revealing the small round of hips and butt I did have. Believe me, it wasn't much, but it didn't matter to these guys.

And I hated how exposed I felt. All the times I've spent in these sorts of places before, I'd been in shabby clothes that hid me beneath them. Now, nothing could hide my body from their unwanted gazes. I openly glared and became hostile to anyone that bumped into me.

As uncomfortable as I was, I could see the appeal of this place to Ryan. This was exactly what Fear fed on, and he was probably getting high off it all now. When I tilted my head up, though, his gaze was hot on mine. I questioned him with a lifted brow. He pushed me forward with his hand against my back. It wasn't this place Ryan was feeding on, but me. I knew it, I *felt* it. I didn't know why he had it out for me tonight, but he did.

And that made me uneasy. That made him dangerous. That made me wish I was disgusted but what I felt was blistering hot.

"You fit right in here perfectly, even more if your horns were out." It had meant to come out sarcastically but somehow sounded more like an opinion. His eyes fell over me with a grin.

"Sounds like an invitation to look the part of the monster that I am." I looked over my shoulder at him carefully. Did I poke the beast too much? The answer was yes as the air around us shifted and darkened. When Ryan was finished, he stood as Fear. I shuddered, but it helped me understand him more. He could become Fear without actually being him, if that made any sense. Which meant Fear could most likely do the same, so I had to be careful.

"Better?" Red eyes preyed down at me with his one word.

We were the center of attention now. A large man stepped in front of us. His gaze flicked over me for a second before smiling at Ryan. "Wondering when you'd show. It's been a few days. That's too long if you ask the whores," the man said and something knotted in my stomach. Of course, he slept with everything coming and going. Bastard. *I don't care, I don't care, I don't care.*

Ryan's grin was directed at me for several long, torturous seconds before aiming it at the ugly demon-man that was no comparison to Ryan's looks. "Sounds like I need to pay them a visit." Someone stabbed me in the stomach, *obviously* not really, but that's what it felt like listening to Ryan speak about fucking other women. I wanted that opportunity, not that he was going to give it up. He'd give it up to anyone but me, though.

The man's gaze fell back to me, eyes clouded with lust. "Who's the doll?"

"None of your concern," Ryan said, his hand on my back heating my skin. "Blue's mine to touch, Darrian," ha-ha, there was really no touching going on in this relationship, "but you will get to see her in the cage." Darrian's eyes widened in surprise as he looked back at me, but not mine. I knew the asshole was going to put me through hell tonight. Did I really want to help this jerk be free of Fear? I sighed, not looking over at him because I knew he wanted a reaction but there was none to give.

"Such a pretty little thing, are you sure?" Darrian asked Ryan with a look that spoke that'd-be-a-waste. "There'll be nothing left of her to touch. She won't survive thirty seconds."

I planted a blank expression on my face while Ryan had a full-on smirk. "I can still take her home dead," he said, messing with Darrian.

Darrian shook his head. "I've seen you do a lot of fucked up things, but screwing the dead? Are your needs growing darker, Fear?" he asked, and Ryan played him with the shrug of his shoulders.

"Get her in the cage, we'll be waiting," was all Ryan told him as he led us toward the seats placed all around the cage. Some were standing, shaking the cage, screaming and roaring as a vampire took on a werewolf. It was ending right as he sat down. The werewolf bit the vampires head off. He shifted back into a man and my heart thudded. *Timber.* What I didn't want to happen, did. I encountered someone that knew who I was. I met Timber when we were both captured by the same demon named Rein. We were stuck in cages for years together, and out of closeness and going through the same experiences, we started sleeping together in between our tortures and cage fights until the night Timber helped me escape… and sadly, I never thought of him again nor did I come back to save him. My priorities had always and forever been for me and me alone. Even wanting to save Ryan was to ease my own guilt.

I scanned the room looking for any sign of Rein. Rein was handsome but sadistic. Similar to Fear, I supposed, which was probably why he didn't like him or me. He was just another demon wanting to be better and more vicious than any other. I couldn't see him anywhere which hopefully meant Timber wasn't a slave to Rein's torture anymore, but if he wasn't then who held him prisoner now?

"Didn't expect you to be afraid," Ryan startled me and I jumped. His eyes squinted as he studied me. I started pulling in all my emotions to hide away but the moment I looked back at the cage, all of it came back when I saw Timber again. Ryan turned and observed Timber before turning back to me.

"Thanks for sticking me in a fight with demons that are three times my size." I swallowed and kept my focus on anything but Ryan's piercing gaze.

"Hmm," that one sound sounded threatening coming from his lips. "The more you try to hide who you are, Blue, the more curious I become at finding out who you are." I ignored him which only seemed to make him worse. "Little Blue, being curious can make me angry, especially if I have to find out what it is on my own."

"I never realized I was obligated to give up anything about myself to the monster that marked me. You also happen to be putting me in a cage fight where the death of one or both fighters is the end game." I turned and batted my eyes at him. He smiled at me in appreciation. "The day you find out my past is the day Hell freezes over." My stomach bottomed out when I realized how true those words were.

"I do love a challenge," he leaned closer and whispered without ever breaking our eye contact. "And I also enjoy when you act like death is the end for you when you've already shown me it's not."

I rolled my eyes before wetting my lips with my tongue. His eyes followed the movement. "And I don't like how you act like that it's supposed to make me feel better. Dying still sucks. Pain still hurts." I said, looking back toward the giant cage. Timber was already out, but he'd see me the moment I stepped in it. "You'd think after a thousand years of it, it would start to feel like nothing but it doesn't. I've learned to accept it but that doesn't make me numb. I feel it all. Every single time." I wished I hadn't given him another part of myself just now, but I did.

"Fear!" Darrian called over to him and Ryan finally moved Fear's eyes off me. Strangely, that didn't bother me as much as it should. It was just a layer of darkness—a new skin, hiding the boy I killed, the touch I craved, the monster I hated, and the man I was now desperate to save alongside with me. "Bring yours up, she's next." I groaned at the way he called me Ryan's, but this mark made it true no matter what I said otherwise

Red eyes, pale skin, and black horns curved from his darkened hair all seemed more threatening than the death I was about to face locked in the cage. He tilted his chin and smiled. "You're up, Blue."

I didn't say a word, I just stood up and walked to where Darrian held the cage door open for me. I could see it in his eyes, he still thought it was a waste for me to go in the cage and die. Luckily, I didn't stay dead.

"How unfortunate that you ran into an entity such as Fear, otherwise, you'd live another day." I ignored Darrian's remark and stepped into the cage. The crowd went ballistic, roaring and screaming that I was a girl—it wasn't uncommon for women to be thrown in fights, so it must have been awhile since their last one. I ignored the catcalls and lewd remarks and stopped once I stood in the center of the stage. My opponent stepped in next and I frowned, quickly recovering by placing my hands on my hips and pretending I wasn't intimated by the ogre walking around me. I wouldn't win this fight even if I stepped into this pit of death willing to put up a fight. Ogres were huge and tough as nails. Most of the time, weapons couldn't even penetrate through their skin. With my bare hands, I didn't stand any chance.

"This isn't even a fight," the ogre laughed as he circled me, eyeing me with amusement and as prey instead of an opponent. "This is a death sentence for the poor child."

I clenched my teeth, keeping a calm face when I was two seconds from losing it. I wasn't a child. I was just slender, but my height was taller than most women. I looked through the bones to spot Ryan. He wasn't in his seat and it took a second to find him standing outside the cage with his clawed hands wrapped around the bones that made the cage. His gaze was on mine, and I couldn't for the life of me figure out what he might be thinking.

"Come on, Darrian," the ogre said. "I need a challenge, not a doll to break apart—not that I mind, but I came for a fight." The crowd laughed at his announcement.

"How about you sit this one out and I'll give you a better opponent after this one?" Darrian asked the ogre. I hardly ever blushed, but I did feel my entire face flush with anger and embarrassment. It was one thing to fight and lose, but it was a completely different matter when you were ridiculed right in front of people by saying you weren't worth the fight.

"Sure, I wouldn't mind watching someone else break her anyway." The ogre took one last look at me before stepping off the stage.

"Saved you a little less pain, Blue," Darrian said and I couldn't help but feel a flare of anger at him for calling me Blue. It only felt right coming from Ryan. Was I dealing with a case of Stockholm syndrome?

"Don't call her that," Ryan yelled through the cage at Darrian. His eyes were bright red and murderous. "And I didn't ask you to make her pain less. I want to see what she's made of."

Darrian looked back and forth between us before he held up his hand in defeat and walked across the ring. He brought my new opponent in the ring. He looked normal, but no one was normal down here. He'd show his true colors soon enough. He was a lot smaller than the ogre, but still way bigger than me.

"I'm gonna sink my canines in you, little one," he said and I suppressed an eye roll. *Werewolf.*

"To make things more interesting and easier for both opponents," Darrian said as two men started placing weapons against the cage. "This fight will have weapons. Choose and let the fight begin."

Once the weapons were hung and they exited the ring, the door was closed leaving me trapped with my opponent. The weapons were my chance, my stomach fluttered with excitement. No, the weapons were my victory. I turned and stepped toward the weapons on my side of the ring. "Don't worry, I'll wait," the werewolf said. "I don't need anything but my teeth to tear you to shreds."

I worked best with swords and daggers. They were the only things I ever used and I was happy to see the daggers lined up. I didn't even hesitate to grab one. Once in my hand, I flipped it around, enjoying the feel of one again before turning around.

"You think I'm going to let you bury that into my flesh while I'm tearing out your neck?" the werewolf asked and everyone enjoyed his jabs at me. "I don't think—"

The dagger hit its mark, sinking into the werewolf's forehead. His eyes widened with death as his body fell backwards. The crowd went silent. Clearly, no one was paying attention to the way I held the dagger when I threw it. Maybe most of them weren't even paying attention just like the werewolf pegged me for an easy kill. I stepped over the dead werewolf and pulled the dagger out of his head. The crowd finally went berserk.

"Well," Darrian stepped back in the ring. "No one expected that. There wasn't even a fight," his tone was disapproving but I didn't give a shit. "Who wants to see her put up a fight?" The demons roared their answer. Ryan rested his head against the cage, watching me intently. I had to look away, it made me uncomfortable. He left the ring again and three more men entered in his place. I squinted, confused until I realized all three were my opponent. I stepped back to the weapons and grabbed a thin sword and another dagger. I had no place to hold weapons on my body so I was stuck holding both. When I turned around one of the men were in my face, then I was being slung against the weapons that were hung. Pain slithered up and down my body as I fell to the ground. I was hunkered down on my knees, playing the part of being in pain when he bent down to grab me and my sword went into the bottom of his mouth and out the top of his head. One of the others jerked me up by the hair and lifted my hand that held the dagger. He was moving it toward my chest. When I tried to let go of the dagger, he gripped tighter so that I couldn't. I screamed and gritted my teeth as the dagger sunk into my chest. I couldn't breathe through the pain. I knew I was about to die but the moment he let go, I bent down and grabbed the dagger I used on the werewolf. He was there to stop me, but instead of him, I aimed at the other opponent who stood and waited. I hit him in the chest and he fell to his knees. So did I.

I sucked in for air. I sucked in for oxygen that never reached until I fell over next.

I was back to life in seconds. My resurrecting process was quicker now that I wasn't going through hell every hour of the day, but if I died again tonight then it would keep getting slower and slower. I raised up and pulled the dagger from my chest and the crowd started screaming at my opponent. He had his back turned, but he looked back at me with a surprised expression. "So, I didn't kill you yet?" He smiled.

"Afraid not," I lied, pulling the sword out of the demon's head and standing up. He was fast which told me he might be a vampire. He had me pinned against the cage. The thin sword was between us and he continued to press it into me. It took everything I had to keep it from eating my flesh while he wasn't even trying hard. I closed my eyes and wedged my leg between us. I kicked him in the groin, it created enough pain that I pushed him away. I swung the sword and it sliced his shoulder. He raised his head and released his fangs.

"Why you—" he hissed.

I predicted his move the moment he revealed his fangs. I flipped my sword backward and aimed it over my shoulder just as he moved behind me. The blade was in his mouth before his fangs could reach my neck. I pushed it further down his neck until it reached his heart then let go of the sword and his body blew out into nothing. I bent over to catch my breath.

The crowd that once laughed at me was now starting to scream for Blue. Darrian was back in the ring. "I think we have a winner," he announced and the demons only grew louder. "What do you say? Want to see if the next demon can take her life?"

They answered with enthusiasm, but Ryan's voice was heard, "She's done for the night."

Darrian's eyes lit up. "Does that mean you'll bring her back tomorrow night?"

Ryan observed me. "Sure," he answered, and I closed my eyes. "Put me up next." I reopened them and met his gaze, dumbfounded. Darrian was happy to hear that.

The ogre stepped in and walked to me. "I'll show you what a real fight looks like," he said with a wink, then he laughed and his whole green belly jiggled with it. I looked away disgusted. Ryan stepped in next and the crowd was a lot crazier now.

"Since Fear's immortal, all you have to do is kill him once and you'll be the victor," Darrian told the ogre with a look of pity. "If he kills you… then you know how it goes."

"Quiet," the ogre shook his head. "Immortal chum will be the one losing tonight." Darrian shook his head and motioned for me to exit the ring with him. I started walking when Ryan grabbed my wrist.

"No good luck kiss?" he asked. I wanted to kiss him, but not when he looked like Fear.

"Like you need it," I said out of annoyance, but I hadn't expected it to sound like a compliment or that if I was betting, it would be on him. I tried to wrench my wrist free and looked away from him. Then his hand was wrapped around my waist and he spun me around. I was pressed against his chest and on instinct, I pushed away but his claws dug into my back. I hissed and finally looked up.

That was when he kissed me. Painfully. Brutally. I refused to give him access inside my mouth, so his hand found my ass and gripped hard. His claws were awfully close to nipping my skin if not already. I gave in and opened my mouth to bite his bottom lip. His blood flooded my mouth and he groaned—the sound brought my lust back to the surface from earlier. I let him invade my mouth with his tongue. And that was enough for him because he released me the second he tasted me.

"Do you want me to draw out his suffering or end him quickly?" he asked, and what an odd question to ask after kissing someone…

"I don't care what you do," I told him. His eyes searched my face before releasing me. The game we've been playing since our encounter was a dangerous one, so why did my chest feel like it had been dipped into a bowl of bliss? Maybe I wasn't much different than Fear. I had my own crazy needs… Needs I didn't even know I had until meeting Ryan.

I walked out and the fight started and ended quickly. Ryan gave him a quick death with his tail. The women were going crazy for him. Which was weird considering he was in Fear's form, yet their panting after him made me restless.

My name was whispered that night during Ryan's fight. I couldn't read Timber's expression as he walked away without another word.

CHAPTER ELEVEN

Ryan

To hurt her or not to.

To fuck her or not to.

To give Fear what we both wanted or not.

I was playing a dangerous game with Fear when it came to Blue. She was impressive, dammit. Even in the fights, she held her own. Even when her dress was riding up her legs as she fought… I found her cute with her I'd-fuck-you-over-in-your-sleep-if-you'd-let-me glares, and she was hardly intimidated by me.

When I kissed her in the caged ring, it had been because I was caving. I wanted her. I liked her cool, moody personality. Not Fear. He was silent tonight, completely satisfied because I fed on Blue alone tonight, even though she wouldn't know. But Blue had many secrets and a name she had yet to give me. Someone had recognized her there. A werewolf and the stench radiating off him was enough to let me know she had been involved with him in some way. He had been surprised yet happy to see her. I was constantly reading his emotions the entire time. I was tempted to go to him and get the answers I wanted about Blue… But I wanted to hear it from her. I knew how women worked. If they spilled their past to you then you were weaseling your way into their mind.

I wanted to stitch myself all through her.

When we ported back to my place, she slipped off her heels and headed through the hallway. She'd been quiet since the kiss. Maybe I shouldn't have kissed her after throwing her into a fight? It was shitty, but I wasn't a good guy. I was merged with a monster that liked when I hurt her, burned in desire when I kissed her and melted every time her body perfumed her desire for me. I was in danger of losing myself to Fear with Blue around, but maybe Fear hadn't realized yet… the obsession he had for her could bring him to his knees.

"You were pretty impressive," I said, breaking the silence with the need to talk to her before she left me in the living room alone. She turned her head slightly to look back at me. "Earlier," I added.

"I refuse the compliment since you were the one that stuck me in there to begin with."

I grinned. "You act like you keep expecting me to be good." I placed my hands in my pockets. "I was once, but I'm not anymore, and I never will be."

She placed her hand against the wall. "I never asked you to be good, Ryan." My name on her lips sounded tempting—valued. "It would be nice to have a choice in what happens to me, though," she sighed and closed her eyes. "I never expected being here would be the most comfortable I've felt in well… *ever*. Maybe I'm just as screwed up as Fear and that scares me."

I rubbed my hand across my chin and watched her in the hall. "I would be offended if I gave a shit," I told her, yet the sound in her voice had me wanting to know why she thought she was no different. "What makes you say that?"

"Because I want to be free." I gave her a puzzled look. She smiled at me and something stirred in my chest that scared the shit out of me. "Molly," she whispered.

"What?"

"Molly," she said again. "My name." She waited there forever to see my reaction until she finally shook her head and slipped into the bathroom.

In the depths of my memory, the name tugged, but I came up empty—or maybe I wouldn't let myself remember.

—

I awoke to the presence of someone standing over me. My first thought was it had to be Blue—should I call her Molly now? I was grinning until I opened my eyes and saw it was Killian peering down at me.

"Having a nice dream?" he asked before grabbing me by the shoulder and forcing me out of bed.

"What the fuck?" I croaked, voice still full of sleep.

"Rise and shine," he said. With his hand still on my shoulder, he faded us out of my bedroom into his giant ballroom. I jerked my shoulder and glared.

“Mind telling me why you disturbed my sleep and stole me from my house?” I asked, and he chuckled.

“Because we thought it was a good idea to fill you in on what we’ve been doing.” Melanie stepped out of the double door between the stairways.

I scratched my head and sighed. “I don’t care who you are sending to the Devil unless I’m the one that gets to kill him.”

Melanie lifted her brows and smirked. “No, that’s not it.” She was excited, pleased about something… it was bursting from her skin. “Ryan, we think we’ve found where he keeps the good demons that couldn’t cross into Heaven before my existence changed that after dying.”

“Huh?”

She groaned. “Didn’t you tell him we’ve been searching for them?” she asked Killian.

“I did, but clearly he’s forgotten,” Killian replied, studying me. “He was a little wired that week with Fear, so maybe that’s why.”

“Just explain,” I groaned, deciding that I didn’t care either way.

“Penny, Ryan, Penny!” Melanie yelled and Penny’s name gained my attention and I looked back up. “And Lincoln and every other demon that deserves an afterlife, if we can find them then we can send them somewhere better.” This was Melanie, full of hope and determination to save others. Her nasty side was just as eager when it came to taking care of the bad guys, like me. Her and Grim knew how to balance their good and evil, but not me. Never me.

“That sounds amazing,” I told her and her smile was so bright. “If I believed you could find them.” Her smiled vanished and her blue eyes studied me closely.

“We will find them, in fact, the place we’re going to might be where they’re at.”

“That’s why we brought you here. We are leaving right now and wanted to see if you wanted to come with us,” Killian said, hooking his arm around Melanie’s shoulder. She was smiling again, hopeful, as she waited for my reply.

“Believe I’ll stay behind,” I said quickly, taking several steps back casually.

"Ryan…" Melanie whispered.

"I don't save people," I told them, "you both know that. I don't even want to save anyone. I've been Fear for a thousand years now, and I only wished I was just saying that but it's the truth."

"Deep down, you're the same guy," she told me. "You've just got lost somewhere along the way trying to please Fear."

I shook my head. "I have two demons and one of them has nothing to do with Fear."

I left. It took a few hours to walk through the woods to get back to my place. I had no portal chip on me and wasn't going to ask Killian to fade me back. I even refused River when he offered his back for me to ride. I'd rather walk and sort out my thoughts. It was hard to be around them the moments they shined so much brighter than me. I didn't kill innocent or good things. I stayed far away from them and instead, took from evil. That part of me I knew was still good, but I had a twisted sense of needs that required pain from others, even my own. Take Blue/Molly for example. All I could think about was breaking her, but then I feared what would become of her once I did.

I opened the door and stepped in the house, Molly jumped from the couch when I entered like she had been anxiously awaiting me. I picked up her emotions… worry, relief, and happiness? She was happy to see me? My eyes fell on her bare legs as my shirt dropped down around her hips when she stood. She tugged on it, obviously aware I was staring. I needed to get her some clothes—her own instead of someone else's. "What happened? I heard you—"

"I had a visit from Grim." Her mouth did a small O and nodded like that explained everything. She placed her hands together and watched me like she was waiting on me to do something or say anything.

I ran my hand against the back of my neck and asked, "Do you want some clothes to wear?" I didn't know why the hell I asked and obviously, she didn't either because the air around her completely changed. Never once had I seen her flustered until that moment. She was full of awkward movements and gestures as she gawked at me. "What?" She shook her head violently. "I don't—"

"You can't keep wearing my clothes when they swallow you whole," I told her, nodding. "Come on, Blue—Molly," I paused, "I think I'll stick with Blue."

She stood there still gawking until her lips curved into a small smile. "O-kay."

After she put on another pair of my jogging pants and slipped on the filthy boots she came here in, we ported to the City of the Dead. We went in one store after the other, often ending up in stores that had no clothes and a bunch of crazy shit that had Molly's eyes lighting up in amusement that I couldn't help but respond to.

Everything she picked out was dark colors and she stuck with pants. While she got the clothes she liked, I tossed in the dresses I knew she'd look good in. When it came to underwear, she chose plainly in that category too, so it was left to me to toss all the lacey shit that would look hot on her on the counter for the hairy demon to checkout. She made no comment about what I threw in the mix, but the scent of her desire filled my senses and had my eyes wanting to roll back it smelled so good.

At some point, while we walked side by side through the street, I couldn't help but say, "Lucky you have me here to bring some color into your life." I opened one of the many bags I carried and nodded for her to look inside. "What is all this dark, gloomy shit. It's like looking at Grim's wardrobe." That made her laugh, so I continued, "It's depressing, you're depressing, Blue. I can't fucking believe how accurate that word goes with you."

"Do you buy clothes for all the women you shoot and place in fights?" she asked with a smile, but I couldn't help but feel the sting. Her smile faded as she watched me.

"Normally the only pain I seek in women is while we're fucking and it's mixed with their pleasure," I said in a hurry. "Or if they come looking for me from Fear's past with Marcus. And I normally stick myself in those fights, but something about you has me extra evil… although, the reason I shot you was because you stabbed me in the neck." I didn't know why I felt the need for her to understand me and the way I worked.

She laughed. "Right." She met my eyes and grinned. "Sorry about that."

I lifted my brow at her. "I wish I could say I was sorry about sticking you in the ring, but all I can think about is watching you kick ass again."

She squinted her eyes at me, disbelieving. "Like you don't enjoy it when I get killed…" she muttered.

"That too," I admitted with a grin.

"You asshole," she yelled, but she was smiling when she said it. "Fighting is no big deal to me. I enjoy it. It's one of the only things I know, although, it pissed me off when you gave me no choice in the matter."

"What's something else you know?" I found myself asking.

"Surviving." She kept her eyes forward instead of on me, almost like she was picturing something. "I know a bit about surviving. Pain. I know all about pain. And I know wants." This time she did look at me with a frown. "Wanting something can take you down a dangerous path, not just for yourself, but everyone you encounter. My want did a lot of damage… and I don't think the damage is over yet."

She looked away when I didn't want her to. I studied her as she walked, wondering how the hell I could get her to spill her secrets and why I was so greedy for them.

"I know a bit about surviving," I started, having no idea why I even chose to. "I chose Fear instead of death. Needs. Know all about that one as well. Can't be the monster if you don't accept your new cravings. Pain. I know all about pain. I need it—can't go without it. If I do, the monster becomes a bigger monster."

"Guilt," she whispered. "I know all about guilt. It's kept me afraid for a very long time."

"The more you speak, the more I want to know about you," I blurted. I stiffened because I hadn't meant to say it aloud.

"Maybe one day," she finally said. "I'll be brave enough to tell you."

I released my breath. "Your guilt. Do you regret whatever it was you did to cause the guilt?"

"Ask me again tomorrow," was her answer.

"You still haven't changed out of my clothes?" I asked her a few hours after we got back from the city. We had bought her a couple of pairs of boots and I chose some heels before heading back home. She was sitting at the table with a book in her hand that she looked up from when I stepped back inside from shooting.

"Are you fixing something to eat soon?" she asked instead of answering my question. I picked up on her feelings… she was hungry. "I'm hungry," she added like she knew exactly what I was doing.

I shifted on my feet. "There's plenty in the fridge."

She looked down at the book quickly then back at me, almost lazily. "I can't cook," she admitted with the drop of a shy smile.

I couldn't help but grin. "You're kidding? And you're how old?"

She huffed and looked back down at the book, but I could tell she wasn't even focused on it. "I've been locked up here and there for a thousand years, I can't cook for myself when I'm in a dark cell with some thrown in scraps." I flinched at her past. That was all she ever talked about was being a prisoner like it was the only thing she knew. I was keeping her here because of the mark, but I wasn't locking her up, was I?

"What about before that?"

She shrugged her shoulders. "I was dead, so I couldn't eat, and I was too young when I did die to have had a chance to learn."

I grinned playfully. "Well, Blue, looks like we have a bit in common. I was a ghost before I became Fear. How'd you end up immortal?"

She kept her eyes on the book. "The Devil."

I hadn't expected that. "That sounds… dangerous."

"It was foolish… and desperate on my part."

"There's sandwich meat in the fridge." I nodded toward the fridge. "Make you one and then come out and shoot with me once you're through." I turned back toward the door.

"Shoot?" I wasn't even looking at her, but I was sure her brows were bending together in the middle with her dubiousness. "Am I being hunted again?" Not being able to help myself, I inhaled and started sniffing out her feelings. She was cautious with a hint of… eagerness?

I couldn't resist twisting my head back around and cocking a brow. "Is there a hint of hope in that question?"

She blew out an irritated breath and sucked in her jaws. I was grinning because no matter how hard she was trying to pretend otherwise, she knew I could taste everything she was feeling. She finally gave up and said, "Stop grinning at me like that or I swear, I'll stab you with a knife again."

"You won't need a knife." I waved my hand around dismissing the idea. "I'll show you how to do it with a rifle."

"So, now not only do you get to kill me in fights but now you want me to kill you?"

I made my way to the door and nodded. "Our next hunt will be a lot better if you can put up a fight. Make things more interesting that way."

"I guess being Fear has loosened a few screws 'cause you're so messed up." She had no idea, but then I picked up the scent of her excitement and lust that she was trying to push away and hide. My dick hardened.

Maybe she did have an idea.

——

"It's uncomfortable," she grunted, adjusting the rifle against her shoulder. "And heavy," she complained some more. "I'd rather use a sword."

"It's because you aren't used to it," I sighed next to her. She smelled good, real good, but that was easy to overlook when her mouth wouldn't stop complaining for two seconds while I tried to show her how to hold the .243 Winchester I had brought out for her. It probably had the least amount of kick and since she had never used one before, that was for the best. "Remember where the safety is?" I asked and felt more than seen her roll her eyes.

"You've only shown me five times in the last five minutes."

After several more seconds of her sighing and trying to throw the rifle down, she finally held it partially right. Her posture was off and she was a little stiff, but that was something she'd ease into as she got the hang of holding it up.

"The scope's the tricky part," I said, leaning into her and she groaned. Her eyes moved over mine and she quietened. "Concentrate," I told her because she filled with lust just like that, the intoxicating scent made it hard to keep my focus. She quickly peeked into the scope as if to pretend her feelings weren't giving me *feelings* down below.

"I don't see anything," she started up again.

I grinned as I watched her shove her eye into the scope trying to see. Her face was equal determination and frustration. "Because your eye is too close. Pull back some and you'll eventually see out of it. You don't want your eye to be too close to it when you pull the trigger anyway." I waited a minute before I said, "Surely, you can see out of it now."

"No, it's black," she answered and my forehead wrinkled. I hadn't aligned the scope in a while, maybe that was the problem.

My hands moved to take the rifle from her. "Here, let me—"

"I can see!" she screamed and I smiled, nodding.

"Do you see the target I placed on the tree?" She nodded immediately. I stood back. "Shoot whenever you're ready. Hold on to it tight or it will blacken your eye when you fire. It's got a kick."

"Okay," she said a little breathless. I inhaled, taking in her exhilaration and resolve.

She fired and the scope clocked her in the eye just like I knew it would if she didn't hold on. She gripped the rifle in one hand and used the other to grab her eye. "Shit." She groaned. I moved next to her and pulled her hand away to look at it. There was a knot visible already but no bruising yet.

"Shoulda listened," I told her, shaking my head and smiling.

"Asshole," she muttered. "Did I hit it?"

I looked at the target trying to see where she hit then looked at her. "Nope, looks like you got the tree instead." I chuckled. "With the way the gun flew back in your face, you're lucky it even hit there. You didn't listen at all when I told you to hold on to that eye-blackener." Still rubbing her eye, she grinned. "Do you want to try again?"

"Do you mean do I want to make my black eye blacker?"

I shrugged my shoulders. "I hardly see the sense in an immortal complaining about a black eye."

"I like my eyes," she argued. "I happen to think it's my best feature other than my legs."

"You're wrong." She gave me a dark look so I continued, "I mean, all of you is pretty damn cute." Did I just call her cute aloud? How lame did I just sound? "I mean, in my opinion." Was I flirting with Blue? Like really flirting, not the kind that got them in your bed, the kind you did when you wanted to keep them? She tugged at her hair and watched me silently. "Of course, I'm a monster that fucks everything so… what's my opinion worth?" That wasn't entirely true, but the need to make my previous words sound less important was heavy on my stomach.

"Then, I guess it's not worth much," she said softly, never letting her eyes stray from mine. And if anything, that was the most irritating and frightening thing about her, the heaviness she placed on me in her gaze. Like she was reaching out and stealing something from me—maybe my soul.

If you don't fuck her tonight, I will.

Fear's words made my heart sink, not because of what he said, but because he was back so soon. *She's not yours*, I thought back to him instead of speaking aloud like I normally did. *Besides, she wants me, not a monster.*

He laughed. *Don't be so sure. There's a darkness in her. Don't pretend you don't see it. You know nothing about Molly… while I know everything.*

He caught me off guard. I had a suspicion that maybe he knew her when he marked her… and the way she looked at me with hatred from the very start, it wasn't just because of the mark. She didn't like that I was Fear… she knew about Fear too, but almost every demon did in the Underworld. *You knew her before the merge,* I said to him.

Yes, immensely. I felt my skin burning with rage. The thought of Molly being with Fear while he was Marcus made me want to rip him out of my body so I could kill him. *I know exactly what you're thinking even when you don't want me to.*

"Ryan," Blue called my name and I lifted my eyes off the ground and rubbed my neck. Blue was mine, Molly would soon be too. If she couldn't be, then she was no ones. I wouldn't even allow her past to hold a claim on her, not if Fear was a part of it. "Do you want me to grab us something to drink?" she offered, her nervousness rolling off her in waves and I found it strange that she was suddenly nervous.

"Did you know Fear before I became him?" I asked and that one question shot fear up her spine. Her mouth fell open and all that bottled-up anxiety came pouring out. I breathed it in out of habit, although it didn't please me as much as her fear once did.

"Why are you asking that?" She sounded small, so unlike my Blue. "Did he say something? Is he threatening to come out?" she asked quickly.

See? was all Fear had to say and I closed my eyes.

Obviously, I see you've done something that has her terrified of you and me. I won't let you manipulate me into having my way with her because I'm going to, just not on your terms.

He cackled inside my head. *Not if I get to her first.*

I bent over, gripping my head. "Ryan?" Blue sounded worried. She should be. Fear wanted out to prove he could take her from me—before me. This game was going to kill me because the thought of him hurting her made me bleed out. For the first time, in a long time, I felt like the boy that faded over time. I didn't want to hurt Blue anymore—at least not right now when the need to protect her was stronger. I hadn't wanted to protect someone since—Melanie and my sister… It felt good.

"Blue…" I gritted my teeth.

Stop resisting, he told me.

"It's probably a good idea for you to leave me. Fear's coming and he wants you," I told her. Her eyes widened and without further explanation, she took off into the house. I knew she couldn't run from me, but I could take him away from her—at least for a while.

I dug my hand into my pants pocket and pressed the portal chip, then I was gone, dragging myself into pleasures, hoping to keep the monster at bay.

CHAPTER TWELVE

Molly

Ryan left. Well, he must have considering I stood at the edge of the kitchen for the longest time, expecting him to come barging in as Fear, but he didn't.

So, I waited and waited for him to come back. Minutes turned to hours and my mind was more like mush from exhausting my thoughts… I should have used the liquid in the vial sooner, I could sense the calmness in Ryan all day but I hadn't because I had been distracted by his company… and when I did remember, it was already too late and Fear woke from his slumber.

Most of my thoughts were of just Ryan, though and what he might be doing. My stomach churned with the possibilities. I did not like the way he made me feel… I wasn't used to feeling weird. Not weird, just different. I felt different around him. Or maybe it was just him and not me, but then these were my feelings, not his so he couldn't be the blame (see what I mean, I couldn't even think normally). I didn't want to feel strange, I just wanted to protect myself, free Ryan from his struggle with Fear, and somewhere during rescuing us I'd like to climb on top of him and have my way with him, but that was beside the point. I'd really like him to have his way with me too, but that didn't look like that was going to happen. It was downright shameful how often I became a dog in heat every time he came near me today and there's no way he couldn't have picked up on my desire, yet he didn't do anything all day. Not that it was terrible... I'd admit I enjoyed our chats and little disputes over ridiculous things. I still didn't see how we managed to argue over every piece of clothing I chose, though. He got them for me, though just not without getting what he wanted me to wear as well.

But of course, the one captor I wanted to take advantage of me, wouldn't.

And then I drifted to sleep on the couch waiting on him or Fear to return and I dreamed memories from a past I thought I forgot.

I stood at the edge of the door listening to Mom and Dad's raised voices. This night should have been no different from any other, they argued all the time, and sometimes Dad hurt her. That's why she always made me stay away when it happened, so he wouldn't take it out of me too. She said Daddy couldn't control his anger, but when she tried to tell him he needed to go to a doctor to get it fixed, it only made him worse, so she was careful with every word she said around him...

I was afraid of Dad. One minute he was yelling at her and breaking her with words and fists, then the next he was cradling her in his arms saying how much he loved her. His anger was never toward me, even that night it was only by mistake. I kind of never existed to him, or at least that's the way it felt.

Dad was still yelling, Mom was crying, then she was at my bedroom door stepping in. Her eyes were wild and full of fear as she shoved me toward the closet. "Molly, I need you to listen to Mommy and go hide in the closet. Daddy's not okay right now, please," she said, all the while pushing me into the closet. That was her first mistake, coming to keep me safe when I wasn't the one that needed to be saved from him.

"Don't touch the fucking kid!" Dad yelled, following her into my room.

At this point, I was nervous, full of words and protests of how much I wished he'd stop being mean to Mom, but like always, I was mute in the face of fear. "Nothing's wrong with me, stop telling our daughter that something's wrong with her father." Then he yanked her back by the hair. In his hands, I saw something I'd never seen before. A knife. Dad liked to use his hands on her, but never anything else. I looked toward Mom, focusing on her eyes, hoping she saw it too, but she was face down so I doubt she did.

My feet were moving on instinct. Dad pulled her up by the hair and I grabbed his shirt sleeve and tugged. He took one look at me and shoved me aside. "Stay out of this. This is between me and your mom."

"Dad, don't hurt Mommy," I cried. "Please stop this."

Mom was right about Dad. He never saw anything wrong with his personality. And when he was called out on something, it only made him worse. "Your dad isn't doing anything wrong, it's your mother that does shit wrong!" he yelled but I never saw her do anything wrong. In my eyes, she was perfect. Her only imperfection was choosing to stay in this house. She could have saved us from this night.

"Claude, please don't do this in front of Molly," she begged him and he shoved her onto my bed in reply.

"Stop babying her," he told her. "She's nine years old!" He was wrong, I turned ten last month, but like I thought, I was invincible to Dad unless it came to using my existence to hurt Mom.

"Claude!" Mom yelled. "Why are you holding your knife?"

"Why? Do you think I'm gonna hurt you?" He was already hurting her. Every single day. I stood there crying. "Stop crying, Molly!" He threw his anger at me, but I couldn't stop the tears.

"Please, Claude. Let's stop. I'm sorry. I'm sorry. Whatever it is, I'm sorry." She reached for his hand and for a second, I thought he was going to let her pull him in, calm the beast inside him, but his knife was also in his hand and once he realized that, he growled and jerked away, thinking she was trying to take it from him.

"Don't play your games with me," he said right before he smacked her across the face. Then he was climbing over top her. My eyes followed the knife. He was so mad, I was afraid he would accidentally cut her with it, so I ran to him and pulled on his shirt again. He hissed and shoved me aside again. Mom grabbed the knife from his hand and everything flew out of control. He went to take the knife from her the same time I grabbed his side again—he jerked his hand back with the knife.

"Dad—". I didn't get to finish the word. Something stung my side. I looked down the same time Dad did. The knife was embedded into my ribs. His eyes told me that it was a mistake, but he was insane and carrying a knife around to threaten Mom was proof of that.

"Molly!" Mom screamed just as I fell to the ground. She was on her knees beside me, her hands shaking as they hovered around the knife. She didn't take it out, but she was crying and screaming.

"I didn't mean to," Dad told her.

"Call 9-1-1!" she screamed at him and when he didn't, she stood and he grabbed her shoulders.

"You can't call. Do you want to send me away?" he asked her.

"We don't have time for this. If she doesn't get to the hospital, we are gonna lose her! You'll lose me if I lose her!" she threatened him, but it didn't work.

She screamed and begged and pleaded with him, but he held her there in the room while I bled out. His own flesh and blood. She kept telling me sorry repeatedly. When my pain stopped, he led Mom out of my room where I stood above my dead body. I could hear her cries as I stood there trying to understand what was happening. A figure stood beside me, beckoning to me with a light—a passage—but a gunshot echoed through the house. I ran from it and found myself in the living room where Mom's lifeless body lay with Dad's gun in her hand.

Dad dropped the phone cord he was yanking out of the wall and ran to her, and this time, he cried. And cried and cried as he clung to her body, something he didn't do for me. She rose like me, dead—as a ghost and when she saw me, she came to me crying, wrapping her arms around me. The light came for me and the dark figure stood next to me once again. His presence called to me, trying to trick me into the passage, but Mom wanted to go so she tugged us toward it. Right when she began to take us inside, I jerked away from her. She screamed my name, but I ignored her, the same way Dad ignored me all my life, and the same way she did when she refused to take us from this house.

I wouldn't leave this way—so I ran.

—

I stood outside Dad's cell and watched him. He was alive and I was dead. As a ghost, I was stuck the same and I clung to nothing but my anger and hatred. The lights flickered because I made them. He stayed cold because I made sure of it, but I could never hurt him.

And, I wanted to hurt him.

The most I've managed to do was push him once, and sometimes I was sure he could hear me when I called to him, because he sat on his bed cupping his ears, rocking back and forth telling the voices to stop, but since he was always crazy, I could never be sure it was my voice he heard.

A prison wasn't only a place for bad people. I walked the halls and I saw things that made my skin crawl. Demons stood behind prisoners, bending down to their ears, I could hear the evil of their voices but I couldn't make out the things they said, but I was sure that these people were being controlled by the monsters that spoke in their ear. And those voices were what put them in this place.

I would wait by Dad... wait for his monster, the one that whispered in his ear like so many other men in this place, but it never came. Dad was his monster so none came for him.

Until one night, the scariest one of all came for him. Even the demons that lived in this place like me hid from him, but I refused to leave Dad. One by one, the horned devil would enter each cell, I'd hear their terrified screams, then nothing. On to the next, he'd go laughing and speaking with a smooth, beautiful voice, unlike his physical appearance. I didn't know what he was doing to them. I stood outside Dad's cell and waited for him.

Dad sat on his bed, rocking, cupping his ears and screaming it was coming for him—and it was.

A long, black tail swayed behind him, shiny and smooth like the horns on his head. His skin was pale and his eyes blood red. He stopped in front of Dad's cell not paying attention to me. "No!" I screamed at him.

He finally looked back at me and grinned. "What did you say little ghost?"

"This one is mine," I told him, pointing toward Dad in his bed.

He arched a brow, studying me curiously. "No, it's not." He turned toward the cell and slipped through the bars like a ghost.

I was furious, my skin burning with my anger. I clenched my fists and screamed. Every light in the place shattered. He looked back at me the same time Dad looked up and saw him. Dad's eyes widened and he tried pressing himself further into the wall away from him.

"No, no, no, no," Dad whispered, then he screamed.

"Do you want me to kill him... what's your name?" he asked.

"Molly," I seethed. "And no, I want to kill him."

"Too bad," he answered and turned. "His self-loathing and regret are beautiful... and his mind is a chaotic mess. I'll take it from him." And he did. He sucked the life out of Dad and once he was done, he dropped Dad's body back on the bed and turned. I looked at his lifeless body and sighed. "You were only wasting away trying to hurt that man, he was already killing himself on the inside. I could make use of you, Molly. Come with me and live like the living instead of the dead."

I snarled and walked away from the monster who killed my revenge.

Now, I had nothing left in this world to cling to.

———

My ghost days became invading people's homes and becoming a voyeur. I was fascinated by all the things I would have been able to do if I had still been alive. I would have been an adult already and being fucked against the dryer looked like it felt good. Or at least the woman in front of me that day made it seem that way.

I even started possessing women just so I could experience what it felt like, but being dead was a bitch, and she refused to give me any kind of feeling other than my own hate. I couldn't feel anything. I couldn't taste anything. Nothing. Nothing. Nothing. Even when I possessed a body.

A hateful ghost made a powerful poltergeist. My body even began to change, I looked less like a little girl and more like a monster. I was rotting away, becoming a plague for humans when the demon found me.

"Molly, I see you've graduated to a poltergeist."

I ignored him because he entered the house I was currently giving hell, putting the woman through turmoil as I drained the life out of her and tore apart her family—it was what I did as a poltergeist. Destroy families.

"Go away, I'm busy." Even my voice was changing. I sounded nothing like a girl.

"Come with me and I can give you what you want." His words didn't affect me because he couldn't know what I wanted. "A body. One that feels."

And I stopped everything I was doing to the woman of the house and turned around to face the horned devil. "How can you do that?" I asked.

"I'm powerful. I can do anything and I could use something like you." Maybe he was the Devil.

"What's your name?" I asked him.

"Fear."

I woke with Ryan's finger pressing into my forehead. I grabbed my head and leaned away from him. He was standing above me, eyes red, expression dark. "What are you doing?" I croaked, still feeling out of the place from memories I didn't want to keep.

"So, that's how you became so destructive." He took his finger to my ear and traced the edges. What was he talking about? Did he— "The man was your dad." He studied me as I pushed away from him.

"You aren't Ryan." My foot found his chest and pushed him further away. He let me and plopped down on the couch next to me. "Were you inside my head?" I asked, feeling exposed to the enemy. "You were the one that planted the memories in my head to begin with!" I accused him.

"You were bad before you met me, Molly." He snatched my foot out of nowhere and I yelped as he yanked half my body onto his lap at once. I raised up on my elbows and glared at him, but made no move to get away from him.

"Your point?"

"You keep trying to blame me for the evil inside you." His hand slid over the jogging pants I wore and I closed my eyes and forced no reaction. This wasn't Ryan even if he looked like him. *Stupid body, do not respond!* "You're good at that, Molly, blaming others so you can ignore the things you've done." I couldn't force myself away from the truth of his words, though.

I sighed, still not opening my eyes. "And you're doing what you do best, getting underneath people's skin. Although you didn't have to get underneath my dad's, you just had to let him see you and what was left of his mind broke."

"Marcus was my biggest mistake, but he did know where to find the best places for fear. Every emotion I took from your dad was worth that trip. Plus, if Marcus hadn't taken us there, I would have never encountered you."

I finally opened my eyes. "I should have taken my afterlife when I had the chance because my *worst* encounter was you."

He grabbed my hips and forced my attention on him. "You never met me, not really. Just bits and pieces. I didn't want the things Marcus wanted." I rolled my eyes and his fingers dug deeper into my sides. I hissed. "Every emotion on you is worth savoring," he told me and I closed my eyes again, but my damn insides were quivering.

I knew this was Fear… why was I responding? I had to get rid of the problem. "Why do you look like Ryan right now?"

"You're fond of his looks… he knows and I know you want to fuck him, but he keeps holding off… so I'm going to."

"Why?" I said quickly. "You obviously marked me for some reason, so why all this waiting. Why not just do what it is you plan to do to me instead of worrying about who I want to fuck." I knew his answer already, I just needed to hear him say it.

"Burying myself in your cunt is exactly what I want," he said as he moved one of my legs off his lap and placed it behind him so that he could climb between them. "Along with your fear, hate, anger, everything. I want *all* of them."

He climbed above me and I didn't fight him. My thoughts were whirling, a jumbled mess. I didn't want to look up at him either because I knew my body would betray me completely, but the moment his hand slipped inside my pants, I reacted, pushing at him. I didn't want this with him. I've despised him for so long. That didn't change just because I found out Fear wasn't who I thought he was. He also wasn't the one I could keep blaming for my own actions. He was right, I was bad long before I crossed paths with him, but ultimately our meeting led to Ryan's death. Everything always came back to Ryan and I didn't know why. I didn't care about my past life, and I didn't feel much guilt toward the things I've done for Fear… just that one. Ryan.

Even now, my body burned for him and his body was right above me, *his* fingers wandering right where I'd beg him to take them, but he wasn't present here. Just his body, one that was filled by Fear. And I didn't want Fear. He had nothing to offer. Everything he had, I carried on my own. We were alike more than I liked to admit, but I was admitting it now and I didn't want his wickedness. I wanted something good. I'd take pain and pleasure—everything with it, as long as it was from Ryan.

I grabbed his hand and tried to pull it out of my pants. "Stop!"

He bent down next to my ear and whispered, "Why? You want this."

No, I wanted Ryan. "I want nothing from you," I spat.

He lifted his head and met my eyes. "Even pleasure?" He didn't give me a chance to respond and he was flipping me over onto my stomach, his erection pressing into my ass. When I tried to raise up, he pressed his palm into my back and held me there. "Of course, I don't need your permission to take it."

I took a deep breath, feeling my disgust and rage bubbling to the surface. "Oh, I know, and it's the very reason I don't want to give it to you." I tilted my head slightly, trying to look back at him. "Just know, taking it from me doesn't mean I give it to you. You'll never taste any pleasure coming from me, my body won't respond." And it wouldn't, now that I came to terms with what I wanted, I'd shut myself down mentally if I had to. "Ryan, on the other hand, I'll let him have it all."

He stilled above me. "Your repulsion for me," he lifted himself off me, "strangely doesn't taste good."

I raised up on the bed and scowled. "You disgust me!"

He sat on his knees and just looked at me. "You think Ryan would even want anything to do with you if I hadn't marked you?" he asked. "What about if he knew you were the ghost-girl that killed him and treated him like a pet when he was controlled by the demon Marcus made him?" I flinched.

"I know!" I hissed. "I know… I stole his life, and now I want his new one." I shook my head in astonishment. "But the moment he learns who Molly really is…"

"You're terrified… I can taste it." He inhaled before closing his eyes. "Even that doesn't please me."

"What?" I glared at him. "Are you going to get rid of me now that my hatred of you no longer pleases you?"

He moved from the couch and backed away, oddly strange. "I still want something from you, Molly… I just don't know what it is anymore."

Then he left.

CHAPTER THIRTEEN

Ryan

I found myself in a bed full of women and men. One of them mumbled something under her breath while I tried to untangle myself from all the limbs on top of me. “Fear?” one of them whispered in that throaty voice that told me Fear had done something pleasurable last night. Which was weird as hell if you knew him. I mostly woke up surrounded in death and carnage when he came out… not something like this.

Don’t get me wrong, Fear enjoyed sex, but he liked it with pain. And he loved to take women in fear of him, but this…

“Where are you going?” someone asked me.

“Come back.”

Jesus, what the hell?

I grabbed my discarded clothes all around the room and ported to my living room.

“Ryan?” Molly’s voice caused me to jump, I still hadn’t wrapped my head around those voices calling to me adoringly from Fear’s doing. Sure, I could make women like that, but Fear, he made them run away screaming.

“Are you still wearing my clothes?” I asked.

I took her in as she stood at the fridge with it open and a bottled water in her hand. Her dark hair was tossed over her left shoulder and she looked beautiful. What was most surprising was that I hadn’t woken up next to Molly… Fear had come out for her.

“At least I have some on.” Her eyes fell on my shirtless chest and unzipped jeans. I quickly threw on my shirt and zipped my jeans up, strangely feeling bad that I came home like that.

“Looks like Fear had a lot of fun without me last night,” I told her and her eyebrows slanted. “Did he… come for you last night?” I had to know. I was kind of afraid to know, but furious at the idea that he did all at once.

She nodded. "He did."

My blood ran hot. I was across the room within a breath and grabbed her arms. "What did he do?" I never felt so possessive before, but I hated the idea of Fear having her instead of me.

"He wanted inside me, but I refused." Despite everything my body must have done the night before, the words "inside me" shot lust into my system.

I shook my head. "Fear doesn't take no for an answer."

"He did last night," was all she said and closed the fridge door. "He did," she said again with a hint of irritation this time. "And he got what he wanted from someone else."

You are what he wants, I wanted to tell her, but I didn't. I couldn't believe Fear.

Fear... what are you thinking? I asked him.

I'm thinking I want her to fucking crave me like I do her... I was stunned at his admittance to me. *It's strange, her hatred of me doesn't appeal to me anymore... but her lust does. Lucky for me, she already wants you, so I can still have it.*

I smiled. *I think that means she's mine, not yours.*

Smell that? he asked and I took in a breath and breathed in Molly's anger. *She fucking hates me, but now she realizes I've gone and fucked someone—a lot of someone's because she didn't want me and it was your body I used and it's eating her alive. Damn, her anger tastes good right now, doesn't it?*

I found myself agreeing with him.

"Why are you smiling like that?" she asked me, and I turned to look at her. Her eyes were wary, but hinted with anger. The longer she stared at me, the stronger it became too. "Seriously, you were just staring at nothing with a creepy ass grin on your face..." Her eyes darkened. "Are you Fear?"

"No, but he was telling me about what he did last night... I think you missed out." I couldn't believe I said that, but when her eyes looked more like lasers and steam might as well been blowing from her ears, I was glad I did.

She's so fucking jealous right now. I told Fear and he laughed in my head with me. I shouldn't be so pleased with her like this… jealousy was a dangerous emotion because it meant attachment, but for some reason, the idea of her attachment felt good. I couldn't remember a time I found myself so damn happy and devious at the same time.

"Are you jealous, Blue?" I stepped toward her and her eyes darted for the hallway. She was planning her escape. She wasn't ready to admit anything to me yet even though she knew I could taste them all.

"Stop looking so damn smug. I turned him down and I'd do the same to you."

Liar, liar… I think we should deny her, Fear sung and I grinned.

"Then, I guess I know where not to go asking for it," I said indifferently.

I loved that she squirmed and couldn't hide that little stubborn gaze from me. "Asshole," she muttered and slipped into her bedroom and my chuckle followed after her.

She came back thirty minutes later looking dejected and annoyed. "I'm hungry," she admitted and I couldn't help but crack another grin. So, her hunger was more important than her pride… I'd do well to remember that for the times I pissed her off in the future.

"I'm guessing you want me to make you something?" I asked. She looked away and nodded. "Say please and I will."

She glared at me for the longest time, seeing if I was serious until she finally dropped her head in defeat and said, "Feed me, damn it…" She lifted her head up. "Please."

"Okay." I stood and walked into the kitchen. "But, come here. It's time you learn 'cause I'm not going to keep feeding us." I stopped abruptly when I realized how that sounded and she did too, so I wondered if she felt as weird as I felt. I no longer knew what this game with her was, but it felt more dangerous than ever before.

"Okay," she answered quickly, almost shyly.

Yes, this was a very dangerous game. Her little meek voice was just as good as her spitfire temper—seemed Molly was just good all around.

CHAPTER FOURTEEN

Molly

Ryan stepped into my room and said, “I thought I told you to get dressed thirty minutes ago.”

I rolled over and glared. “Go away.”

He smirked. “Are you still mad about earlier?”

Yes, I was. You didn’t make fun of someone trying to learn to cook. I did not know oil shot up and attacked you like that. He told me to stick the sliced potatoes in the hot oil… and I did, and I was attacked. And I jumped when I was burned and dropped the potatoes I hadn’t yet put in there.

“I refuse to even try to learn to cook if you’re just going to make fun of me.”

He nodded. “Come on, I couldn’t help it,” he sounded pitiful and earnest, and damn it, I no longer felt mad about it. “If my sister learned how to cook, then I know you can.”

I sat up to a sitting position on the bed. “Your sister?” That’s right, he had a sister if I remembered correctly.

“Yeah, she’s human.”

“Is she still alive?” I asked surprised.

He nodded. “Yeah, she’s an old woman now, but yeah, she’s still kicking.” He leaned against the doorway. “And growing up, she couldn’t do anything for herself which was probably my fault. I might have spoiled her too much—she was my twin.”

I smiled, anxious to continue this conversation, feeling like he was opening up to me in some way by talking about his sister. “Do you go see her often?”

He shook his head and straightened himself back up. “No, she thinks I went onto my afterlife—ya know, Heaven. There’s no way I could tell her the truth of what I’ve become.” Then he raised his head and realized what he was telling me because his eyes got that startled look in them and he stepped out of the room. I climbed out of bed and followed him.

"And all this time, you've not even gone to see her?" I trailed behind him.

He sighed. "Of course I have." He turned around to face me. "Penny would bring me and Grim's wife, Melanie pictures of her over the years, including ones of my niece and nephew before Penny passed away, and I've also made my way into the human world to sneak a peek at them every now and then—"

"Penny?" I interrupted him.

"She was someone that stuck by my side despite everything I'd do," he said sadly.

There was a lump in my throat the size of golf ball. For some reason, the thought of someone being there for him, making him have an expression like that as he thought of her, bothered me. "Sounds like you two were close."

"We were," he told me, then his eyes came together as he watched me. "Are you getting jealous again, Blue?" He drew closer and inhaled me over my shoulder.

I shuddered. "I'm not," I said a little too defensively.

He leaned back and arched a brow, making a tsking sound. "What am I gonna do with you?"

"Any other women I should know about from your past?" The words were like dynamite forced off my tongue. I couldn't even be ashamed I said them because in my head, Melanie's beautiful face appeared telling me the answer I waited for.

"I don't get attached to anybody," was his answer and even then, I knew his answer was a lie. He didn't know I knew he was in this dark place because of his love for Melanie. Now I wished I never thought about it, my chest squeezed—a sweet, beautiful ache, maybe the realest thing I've ever felt, and it was suffocating. I didn't like it, I hated it, and I hated him for probably still loving her. "Your mood is murderous, Blue, why is that?" he teased me as he walked away from me.

I no longer knew which direction to save him or me anymore. I feared I was setting myself up for the biggest payback of all, and even though I knew I deserved this hurt I was walking into, I couldn't help but want to reach up and pluck all others from his dark, dusty heart and place myself there…

And I'd call it home.

———

"Don't worry, Blue, I'm not sticking you in the cage tonight." Ryan pressed his warm palm against my back and led me through the crowd at The Den and I let him, still drowning with dark and possessive thoughts. "I know you said something about *asking* if you wanted to be thrown in there, so I'll give, only because the shit you're feeding me right now is the best of the best… want to tell me why your emotions are so dark?" I chose not to answer.

Darrian weaved his way through the demons and moved in next to Ryan as we walked. Anyone could see that he came to Ryan like he was a little, pleased puppy, glad his owner was returning to make him happy—in Darrian's case, Ryan helped fill his pockets from the bets and his whores… not anymore, if I had something to say about his hands on other women. "Are you sticking her in the cage again?" His eyes shot to me, sliding down the tight little black dress Ryan picked out for me. "She was a big hit; the crowd will be happy to have her back."

Ryan stopped abruptly, so I did. He grabbed Darrian's neck, surprising me and Darrian both. He wore Fear's skin so he was already intimidating, but I'm sure it was worse when he was breathing down your neck. "What part of her are you looking at?" he asked him.

Darrian looked toward me then quickly averted his gaze. "Is there a problem with looking at her? I was just asking if she'd be fighting—"

"And that requires your gaze to trail down her body?"

"Fear—are you messing with me? You know everyone will be looking at her." Darrian tipped his head toward me as Ryan gripped his neck and Ryan's head turned.

"He's right," I told Ryan, scanning the crowd and trying to ignore the buzz coursing through my body at Ryan's reaction to one demon looking at me—it wasn't even one of lust. "You're the one that dressed me to be looked at and now you want to get upset?" I let out a dramatic sigh and Ryan shoved Darrian away and wrapped his arm around my waist and all that buzzing I tried to ignore burned to the surface.

I couldn't play off my desire as nothing when his breath fanned my neck as he leaned over and inhaled, taking it all in. I expected some sort of reply, but instead, he pushed us forward. Darrian studied us quietly as we left him rubbing his neck. A squeak escaped my throat as I felt something slithering up my leg. When I looked down, I saw that it was his tail.

He shoved my body into his and spoke into my ear as we walked, "Careful, Blue, you might end up drawing attention to yourself, and I don't think you'd want that right now." My entire body heated, from the tips of my toes to the hair on my head. His tail wrapped further up my leg and I was so bothered by it that Ryan was practically walking for the both of us.

All I knew was I had seconds to figure out how I should handle the situation. Was I really okay with him handling me this way when his horns and tail were out? "What's wrong?" he whispered cruelly.

Oh, hell. I. Did. Not. Care.

I let him lead us toward the fights as his tail slid closer to my dress, closer to slipping between my thighs. He grabbed a seat, carried it while shoving through demons, and placed it a foot from the cage. He sat down and I stood anxious and wobbly next to him. He grabbed my wrist and pulled me down. "What—" I squeaked as I fell in his lap. What little was left of my hesitancy fizzled out with the hard press of his dick poking my ass.

I slumped back against him just as his tail weaseled its way further up my thigh. I clamped my legs shut, denying it any further access. He wrapped his arms around my stomach and arms and pressed his face into my back. I arched, his breath on my back alone made my body tingle. "What's wrong?" he asked innocently like he had no clue. He was every bit the monster right now, proving the horns to be a nice touch to his scheme.

I placed my hands between my legs, shoving the thin black material between them like that would save me… I didn't want it to save me. I studied his tail as it moved around my leg. It was black and thick… the same width of a dick, and smooth… I also knew he could change it into whatever he wanted. "I don't know what you're planning, but the tail is out," I said, but I wondered why it didn't sound convincing.

"You're more worried about my tail than all the demons that'd watch?" I was shaking, his voice against my back was killing me. His hands moved over my hip bones where he pressed me into him desperately. "What was that? I think I heard a moan?" He bit into the exposed skin of my back and this time the sound did escape my mouth. I dropped my head in defeat. Why was it so easy to feel with him? Every orgasm I've ever had I've had to concentrate and work my body hard for, but with him, it already felt like it was about to be triggered when he hasn't even started.

"You're strangely quiet, Blue," he added.

"What do you want me to say?" I whispered, head still hung in my lap.

"That you want me to fuck you with my tail."

I was on fire, but the thought of admitting that was hard to swallow because that part belonged to Fear even if this was Ryan. I turned my head slightly even though I couldn't see him since his face was pressed into my back. "This is really you, right… this isn't Fear?"

He chuckled. "It's me, but Fear's right here inside my head, watching like the depraved monster he is." One of his hands slid down my thigh. "If you don't want to say it with words, all you have to do is open your legs," he mumbled against my back.

He straightened his back out until his head was at my shoulder. I leaned my head back and closed my eyes, then I parted my legs shamefully. "Do you have to close your eyes to let the monster in?" His words did nothing but feed my lust. "I can't be the only one that can smell your sex. I wonder how many are already watching us?" I wouldn't let myself open my eyes. He put us front and center for a reason…

His tail slid up my leg, slipping between my legs, and when the tip of it pressed into my panties, my eyes shot open and I bit back the sounds I wanted to make. He wrapped one arm around my waist and used the other on my breasts. They weren't big enough to palm, so he made use of my nipples and the fact that I wore no bra. They pebbled against the dress, all he had to do was pinch one between his fingers and I cried out. His tail rubbed against my clit and my senses were going crazy, then his tail slipped inside my panties. He bit the back of my neck and one of my straps fell off my shoulder. His hand left my nipple to force my legs open more, letting them dangle off both of his. The fighters in the ring could most likely see me if they'd take the time to look. I wiggled my shoulders, letting the strap down completely, revealing my breast, then I grabbed Ryan's hands and placed it there, wanting his skin on mine. I panted and squirmed, but he placed the strap back on my shoulder and covered me back up. "None of them get to see any more of your skin." His voice was raspy and beautiful when spoken through desire.

Without any warning, he pressed his tail inside me and his arms barricaded my body from moving whatsoever. The only thing I had control of was my head and I let it fall against him, and even then, he bit into my neck like he wanted control of that too. He moved it out, then back in, before he started moving it in every direction. It felt unbelievable, unrestricted to the ways of a man. I lifted my hips up when the orgasm hit me. I didn't care that I cried out from the pleasure. He kept rubbing the same spot relentlessly to the point that my body was jerking, and then another one came.

And I came and came in such a short amount of time. "Ryan," I pleaded and begged, over and over for it to be over or to never stop, I didn't know. He was thrusting against me, caging me in with his arms as he ruined me with Fear's tail. He slipped in deeper, but he sensed my body's limit on how far he could take it and repeated his movements. My face was wet and I knew it was because my eyes were leaking. It couldn't have been but a short amount of time that he'd been fucking me this way, but it had me unhinged—lost, falling into a place that might even have me beg Fear for it if this pleasure was ever taken from me.

"Fuck, Blue," Ryan groaned. "You aren't ever going to stop, are you?"

"No… don't stop."

"Molly." someone called my name. "Molly." Louder this time and that's when I finally recognized my name. I lifted my head and stared at Timber standing a foot in front of me inside the ring. His expression was unrevealing, but my legs spread open and Ryan's tail between my legs, revealed everything to him. I closed my legs quickly, lust draining from my body. Ryan gripped me tightly, he didn't want to stop, and I tightened around his tail, wanting the same for him, but not anymore in this place.

Then he must have noticed Timber. His tail stopped but made no move to leave. Darrian stepped next to Timber nervously, obviously terrified to even disturb Ryan after earlier. "I know you said she wasn't going to fight tonight," he said, glancing toward Timber. "But he keeps insisting that she be added in this gang fight."

Ryan blew against my neck and goose bumps spread over me. "You already know my answer."

"It's fine, I'll join in," I said quickly as I straightened out my throaty voice with a cough or two.

I couldn't see his face to guess what he was thinking, but his arms gave around me and I stood, waiting for him to remove the tail. And he did, finally, slowly, deliberately trailing it down my leg, so that my desire glistened against my skin. I felt it drip onto my leg. I was wobbly on my feet, my body still wrapped in everything he'd just given me. I didn't even look back, I was afraid to because I might have crawled right back onto his lap if I did.

Instead, I focused on Timber, letting his presence bring me back to who I really was. He was more focused on Ryan than me. By the time I entered the cage crawling with several disgusting demons, I felt more put together. I sucked in a breath and met Timber's gaze from across the ring. He made his way to me. "I see you're doing well for yourself." I couldn't tell if he was being condescending or not. Considering I had a tail in my vagina, I'd say he was. At one point in the past, I probably meant something to him, though… before I chose not to go back and save him. Even forgetting about him. "Since when were you so intimate with those that captured us? I don't recall you enjoying the one from our past."

I couldn't remember if I had shared anything of my past with him. I trusted myself that I didn't, though. I never gave secrets. "You know I can't die… are you asking for a death wish?" I asked him.

He smirked. "I only have to kill you once and I'll be named victor. I'm undefeated, you know that."

I smiled. "I'm well fed right now; my recovery time is fast… fast enough for me to convince others that I was never dead."

"You never play fair." He yanked a sword off the cage and tossed it to me.

"When has life ever been fair to us?"

"When you put it that way…"

And the fight began, I took out two easily before getting thrown against the wall by another. Timber took care of him for me, though and I grinned in appreciation. We ended up sticking close to each other. "Takes me back," he told me over his shoulder as I cut into a demon.

"We always did make a good team," I told him.

Getting rid of the others wasn't a problem for us and soon, it was down to just me and him. He circled around me, flipping his sword cockily, and I rolled my eyes. “I have to make you stay dead for a while… any pointers?” he asked with a smile.

I wasn’t a good person. I’ve done a lot of bad things in my time and I’ve only ever thought of myself, but Timber knew I wasn’t going to kill him. He had only one life, I had many.

But, even though I didn’t kill him, my presence did. I dropped my sword as the tail that had delivered my orgasms just minutes before ripped into Timber’s chest. Blood dripped out of his mouth and he met my eyes for the last time… his body fell at my feet, and Ryan stood in his place.

And it hit me, the boy I killed, the man I both needed to save and desperately wanted for my own, was already trading his soul with Fear’s. And maybe, in return, he was already giving his to Fear.

CHAPTER FIFTEEN

Ryan

Red was my vision.

Fear's wrath was overlooked by my own. The werewolf's body dropped to the floor and I still wasn't satisfied. My vision was still bleeding. Several emotions ran through Molly as she watched what I did. She started out shocked and confused, then she saw that it was me and anger and fear clashed around her.

Inside my chest, something twisted like a knife and it controlled me. I didn't have to say anything to her, I just stalked over and grabbed her, forcing us both to port back to my place. As soon as we arrived, she jerked away from me and turned on her heels. Her anger was still growing and I bet she had a ton of hateful words to spew at me… so why wasn't she letting them fly?

"I don't think so." I grabbed her by the arm and yanked her back. She stumbled backward into me and a growl rose from her chest. She was mad… but I was furious. Not too long ago she had been in my arms, shaking and falling apart with the pleasure I gave her, but she left that and went in the ring with the werewolf… the one from her past, the one I should have killed sooner.

"What?" Her voice was surprisingly calm for all the anger she carried. "What?" she said louder this time.

"I fail to see why you're pissed." I grabbed a handful of her hair and tugged her head back. She hissed before I added, "We were in the middle of something when you stepped into the cage to help your werewolf pal." At my words, her desire collided with her anger, and THAT was exactly what I wanted, but she belonged to me. She needed to know that or my monster would never be able to quieten. "Who was he?" I asked, completely ignoring the fact that I wanted her to open up to me about her past without asking, but we were past that. She made me like this, now she had to handle me this way. I released her hair and trailed my hand down her back.

She tilted her head back and smirked. "What is it you want to know... how I knew him or what I did with him?" The red was back and this time, she was seeking it from me. I growled and pushed her from me, but only so that I could rip the dress off her body. The material was thin and useless, tearing easily for me to reveal her smooth skin.

"What'd you let him do with my body?" I asked, jerking the rest of the dress down her legs. She stood there and let me because it wasn't her that I was torturing but myself, thinking of all the others who had her before me and disgust for all those that took her against her will.

I pushed her against the wall and she stepped out of the dress, leaving her in only her panties. She grunted as her body smacked against the wall. I pressed my body into hers and she looked back and her desire went up a thousand degrees, losing the horns and tail had been a good idea. "We fucked every night in the dungeon we were kept in," she told me as I slipped my hand between the wall and her and pinched one of her nipples. Her tits were small just like the rest of her, and her body type was quickly becoming my favorite one of all.

She gasped. "We'd release our frustration out on each other every night—the only thing that made being trapped there tolerable."

"Are you trying to tell me you loved the werewolf?" I bit the words out trying to control my hatred of the very thought.

"It wasn't like that." She moaned when I went to her other breast. "At least not for me but... he did try to mate with me more than once, so maybe—"

I yanked at my zipper and Molly went silent, except for her heavy breathing. I knew she was listening for the moment I freed my dick. "I want to see your little ass shimmy out of that red lace." She didn't even wait for me to finish the sentence before she was moving her hands between what little space I gave her. She wiggled her hips and slid them down until she couldn't any more.

She huffed in frustration. "I can't get them any further down if you don't give me some room between you and the wall—"

I went right back to trapping her against the wall with my weight, but only this time my erection met her skin. She gave a hopeless sigh in the process and I swallowed up every bit of her hunger—that was for me, so it was mine to take, mine to keep. Even after all the times she came earlier, I could taste the ache resting between her thighs, the yearning for more of me. She wasn't trying to hide it, but she wasn't the only one that lost control. Mine was lost the moment I took her to The Den and had the first drop of her spill on my tail.

I grabbed her by the hips and lifted her feet off the ground. She knew what I was doing and thrust her ass against my dick. Her hands palmed the wall as she lay her cheek against it. I positioned myself and she finished thrusting the rest of the way.

"Yes!" she cried out and I groaned as she covered me in her slick heat. She was beautiful torture; one I didn't know whether to destroy or savor.

I wasn't slow or gentle; I was rough, bruising as I pumped into her. She took it all in screams. I covered my hands over hers against the wall and caged her, kept her trapped while I fed off her pleasure and mine. She tightened around me as she came undone, smacking her head against the wall in the process of her orgasm. I didn't even try to hold off mine, that would be impossible, not when I was so over the edge, and not when I wanted to join in with hers. I bit into her shoulder when I did and that sent her spiraling into another one. She let her head hang over my shoulder this time as I gave one more violent thrust before giving her feet back to the ground.

I finally let her body have distance from mine as I pulled out of her. She dropped to the floor a quivering mess and something about her vulnerability, her unguarded passion with me, left me feeling strange. Not unpleasant… just unsure. And when I reached out to Fear inside me, something I never did, he only purred like a helpless moron who finally got what he wanted. And it was just as I thought, she brought down the monster I've been fighting for a thousand years in a matter of days.

She turned around slowly leaning her back against the wall and looked up at me. Cheeks colored, eyes glazed, and a pleased look on her face, she smiled—and my heart stuttered in its wake. Like I thought, unguarded Blue was the most dangerous. She placed her hands between her legs to cover herself and after the tail-play and fuck against the wall, her bashfulness finally came out. "We can do it again," she said immediately, eyes glancing toward my growing erection like it was begging for her to open up again already. Her arousal invaded my senses telling me it wasn't an empty promise, and when I bent down to get her, her arms automatically opened for me, and something about her giving herself so freely to me had me shaky and nervous. Women gave themselves to me all the time, but something about this with her felt scary and new.

Her legs wrapped around my waist as I carried her to my bedroom, but I didn't place her on her back. I untangled her from me and shoved her face into the pillows. I wanted her and I'd have her, but having her eyes on me while I took her felt too intimate, so I took her from behind. The red was gone from my vision now, so when I pressed into her this time, it was for no one but me and what I wanted.

Blue was loud and very responsive. Her body responded to me in a way that was almost too perfect. And when I spilled myself in her a second time, I was beginning to wonder if she was stealing a part of me like she did to Fear.

We fell asleep afterwards and sometime later that night, I woke up when she climbed out of bed. I lifted my head and watched her naked silhouette disappear into the hallway. It sounded like she was in the bathroom. I heard the toilet flush and when she came back out, I thought she'd go sleep in the other room, but instead, she tiptoed back into my bed and slipped underneath the covers. I lay there stiff as a board as I waited for what she was going to do, but when she pressed her body against my back and placed an arm over my chest and got comfortable, she was back asleep within seconds.

And with her comfort, a tingle in my chest formed.

———

The second time she woke me up, it was her hunger that stirred me to wake. She ran her hand over my ribs lazily and I leaned into her. She hid her face in my back and I sighed. "You're hungry, right?"

She lifted her head and dark eyes peered into mine with a cheesy grin. "Yeah," she answered.

Let her drink your semen, that will fill her up. Fear stunned me with his words. Jesus, this was exactly the reason she didn't want anything to do with him, although… I might have to add that on my to-do list today, not that I had a to-do list, ever. Kinda just did whatever I wanted every day. I was grinning… those lines with Fear were blurring more and more, I was just as depraved.

I dropped my feet out of bed and wiped my eyes before standing. I turned back when I heard the bed creak as she climbed out. She stood in front of the window—the light was strange here, it never actually got earthly bright outside other than the glow from the plants, but it was enough to send a radiance around her nude body. Her black hair was bluer and it fell over her breasts… she was lovely… who the hell said lovely?

She glanced down at my growing erection and pointed toward it as she pranced out of the room. "None of that until you feed me," she hollered.

I smiled and went to the closet to find some clothes. "You're helping," I shot back. "I still haven't given up on teaching you to how to cook." I could hear nothing but huffs and groans as I put on my clothes.

And that was how my day began with Molly—little Blue. She'd never heard of gravy and biscuits until that morning when I showed her how to make them, and she loved them, but I was beginning to think she'd eat anything despite how her nose wrinkled up at everything before I made her try it. Her appetite seemed to be growing now that she wasn't locked up and left to starve. A few times I wanted to ask her about her past as I watched her scarf down the food, but then I decided against it. I didn't want to hear what she'd been through; all that mattered was she was here now and protected from everyone but Fear and me. But the longer Fear let his feelings drift into me, I was starting to think that the monster might be capable of caring for at least *one* soul instead of forcing them into fear. And that soul was standing across the table from me.

Fuck her again, Fear said multiple times while I was trying to eat. I slammed the fork down and Molly jumped. She lifted a brow and I shrugged my shoulders, not wanting to look at her for too long or I'd give in to his words just because I wanted the same. But I could control myself, *occasionally*, and right now felt like a good time to work harder for that control more than ever. With Blue around…

How long would I get to keep her before she'd go running from someone that was half-man, half-monster, sometimes becoming one more than the other? The bigger question was why my chest tightened at the thought of her running from me one day… like she tried when Fear first brought her here.

Forever, Fear listened to my thoughts and said it like he was making it a promise.

Killian faded next to the table and Molly's body filled with fear and worry at the sight of him. He nodded toward her before looking at me. "You're really going to have to start knocking." Especially now that Molly was here. Melanie was always getting on him for that kind of shit too, but it never seemed to stick in that thick skull of his. "What if we had been fucking?" I asked casually and Molly lifted her gaze to mine and a grin formed on her lips.

"Since when have you cared before?" he asked me.

"What is it?" I stood up and Molly shifted uncomfortably in her seat.

"Can't I come to visit without it being about something?" He crossed his arms and I arched a brow and he sighed. "It wasn't the right place," he finally said and I knew exactly what he was talking about. My stomach knotted even though I had already known not to have hope to find our deceased friends… and Penny. She deserved that afterlife, but because she was born a demon she'd never get it.

"I never thought you would," I said coolly.

"That doesn't mean we are going to stop looking for the place he has them kept." He placed his hand in his hair and muttered, "You know Melanie, she's not ever going to stop until we find those lost souls—all the millions denied entry to Heaven because they were demons. With Melanie, they have the way to get the afterlife they deserve, we just have to find them. Every single lost soul."

"What makes you think the Devil hasn't already destroyed them? Every demon soul might as well belong to him." I turned and grabbed my plate, needing something in my hands and tossed it in the sink. Molly cast me a worried look.

"That's not entirely true, he can't touch a good soul. The only ones he can taint are the ones that give in to his darkness, which means he has to have somewhere where he keeps them all trapped, waiting for them to give in so he can have them."

"And what makes you think there are any left that clings to the good when it only led them into his hands regardless?" I yelled.

"You of all people should know how strong someone will cling to their good side—"

"Don't." I raised my hand to stop him from saying any more. "I'm not good. I wish you and Melanie would accept that!"

"We do," he replied effortlessly. "We know exactly what you are—we know everything you do, fuck, Ryan, I'm Grim Reaper and she's my better! Some things we just know!" He took a deep breath and spoke calmer this time, "You're the only one that refuses to accept what you are, always fighting it, always trying to hide it from us all the while telling us you aren't good." He placed his hand on my shoulder and I staggered back. Small hands ran against my back and I hadn't even realized Molly had left her seat. His eyes fell on Molly behind me and he let go of my shoulder. "Maybe we should walk outside so we won't frighten your guest any more than what Fear does."

Killian headed for the door and Molly gave me a nudge. I turned back to her and she just shook her head, smiled, and shooed me to follow him. Her nerves danced along her skin and I breathed in her sadness, and I didn't like the taste of it. I hated it in fact, so I turned around and followed him out the door.

"Why did Fear mark her?" was the first thing he asked the moment I shut the door behind us.

"I don't know." I scratched my chin and looked the other way.

"I can't sense her death—I can't even get a name from her," he said glancing toward the window as if he'd see her peeking out.

"She's immortal." He turned his head surprised and I added, "The Devil did it to her."

His eyes drew together. "And she doesn't seem suspicious to you?"

I shrugged off his worries. "She tried to escape the day I brought her here. She absolutely despised the fact that she was marked by me, so believe me, she's not out to get me if that's what you're implying."

He grinned. "And now?" He cocked a brow. "Doesn't seem like she's trying too hard to leave… the mood looked intimate in there earlier."

I laughed and gave him a ridiculous look. "We were eating at the damn table, how was that intimate?"

He shook his head. "Some of the closest intimacies is what you guys were in there doing when I interrupted."

I scoffed. "At least you know that you were interrupting—really, you got to stop doing that," I told him.

He nodded. "All right, I will now that there's a lady living in the house." I opened my mouth to say something, but he held his hand up. "If you are as bad as you think you are then why did she come to you naturally when she saw that you were hurting in there earlier? It bothered her to see you upset."

"She has a dark past. I'm the nicest monster she's encountered so far. She's a prisoner with my mark, it's only when she tries to leave that she'll be reminded that I'm her captor."

"What makes you think she'll leave?" he surprised me by asking.

"Why would she want to stay?"

"Do you want her to want to stay?" he attacked me with another question.

"Stop." I didn't want the conversation to go any further.

"That's probably a good idea." He turned around and peered into the woods. "There's another reason I came to see you." I stepped next to him. "Come on, let's go see my love." I rolled my eyes and he faded. I ported after him and landed myself in their ballroom.

Melanie hurried down the stairs when she saw me with a smile, but once she was in front of me, it slowly faded like I knew all good things did. "What is it?" I grinned to ease the tension.

"It's about Tess."

CHAPTER SIXTEEN

Molly

I paced back and forth through the house, waiting for Ryan to return. Something in the way he spoke to Killian like he was desperate to convince him to understand that he wasn't a good guy, only proved to me how much he *still* was. Bad guys didn't feel pain or remorse like he did—it was clear in his expression, the fall of his shoulders. Ryan was a good guy who spent all this time struggling until eventually, he began to hate a part of himself for liking the things he did.

Ryan wasn't a saint—a few days with him was enough to know that. He carried bloodlust in his eyes, he had no qualms in killing. He had no problem mixing pain with pleasure, but without even having to know or ask, I already knew he was a man that struggled with everything he became, and I was sinking—soon to drown completely in the depths of him.

He spent his whole life fighting for the last bit of good in him while I spent my whole existence running from that tricky goodness. I knew what it felt like to feel bad about something, Ryan was proof of that over the centuries, but unlike him, I did what I had to because all that ever mattered was what I wanted.

Until now.

Until I let myself fall in love with him.

I didn't know the first thing about love but every part of me believed that this was me learning what it was. I didn't want another woman, demon—anyone! to touch him, or him to touch another in the way he touched me last night. What we did was no different than what I've done with others, yet nothing compared to the feeling I got with him. My body liquefied for him and his touch so much that I fell apart and didn't come back together for the longest time afterward.

Two things were in the way of what I wanted.

My own secrets… And Fear.

The things I left unsaid were harder to swallow now. I was more worried than ever about telling him who I was. No, I was terrified. No matter how I told him, I couldn't see it ending the way I wanted. Who could overlook their killer? Not to mention all the things I've done to Melanie and the fact that I continued to keep it from him… The night I told him my name, I'd hoped there'd be some sort of recognition and it would all be over with that night. He hadn't remembered the name of the ghost-girl that stayed by Fear's side, I was forgettable that way… but I guaranteed the moment I told him who Molly was, he'd remember the dead girl that petted him like some sort of animal while he was shackled to Fear.

I sat down on the couch and pressed my fist against my chest. So much pressure was there and it hurt. Why did I do that to him? To make it easier to cloud my guilt with meanness? No, I was truly bad and for the first time in my descent into the wicked, I let my mind swallow me whole. The pain came first and all the guilt. Ryan wasn't the only person I destroyed, even before Fear came to me, I had already destroyed countless families as a poltergeist, but I wasn't hiding behind Fear anymore and I was accepting all the things I've done. Ryan just stood out more than the rest, from the very moment I climbed atop his broken body—also because of me—in that hospital and set him on the path that forced him into an eternity as Fear. Maybe it was because I thought he was an idiot for getting himself into this mess over a girl—he could have stayed away, but he wouldn't. And even then, her life was still the most important to him and that had the woman in me trapped away in a childlike ghost body thinking… *ah, so guys like him exist?*

So, yeah, even then, Ryan engraved something in me that would haunt me all these centuries.

Next came the tears. Damn, they were a lot. Those were the first tears I've released since the last time I cried for Mom the night we both died. I could have saved myself from this pain right now if I would have walked into my afterlife and forgot all my worries, but I clung to my hatred and anger… and even so, I found myself understanding that I'd repeat the same mistakes all other again, even the ones against Ryan, because all the things I've done has led me to here, right now with him and even the guilt, couldn't wash away how much I wanted to keep him.

If that made me the cruelest bitch to ever walk the Underworld and human world, so be it.

I held the vial in my hand, twisting it around as I watched the clear liquid move from side to side. Even this vial no longer held the same meaning. My intentions kept shifting while I was here. Fear no longer felt like my enemy, but I also didn't feel like sharing Ryan with him. All Ryan's anguish was because of the monster, yet...

Fear wasn't hurting me or exacting revenge on me like I had thought. He was different than who I knew him to be...

Why did he merge with Ryan? Why did the question suddenly feel urgent? I had my own suspicions about the why he chose Ryan.... But the bigger question was why I was even trying so hard to figure out the monster... I was my own demon, I didn't want to deal with another.

Now that I thought about it, I should be mortified that I let Ryan use Fear's tail... I shoved the vial back between the mattresses and placed my face into my palms and sighed. I didn't know what I was doing, but above all, I needed to tell Ryan. If I hoped to stay next to him in any possible way, he needed to know before Melanie saw me and revealed my identity. My skin crawled when I thought of the possibility of her fading into Ryan's house instead of Killian.

She'd remember me. She'd ruin everything, and she had every right after everything I did.

I was on my feet, hurrying from the room. My body had a will of its own, but I knew what it was doing and where it was taking me. I grabbed the portal chip off the counter—my chest tightened, Ryan never once tried to hide it from me—and gripped it tight in my palm. I took a deep, solid breath and ported in front of Melanie and Grim's castle. It was showy and dark and mysterious, completely suited for the two. I would never be like them, nor did I want to, but they still managed to somehow make someone like me feel a hint of respect for everything they were and did as God's entities.

I knew there was a chance Ryan was in there, so I stood outside and waited, too afraid that I'd ruin it all by running into him and her together. I didn't know how long I stood out there before Killian faded in front of me. I was nervous and scared as hell, but I didn't show it. He cocked his head to the side like he was trying to figure me out. "There is something about you, isn't there?" he asked me.

I had no idea what he was referring to. "Looking for Ryan?" he asked another question.

I might have turned ghostly pale at the mention of Ryan. "I don't want him to know I'm here," I said quickly. "I need to see Melanie without him being there."

"What are you up to?" He stepped toward me and I fought my instinct to back away.

"Nothing," I retorted, "but you'll know everything soon enough if you bring me to Melanie without Ryan being there." I waited a few seconds before I grew desperate. "Please, I need to see her. It's important."

His eyes darkened. "If you so much as touch her—"

"—she's gonna wanna kill me," I interrupted, placing my shaky hands behind my back hidden from view. I wasn't afraid of her, but by doing this, I was placing everything into her hands. She could ruin any chance I had at Ryan's forgiveness if she decided to run and tell him. That was why I needed to see her before that happened and if she still chose to, there was nothing I could do. THAT was why it was so damn scary, but facing her first seemed a lot less frightening than telling Ryan. I was being a coward, I knew, but only because I knew Ryan couldn't care for me like I did him, so if I further crushed what little he might care for me, then I'd lose him.

"Ryan's been gone a while after what we told him about his sister—"

"What news?" I interrupted him again.

He arched a brow. "I'm getting this feeling you might care for Ryan..."

I shrugged my shoulders. "He's hard not to like."

That earned me a smile. He turned and beckoned me to follow him. "I can't wait to see what this is all about," he said while my insides churned in response.

I didn't make it three steps into their ballroom before I was thrown against the wall. I didn't have time to rub my throbbing head, I was too worried about getting on my feet, but even then, Melanie had her scythe pressed against my neck when I stood. She pressed me into the wall, a murderous glare planted against her pretty features. "I take it you know her?" Killian asked her at ease.

"Mind telling me why you let Molly step into our home like she didn't hand deliver me to the Devil himself."

"Molly—" Killian went from startled, eyes widening into a hard stare aimed my way that fell into recognition as he pieced together the ghost I had once been. "She's been here for days." He threw me to the tiger, the almighty Grim Reaper succumbing to his wife's will. Melanie had a talent for making men love her.

"What!" She glared at him then aimed it back at me.

"She's the one I told you about that's been staying with Ryan—"

"I came to tell you myself—"

She sliced my throat open and stepped away. I clutched my throat and dropped to my knees, then—

I sucked in a lungful of air when I came back to life. She squatted next to me waiting for my revival and I quickly pressed my face off the floor and met her eyes. "I deserved that," I told her, waiting to see if she was going to let me talk or kill me again.

"Feel better now?" Killian asked, standing next to her. "I'd like to know what the hell she's doing here."

Melanie sighed. "What are you trying to do with Ryan?"

"Nothing!" I snapped. "Fear was the one that marked me and brought me here. Believe me I would have stayed far away from the three of you if he hadn't known it was me."

"I knew there was a reason," Killian said.

"Makes sense." Melanie scowled at me. "After everything you've done, I'd stay away too."

"Does he know who you are?" Killian asked.

"Of course, he doesn't," Melanie answered. "There's no way he'd let her stay if he knew." Her words only reminded me of all the reasons why I didn't want to tell him.

"That's why I came to you first," I spoke calmly, trying to sound at ease. "I was afraid of you seeing me and telling him who I was—"

She scoffed. "And you think I'm not going to tell him now?"

"I can't stop you from telling him, but I came to tell you first, so that I could have the chance to tell him—on my own terms," I said, voice painfully low.

She stood and placed her scythe against my throat. "What are you and Fear up to?" she asked and as bad as it pissed me off, I knew everything I've done to her in the past warranted this kind of behavior from her. "I won't let you hurt him."

I stood and her scythe stayed against my throat as I did. "I don't want to hurt him," I swore. "I don't have any plans with Fear. The only reason I stayed by Fear's side… I got already when I handed you over to Satan," I gave her the truth.

She smirked. "Oh, I remember clearly."

"I have no power—nothing to gain coming to you like I am right now or trying to hurt Ryan, who's also stronger than me!"

I could feel the tension coming off her as she gritted her teeth and reluctantly moved her scythe from my neck. I grabbed my neck. "Then, tell me, why are you asking me to give you the chance to tell him who you are yourself?"

This was the part that made me feel uncomfortable.

"Come on, Love," Killian said, sliding his hand around her waist. "Even I know the answer to that." I studied him nervously as he met my eyes. "She loves him."

My face grew warm when he said it and I twisted my neck around awkwardly, then I swallowed and decided to be honest and get it over with. "Because I can't bear the thought of him finding out by anyone other than me, not when he's going to have the same disgusted reaction as you have right now." Tears messed with my vision, so I looked away and wiped them from my eyes.

Melanie's expression was no different, hard and full of venom. "What makes you think hearing it from you is going to make it any better?"

"I know!" I yelled, tired of hearing what I already knew. "I know," I whispered.

She closed her eyes and shook her head. "Why did you keep it from him!" she was suddenly yelling and this time, she looked sad. "You're scared of him hating you, but how do you think he's going to feel when you tell him he's been letting you in his home…" She let the rest die off her lips because I already knew what she meant.

I wiped my hand over my face. "Because I didn't know what Fear was going to make him do to me at first and then when it became clear I was safe, I became terrified of him knowing the truth of who I was," I panicked. "He doesn't see me like you do. He only sees me as this pain-in-the-ass woman that Fear marked and brought home and as shitty as that sounds, I like how he treats me as Blue!"

"Even now, you worry only for yourself." Her words had me feeling sick. I could only shake my head denying the ugly truth about myself. "Don't worry, I won't tell him, I'll let you. Ryan's my best friend, but he's a grown man and he's capable of making his own decisions."

She turned and walked off. I left feeling worse than what I did when I went.

It'd been hours and Ryan still hadn't returned. I spent them mulling over when I should tell him while Melanie's words ate a hole in my stomach, but the longer Ryan was gone, the more that worry transitioned into worry for him. Killian had said something about his sister—had something happened?

As night moved over Grim's woods, I changed into some black jeans and a shirt and gave into the idea that he might be blowing off steam or feeding Fear; or Fear was out. The thought of him going to another woman after last night hurt, really bad. I ported to The Den, hoping he chose this place if that was in fact what he was doing. I felt even worse when I couldn't find him there. Darrian came up to me, a lot more aggressive and nasty now that Ryan wasn't there to scare him away. I shrugged off his advances and asked him if he'd been there. His answer had been no, but when I had said no to his advances toward me, he didn't know the meaning of the word. I might have broken his wrist before porting back to Ryan's.

It wasn't even a minute later when Ryan ported into the living room. I breathed out a sigh of relief and my feet started their destination to reach him and halted when I saw the unhappiness all over him. His head was hung and his shoulders were dropped. I stepped closer, feeling horrible that I was worried about him chasing after women when he clearly hadn't. "Ryan?"

He lifted his head, met my eyes. "Do you have any siblings?" he asked.

I was already shaking my head before I said, "No."

He waited. "… Even before you became a ghost?"

I nodded. "I was an only child." I moved closer. "Is something wrong? You've been gone awhile." I placed my palm against his chest. He closed his eyes and took a deep breath and let it out.

"My sister's going to die tomorrow night. It's going to be from a heart attack," he said shakily. "And they want me to see her before she goes… into Heaven."

"You should."

"No, I can't," he croaked. He looked so broken about it that I felt it cloud my eyes. "If I go see her, she's going to know what I am—what I've become. I told Melanie to tell her that I moved on after I died, I didn't want her to know then and I don't want her to know now."

I ran my hand up his chest before I placed it against his cheek. He watched me with no hidden desire or lust, this was purely him needing an outsider's ear. I didn't want to dare hope that maybe he came to me because it was me. "You have to go see her." He shook his head like it didn't make sense to go see her. "What do you think's going to happen when she gets to the other side and you're not there?" He frowned. "Once she crosses over, that's it. You don't ever get another chance to say goodbye or see her again." I looked down for a moment. "Take it from someone that screwed up in that department. Heaven opened up for me the day I died, the same day my mom killed herself because my dad accidentally stabbed me while they were fighting." Ryan's eyes darkened and his lips slanted—I had no doubt that expression was for my dad, whether it was more Fear or him, but I ignored it and continued, "Mom was walking us toward the light, but right at the last second I pulled away from her. I didn't say anything, I didn't have to. She had to know I was upset that it took dying for us to finally get away from Dad. That was all it took to change me completely. I loved my mom, but I left her without giving any sort of goodbye because I was upset with her in that one moment."

"Fear killed him," I blurted. Ryan lifted his eyebrows waiting for me to continue. "My dad, I mean, something that I kept trying to do and couldn't because I was a ghost… it wasn't until he died that I wanted to go back to Mom, but she was gone, Ryan, gone forever. Somewhere good and safe, somewhere I could have gone if I had chosen peace over my anger."

I froze in place when he lifted his hands up and wiped my tears away. I didn't even realize…

He lifted my face. "I'll go," he promised. "I'd feel like an ass if I don't go say goodbye after you shared something like that with me." I smiled and nodded feeling too exposed and opened now that I shared something else with him about my past.

"You'd still go say goodbye to your sister even if I hadn't told you how I died," I whispered, placing my hand back on his chest. "Even with Fear, you're good in here." I pressed against his chest. "Good guys like you always make the right choices in the end, unlike the villains."

He laughed. "Are you trying to tell me you're a villain, Blue?"

I didn't smile. "I am, Ryan, you just don't know yet."

My heart broke a little more when he shrugged what I said away. *I keep giving you reasons to be wary of me, make you wonder why I've been in so many prison cells, yet...* "At least Fear got one thing right before me, sounds like your dad deserved death."

"It was his mind," I replied. "Mentally, whatever lurked there only continued to fester in him."

Ryan was quiet for a long time, so I finally lifted my head to see his expression. He smirked when I did. "I don't know about you, but I need to blow off some steam." I perked up at his words, body already tingling. I used the hand that was on his chest and twisted his shirt into my hand and pulled him closer.

He smiled and I said, "Oh?"

He placed his hand over mine and pulled his shirt from my grip. "Come on." He tugged on my hand and pulled me into him.

I frowned, clearly expecting a different sort of steam-releasing activity than what he was as he removed the portal chip from his pocket. "I thought—"

He grinned. "I know what you thought." I gave him a heated glare. "I kinda wanna kill something—definitely wanna fuck you, but I don't want to have to kill you just so we can get to the fucking," he said.

I gripped his hand. "I get it, you're Fear now despite being your own person, his needs are yours." I moved into him impatiently. "So, who are we killing?" He grinned.

CHAPTER SEVENTEEN

Molly

"This is not what I had been expecting," I grumbled, smacking whatever bug was crawling on me in the godforsaken place he brought us. It was dark, not Underworld or Grim woods dark, but actual *dark.* We were somewhere in the human world, of course. Sitting in grass that made me itch, in front of a pond with a lantern between us as a frog croaked nearby and the never-ending sound of bugs only seemed to get louder and louder.

He snorted as I smacked another bug off my pants and cast his line into the water—that's right, he took us *fishing.* We were killing fish… that he was most likely going to make us eat. At least I had changed into some pants before I had gone to The Den because Ryan sure wasn't about to tell me where we were going or that it would be a good idea to change into something comfortable. He took us to some random house and took someone's lantern and fishing pole out of their storage building, even opening the miniature fridge in there and grabbed the live bait like he'd done it before.

"Tell me again what we're killing," I complained and watched him while I did it. He sat on the ground a foot away from me, watching his line, eyes completely focused with his elbows propped on his knees. The fishing pole rested between his legs, propped up on a stand made from a stick he found lying around. My insides quivered just looking at him. He was drool worthy. I'd hump his leg and I wasn't just saying that. I wanted to do a lot more than that but he wanted to *fish.*

"I might have over exaggerated a bit with the killing," he replied. "But if I catch a few then they are dead because we're gonna eat them." I knew it.

I nodded. "And what if you only catch one?"

"Then we let him go."

I sighed, staring into the water. This was kind of peaceful and relaxing. The frog was irritating and the bugs were chirping, but if I let myself get lost in the sound and feel of it, it kind of sounded pretty. I took in a deep breath and it smelled like fish water, okay, that part was bad but I could get used to this.

I looked back over to Ryan and lost all other thoughts. He was still completely focused on the water, oblivious to the needy, wanton woman next to him.

"You're distracting me, Blue," he said without looking my way.

I let out a breathy sigh and kept staring at him. "I'm not even doing anything."

"You might not be." He finally looked at me. "But your desire is wrapping itself around my neck, pulling me in so that you don't have to." I had my natural ability to get wet in his presence to thank for that. He grinned like he knew I was happy about it.

I pretended pity. "It must be horrible to taste everyone's emotions and know what they're thinking." I turned toward the water. "It's why Fear's so good at crawling under people's skin."

He was quiet for a while. "Fear's different with you." I tilted my head and met his intense stare. "Is it because he knew you from the past?" He waited for some sort of reaction, my stomach tensed up and I knew he probably sensed my worry. He shook his head and turned back to the water. "I'm telling you, he's a monster and I'm a monster because I'm him, but—" he paused, wiping his hand over his mouth. "With you, I—I don't know what you've done to him."

I scooted my legs up, placing my chin on my knees. I should tell him now, get it over with so that if he wanted to throw me into the water, he could. I glanced over at him and knew I couldn't, though. Not when I wanted him so much. Melanie was right, I was selfish, but I already knew that.

Thirty minutes or more ticked by when Ryan's voice filtered through the insects. "Come here, Blue." I perked up, lifting my head from my knees. He moved the fishing pole to his left.

"What is it?" I asked, hopeful.

He took one look my way and grinned because he just knew. He motioned me with his hands. "I said come here," he said again, and I happily did as he told me to. My stomach was tight with expectancy. He wasn't even looking at me when he added, "And leave your pants." I don't think I ever tore out of jeans as quickly in all my centuries.

When I stood next to him, waiting, he grabbed my hand and pulled me down onto his lap, straddling his waist. My bare legs touched the damp grass the same time my panties met his hard-on, and my heart did a little happy dance that he wanted me this way, at least. I know, *pathetic,* right? His warm palms pressed against my back, and I hesitantly placed my arms around his neck then met his eyes.

"So needy," he murmured as his hand slipped underneath my shirt. Chills broke out over my skin wherever his fingers traced. He pulled at my shirt. "Off," he ordered just as I lifted my arms. He tossed it somewhere and his head dipped into my chest. I cried out when his teeth bit into one of my nipples. I ground into him as the pressure built between my legs.

I lifted his head back so that I could stare into his eyes. He averted his gaze and bit into my neck. I bit back my moan and ran my hands through his hair. I slipped my hands between us and started tackling his zipper with all the urgency coursing through me. "Here," he whispered when I panted in frustration. He parted our bodies enough so that he could help me. Ryan had to wrestle with my fingers almost as much as the zipper, and the moment he freed himself from the confines of his jeans, I gripped him hard. He hissed and grabbed a handful of my hair, exposing my neck so that he can bite into it, then his hands traveled down to my ass and gripped it tightly before one of them slipped into my panties. I pressed my ass back, giving his fingers access to my needy flesh.

He groaned when his fingers found my slick heat. I gripped his shoulders and wiggled further into his hands. He gripped my ass again, this time spreading my cheeks apart while sliding his finger over my heat. I leaned my face into his so that he'd lift his. His breath fanned my cheek before I covered it with my mouth. I kissed him, I breathed him in, all the while hoping my feelings weren't pouring into him in the process.

Coating his fingers with my arousal, he slid a finger against my back hole. Pleasure flowed through me in the process, but I stiffened as the unease crept in. I'd been raped anally a lot over the years, never once had it been about pleasure. He moved his mouth from mine and met my eyes. I tried to suck in all the bad emotions I was feeling so he wouldn't sense them. He slid his finger back down into my heat as if to ease my discomfort. I relaxed somewhat but felt bad that I messed up the mood.

He stole my lips while I was drowning in bitterness. His hands were all over me, pinching and pressing into my flesh, and soon I was back where he had me before, writhing in his arms. I stroked him hard and rough like I wanted him inside me. He pressed a finger into me and I cried out, but he muffled the sound with his mouth and tongue, invading another part of me. I brought my legs up and started lifting myself. I needed him inside me and he seemed to be in no rush.

Then right when I was taking matters into my own hand and inches from having him inside me, he jerked to grab his pole. He held me to his right side as he jerked the pole back. "I got one hooked," he told me with a smile. He patted a hand against my ribs like he expected me to get off him while he reeled it in… I had no intention of doing so.

I was horny, and now pissed. Without thinking—and letting desire control me—I leaned over and yanked the pole from his hand. "What are you—" He didn't finish the words and I chucked his pole into the weeds next to us. He let his mouth hang open as he looked at me. "Blue," he swore as he started lifting me off him, but I held him down. I could hear the pole moving around where I had thrown it. He faced me again, only this time there was a storm in his eyes. "Damn it, you crazy woman. What the hell?"

"Don't 'what the hell' me!" I barked back, fighting to keep him on the ground. He hadn't tried any forced yet but I knew it was only a matter of time. "We are in the middle of something. The fish can wait, but my pleasure cannot."

His head tipped back as he looked at me like I was insane. "We came here so I can fish and that's what I was doing so, no. What we were doing was messing around until I got a bite." I huffed and felt the anger cross into my cheeks. He tried to raise up from underneath me, but I still put up a fight. He gripped my shoulders and shoved me to the side. I came right back and he kept shooing me away. I didn't know what the hell I was doing at that point.

I ran past him for retribution and a grin so evil it'd put the Devil's to shame. "Molly," he cursed as I dived into the weeds to grab the pole. He was right behind me. "Oh, no you don't!" He lunged for me and I squealed the same time I bent down and grabbed the pole. He yanked me back. I tossed the pole and he jumped to catch it. I cried in frustration when he caught it before it could greet the water like I had so desperately wanted.

He started doing something with the pole, but my guess was the fish was long gone because his gaze turned on me—all pissed off and sexy. I swallowed and stood in place, hoping he planned to retaliate. He watched me for the longest time before he smirked and stepped out of the weeds and plopped back down on the ground. My plan just blew up in my face.

Bitter from rejection, I scratched at my legs and stepped out of the weeds that were making me itch. I sulked while putting my pants and shirt back on, and sat down next to him afterward because I still wanted to be next to him.

"Is there something you wanna do?" he asked out of nowhere.

My immediate thought was *him*, but I didn't think that was the answer he was looking for so I shrugged. "I don't know what you mean."

"What do you do for fun?" he elaborated. Before I could say anything dirty, he added, "Besides fucking."

I sighed. "I don't know." With the look he was giving me, I felt compelled to go on, "Honestly, I don't know. Me and fun don't have any sort of relationship unless…"

"Unless what?"

I met his eyes. "You."

"Me?" He squinted his eyes.

"I mean, I don't mind arguing and fighting with you," I said quickly, tossing my head back. "Ya know, I think I probably… have fun with you because I don't mind what we're doing when we're together, I just feel good." His gaze could have swallowed me whole. I couldn't believe I admitted to something like that. I turned my head and concentrated on the water.

He snorted and I looked back over at him. "Are you trying to be nice after you tried to throw my pole in the water?" I groaned and dropped my head.

"You shouldn't keep a woman from an orgasm," I muttered, defending myself.

"So, you were just going to use my cock to get off? And attack me and the fishing pole, and probably anything else that would have got in your way?" He smiled.

I grinned slowly. "I don't know what you're worried about. I was gonna use you real good."

He burst out laughing and my stomach quivered in response. "Damn, then get back over here and ride me real good," he hollered.

I hmphed and didn't comply. "No, thanks. Like I'd come back when you chose a fish over me the first time." I stood up and dusted off my pants. "Actually, I think I'll go ahead and head back." I made the mistake of looking over at him and seeing the smirk resting on his mouth. Why was he so infuriating…ly handsome?

"Get your ass over here," he ordered.

"No."

"Blue," he warned.

"Ryan," I mocked.

"I said come here." He waited. "If you don't, I'll take you instead." Should I run and let him catch me, or give in and have him like I want? "Look, I'm reeling in the line right now." And he was. I found my feet moving, my heart was already there but my mind wanted to fight him some more.

Once I was next to him, he reached up and undid my pants before sliding them down. I stepped out of them and he pulled me back into his lap again. My chest had this little fuzzy feeling in it. Something as simple as getting my way with him had me giddy. He smirked right before taking off my shirt—everything was happening again, and this time I knew we wouldn't stop because he went straight for what I wanted.

He freed himself from his jeans and took the edge of my panties, ripping them. I watched everything his hands did underneath the tinted glow of the lantern. "Is this what you want, Blue?" he asked me, and I nodded with a deep throaty moan. I lifted my ass and he gripped it the same time, slamming me down onto him. We both cried out before he covered our sounds with a fierce kiss. His tongue claimed my mouth, and I wrapped my arms around him, desperate to feel every part of him.

He tried to control my movements with his hands on my hips. "Let me," I whispered before taking over. I rode him, wishing I was a succubus who could make him want me as much as I wanted him. Every time my body took him completely in, he groaned, and his reactions were what spurred me on. I started grinding my pubic bone into him before moving up and back down all over again. "Jesus," he muttered. His hands were all over me, taking each of my nipples into his mouth and biting down. My body was on the verge of tipping over, but I wanted—no, I needed it to be him this time. I wanted him to fall apart with me like I did with him.

My legs were shaking as I drew my own pleasure near. The orgasm was only another slide down his dick so I stopped and rocked into him instead to prevent it. But it was no use, all I had to do was meet his lust filled eyes as he tipped his lips to my neck and I cried out in frustration because I was fighting a losing battle. I couldn't make him feel what I felt between us, and that ripped me open. "Give in," he said as my body shook and I could barely move because my orgasm was all through me, and Ryan always shattered me until I no longer existed afterward.

"No, together," I moaned, and stopped myself from moving on him anymore so that I wouldn't without him. As I shook, I dragged my hands to his face and lifted it so that I could kiss him. I savored the taste of him slowly despite the chaos my body was going through. He brought his hands to my hands and kissed me back before lying back.

I leaned down to join him, but he stopped me with his hand. "No, I want you sitting up." Even I didn't know what kind of look I gave him, but he added, "Don't come until I do." I nodded vehemently. "*Together,*" he promised.

"Yes," I cried, straightening up my back. This position brought him into me deeper. Ryan's hands moved to my hips. This time I let him control my body's movements. He lifted me to where he was almost completely out of me before forcing me back down in a painful thrust. I whimpered and let my body fall onto his.

"No, Blue," he said with a throaty voice. "Sit straight up."

I sat back up and he began pounding into me, his grip tightening on my hips. He was hitting me deep and he held me in place so that I couldn't move. I arched my back and took it all, the pain and the pleasure. The pain of every thrust brought a dark, pleasant ache that spiraled all through me.

"Ryan." I dropped my head so that I could gaze down at him. His pained, lustful expression only heightened my approaching orgasm. "I'm gonna come," I told him. "Come with me."

He groaned, tossing his head back onto the ground. "Fuck," he muttered. He thickened inside me and my tensed stomach finally began to relax and let my orgasm go. My whole body loosened as I let his ongoing thrusts push me into what I kept denying myself. "Fucking come now, Molly," he ordered, and I did the moment his own release hit him. My body shivered and rippled as he spilled into me. He buried himself deep, neither of us moving. We didn't have to, our bodies gave in so easily, all we had to do was absorb it from each other. I fell against his chest, our breathing heavy, and our bodies sated.

"You like getting your way, don't you?" he asked through pants. I smiled against his shirt, still a little loopy from sex. He wrapped his arms around me and squeezed. "Shit, I think my head's in the mud."

I laughed and lifted my head. The moment ours eyes met he hardened inside me and my laughter died out. "Again?" I asked, and he smirked.

One of his hands trailed down until one lingered around my back hole. "I can show you a whole other world of pleasure if you'd let me," he teased me with words.

I shrugged my shoulders playfully before meeting his eyes again. "I don't think there's anything you can do to me that I wouldn't find pleasurable." I was embarrassed by my words so I placed a kiss on his chest to keep from looking at him.

He brought his hand to my hair. "I think you're right," he agreed softly. "You kinda fade away on me for a while after that first orgasm hits, except for this one."

I nodded. "Well, believe me, I was holding on for dear life so that we could let go together."

"Why?" He chuckled.

"Because, I just wanted to." I placed my arms on his chest and laid my head over them. "Damn," I huffed. The scary thing about falling for something I realized was you couldn't control some of the things that came from your mouth, just like you couldn't control the emotions that came with being around him.

His fingers were still messing around with my back hole, and he was still hard inside me, but we lay there absorbing the peace until I finally said, "We should probably go shower. I'm pretty sure something's crawling up my leg, and I might let out one of those girly squeals any second now if we don't."

"Women and bugs," he muttered as he sat up with me still in his arms. I reluctantly disconnected our bodies.

I didn't even bother to put on my clothes, I just picked them up and ported before him. I walked into the bathroom and turned the water on, letting it warm up. I switched it over to the shower and stepped inside once the water was scalding. I smiled when I heard him step into the bathroom a couple minutes later. I busied myself by grabbing the washcloth I brought in, lathering it up with soap. I tried not to look too happy when he opened the shower curtain and stepped in behind me but I probably failed.

"Scoot up," he nagged behind me. He leaned into my back, letting his erection poke my ass. He brought his arms around me, letting the water pour over them. He wanted to steal the hot water from me. "Share the wealth," he said, pushing me forward.

I laughed and turned around. "I was here first." Then I looked up at his hair. The back of it was covered in chunks of mud, and I sniggered some more. "You have mud all in your hair."

He nodded. "Yeah, I noticed in the mirror before stepping in," he replied. He grabbed my shoulders and started maneuvering us around the shower.

"I don't think so," I grumbled, and grabbed his arms to stop him. He smirked and I huffed. "Just stay like this. That way we both get the water," I told him. The water sprayed between us so that we both got some of it.

He cocked an eyebrow. "There's no room for me to wash off," he complained.

"Stop holding my shoulders." I pushed his hands away. His dick started poking me as he leaned down to grab the body wash. "This is my side, stop crossing over," I said, right before I shoved it away, only for it to slap right back at me.

He stopped what he was doing and just looked at me before laughing. "Did you just smack my dick?"

I started washing off. "He won't stop poking me," I mumbled, and even I knew how stupid I sounded.

"You don't usually have a problem with him 'poking' you."

I rolled my eyes and took another look at his hair. "Here, turn around and I'll wash your hair."

He did as I told him. I filled my palm full of shampoo before leaning into his back and washing his hair. I enjoyed my body resting against his. My nipples were too as they slid across his back. He tilted his head back and groaned. "This is nice," he murmured, and that alone made me happy.

For fifteen minutes, we fought over the water and took turns washing each other up, and even though he was hard the entire time, we didn't jump each other. It was new and refreshing. When I stepped out, he asked, "Are you hungry?"

And I replied with, "Always."

We ventured into the kitchen and furthered our conversation. He made us hot ham and cheese sandwiches as I found the chips and drinks. I planted myself on the floor against the kitchen wall with my food, and he looked down at me with a smirk. "You know there's a table, right?" But he sat down on the floor next to me nonetheless.

"I don't know why I sat down here," I told him with a playful shrug, placing the bag of chips between us as I crossed my legs Indian style.

"Who knows with you."

"What the hell is that supposed to mean?" I asked.

"See." He pointed at me. "You get riled up so easily."

I sighed. "Don't even start. You're Fear. You're the one that takes everything too far." He grinned wickedly and I rolled my eyes. "About Fear…" He watched me curiously. "Is he, ya know?" I brought my arms out.

"Present?" he offered and I nodded. "Like he's going to disappear when you're around." I arched my eyebrow and he continued, "He's obsessed with you."

I straightened my back and studied his expression. "I don't think that's what it is."

He nodded. "It is. He's quite into you."

I didn't know what to say to that so instead, I asked, "Don't you need to go kill something… ya know go cause something pain and scare the shit out of them?"

He laughed. "I'm okay, for now." He took a drink of his Pepsi. "But yeah, I'll have to eventually, just not at this moment. I'm strangely… good."

"Okay." I smiled. "Am I gonna be one of those that you go after?" I couldn't help but ask.

He cocked a brow. "Most likely."

I tugged my wet hair behind my ear before taking a bite of my sandwich. The heat pooled between my legs at the thought of him hunting me before it turning into something else, something better. I needed to think about something else before he called me out on what my body was doing on its own. "Don't you want to leave now and spend time with your sister before she moves on?" I asked.

"I don't even know what I'm going to say when I do see her again."

"I'm sure she'll have a lot to say when she sees you."

He laughed, looking down at the floor before nodding. "I'd say you're right."

I didn't notice at first because I was busy eating but Ryan's eyes were on my body. I wouldn't have thought anything of it if it weren't for the fact that he'd been staring at my chest for minutes now. Had he zoned out? I had on a white spaghetti shirt, and my nipples were poking through the longer he stared. Finally, I couldn't take it any longer and asked, "What is it?"

He lifted his gaze and seemed to snap out of it. He shook his head and straightened his back. "I was just thinking… there isn't a need for so many marks on your body."

My heart skidded. Suddenly I feared he was done with me already. "What do you mean?" I whispered quickly.

He placed his chin on his knee and kept staring at me. "I only need one mark, don't I, Molly?"

"Huh?" I was frustrated and scared that he might want to get rid of me so soon.

"Because you won't leave even if there's none."

Slowly, I was becoming exposed to him.

But I couldn't make myself care.

CHAPTER EIGHTEEN

Ryan

Molly slept like the dead. She never stirred when I carried her to my bedroom after she fell asleep watching a movie on the couch. We had showered and ate on the floor of the kitchen the night before that. She never stirred when I slipped my hand underneath her shirt, wanting to take her body one more time before succumbing to sleep. Even when morning came, she never stirred when I tried again, or when I sat over her shoulder and watched the vulnerability and peace in her expression as she slumbered. She never stirred when I climbed out of bed either.

Even though I adored something about her being so relaxed, another part—the darker part of me—wondered what hell had she been through before getting stuck here to sleep with a monster like she was perfectly safe. The ugly in me was growing, I felt it, and soon it would consume me if I didn't get relief soon. It didn't help that I had to face my sister today who would know the truth of what I've become, and it didn't help that I was keeping Molly here, treating her nice and making her comfortable when it was only a matter of time before I broke her. She was scaring the shit out of me because I *wanted* her to stay.

So did Fear.

Together, we didn't make a right—we made a very messed up fucker. I was good when I could be good, but when I was bad, I was very bad. How could I keep someone like Molly around when she was so accepting and willing to take me inside her any and all the time—except for the moments she fell dead to hibernation. I don't know, the way she looked at me, the way she smiled, and waited and cried out for my attention made it feel like I was the only thing she wanted.

It felt good. No, it felt damn great.

She no longer looked at me with hatred and uncertainty… even Fear was weird. We were all *weird,* and I didn't know what to do about it.

You should wake her up before you leave, Fear filtered through my head.

"I've tried once last night and again this morning," I grumbled as I grabbed the portal chip off the counter in the kitchen. "Believe me, when she sleeps, she sleeps."

He was quiet for a second. *Did you make her like that?*

I frowned. "What do you mean?"

Calm… quiet. Rested and content.

Fear was way strange lately. I shrugged my shoulders. "I don't know. Considering she told us about being locked up over the centuries, I can imagine this place is nice compared to what she's been through."

If you keep her that way… does that mean she'll stay?

Seconds from pressing the portal chip, I stopped at Fear's words. It was as I thought. Molly was bringing the monster to his knees, and she wasn't even doing anything. He wanted to keep her. I wanted to keep her.

"Yes, normally when you treat a woman right and woo her, she'll stay," I told him.

Woo her? he muttered, confused.

"It means we go after her with charm and interests other than what's between her legs so that she knows she's wanted."

Then you woo her, he said, *so I can keep her.*

I dropped my head and clenched my teeth. "I can't keep her, and neither can you."

Why? You can't stop me—

"Because I'm you, and you're you." I gripped the portal chip. "You don't even know how to care for someone. The only thing you know is pain, and now that's all that can keep my interest in the long run."

———

"You ready?" Melanie asked for the hundredth time since I got here *twenty* minutes ago.

"I'm ready," I muttered, lifting myself off the couch. "You're the one that seems nervous." Which was true, I breathed it in all around her. I didn't know if she was nervous to see Tess again or if her nervousness was for me meeting Tess after all these years. It was only a lifetime for Tess but for me, it'd been several.

I raked my fingers into my scalp and took a deep, silent breath to calm my own nerves. Honestly, I wasn't okay. I was on the verge of running. I broke into a cold sweat, clammy hands and all. I was good at hiding it from Melanie though, or at least I thought so. Killian, on the other hand, probably sensed it all but didn't say anything.

"Let's go," I finally said. "I wanna get this over with before—"

"It eats you alive?" She smiled softly and all I could do was nod.

There was another scent in the room that I couldn't ignore either, and although it was something I could always smell on every other male or female, it was the first time smelling it from Killian. Melanie, she was always heavy with the scent of being fertile but Killian, he kept his closed off. Until now. As Fear, it was something even I could control so that I wouldn't impregnate someone and the fact that he wasn't controlling it anymore told me all I needed to know. They wanted a family. I couldn't congratulate them or bring it up until they did. I was left with the awkwardness of knowing but keeping quiet until they wanted to share the news with me. Which would probably be after she became pregnant.

I was happy for them, honestly. But I couldn't change the fact that being around two people so happy and in love, and about to start a family reminded me of what I'd never have. I had once wanted those things with Melanie. Growing up, I had pathetic dreams about our future together. One that never came to pass, and although I was over that hurdle and was happy for her and Killian, it didn't mean I forgot how much I wanted a family. Kids. I couldn't believe how much of a family guy I dreamed of being until I realized, sadly, I still was one underneath all the layers of darkness.

And it was another thing I could never have as Fear. Molly's face filtered through my thoughts and I knew why. But even that possibility was shut down. Molly was infertile. It wasn't something I wanted to sense in people. I didn't want to know if they could make babies or not but I could. A monster could sense a lot of things.

I didn't even know why I thought of her in that moment of reminiscence.

She'll stay, Fear started up again since he knew my thoughts and knew I was thinking about her. *If you make her want to.*

Why don't you just force her to stay? I snapped back in my thoughts. *When have you ever asked me to do anything, including asking someone to stay next to you knowing you're poison. You take what you want, even if I tell you Molly deserves a chance to run from us. I'm sure you'll bring her back. I mean, that's why you marked her, to begin with, right? So, she'd never get away? I'm done playing with her. I don't want to fucking hurt her, and I don't want to hurt when one of us finally do hurt her.*

"Are you okay?" Killian's hand gripped my shoulder and I escaped my mind to focus on his hard stare.

"I'm fine," I reassured him with a grin. "He's not coming out if that's what you're worried about."

He sighed in relief and dropped his hand. "Good, I was worried he might mess this up for you."

Why are you buddies with him again? Fear growled. *And why the fuck did I let you live so close to these two is beyond—*

"Fear's been preoccupied lately," I said quickly to shut Fear up. It was irritating as fuck trying to have a conversation with Fear blaring in your skull. "Freaking the hell out of me as well," I added, and Fear made a grab for my body in response. I tensed up, worried that maybe he was going to force himself out, and me in. But he didn't. It was only to worry me after talking about him.

Melanie's head lifted at my words and she walked over. "Is that right?" she asked, curiosity and worry slipping out of her. "So," she exhaled, crossing her arms nonchalantly. "How's it going with your new houseguest?"

I smiled. "Ah, it's interesting," I gave a bit.

She wanted more. "Oh?"

"Yeah, Fear might have delivered her into my arms, but it's me that she wants." I slid my hand against my chest and just knew I should keep my mouth shut. Fear and I have never gotten along, but with Molly, we came to an agreement then to disagreement again. Point was, things were strained between us and I didn't need to go poking the monster, but it was the only thing that relieved me of the fear of seeing my sister again. "She won't even let him touch her." I doubled over, grabbing my stomach as Fear did something to me from the inside.

"Ryan!" Melanie panicked then it was over.

I lifted back up and smiled. "It's fine. He's a little sore about it."

Killian smirked and Melanie shook her head like I'd lost it. "I think maybe you shouldn't go making it worse," she scolded me. "Fear has the power to take you from us, Ryan." I stopped smiling, the truth of her words I already knew. "I'm worried there will come a day when he never lets you come back out." Her words, face, and emotions reached out. She was sincere about the worry.

But it didn't matter because I was starting to think I should have died when I was supposed to. I didn't care how weak that made me sound to Fear. I didn't understand why he chose me.

Maybe just like Molly had told me about her chance at peace, I should have tried harder to fight the link that drawn me into Fear. I should have tried harder for my own peace. Or died as nothing.

Now I'd never find peace or death unless Fear decided to give me one or the other.

We stood outside her bedroom door to wait for her death. I wouldn't cross over into her bedroom where she was lying peacefully next to her husband. I didn't want to witness the pain that took her life. Her death already fogged the air around us to the point that it was stifling. We should have waited until it was already over.

I looked over at Grim and Melanie and wondered if this was what it always felt like for them. Two beings that carried death everywhere they went—waiting on it, trusting it, guiding it. Suddenly, I wasn't so envious of them anymore. This dark cloud floating around in the air—Grim, more like it—was suffocating. And now he was here for my sister.

Then I stumbled away from the door when I heard it—yes, I fucking heard the huge gasp of air she sucked in. It filled the quiet room, the empty house. It was just her and her husband, now that their kids were grown. And the gasp came, but the exhale never came after. It was a constant wheezing sound. Grim slipped into the room. Melanie stared at the door, conflicted before turning to me. "There'll be no more pain for her after this," she said it like it made this part better. But she knew it didn't. She experienced this all herself so she knew exactly what it felt like.

I heard the sound of someone flipping the light switch—her husband started panicking, "Tessa! Tessa!" I imagined him placing his hands on her body somewhere, maybe shaking her—checking her somehow since he was a doctor. Even through the fear, I could sense the love tumbling off his body for her. It made me smile, only for a moment. But she kept gasping, gasping—

"Come on, we can't be there for him, but we can be there for her," Melanie said right before taking my hand and walking me through the door with her. The worst part was already over—her pain, I meant. As for husband and family, theirs had just begun.

Penny kept me updated with pictures of everyone while she was alive, and when Melanie came back, she started giving me pictures of them instead. I would occasionally go see her or my niece and nephew from afar, but only for a few seconds before I'd cave and port away.

But looking at my old and frail sister rise from her body as a ghost, something in me regretted all those years I wasted because of my own fear. Her husband had already dialed 9-1-1 even when he knew it was too late. He just sat there crying with her in his arms, waiting, knowing he would have to call up his kids soon.

My heart twisted, and I was full of regret. She noticed Grim at first, and since I was a ghost before I knew that you automatically knew of Reapers the moment you died—it just planted itself in your brain to know so you're prepared for what's to come.

She nodded toward Grim then her eyes landed on us. "Melanie," she gasped, her voice raspy and aged. Tess had aged. She wasn't the girl I left behind, she was an old lady I was saying goodbye to. Her wrinkled face looked even more shocked as she locked eyes with me. "Ryan." She cupped her mouth then brought her hands to her ears, confused. "What—"

"I've missed you," Melanie choked out as she tugged at my hand before stepping in front of my sister and wrapping her into a hug. Tess went from shocked to a happy, warm smile as she closed her eyes and hugged her back. "And, I'm going to miss you even more with our last goodbye." Melanie's words brought me back to why we were here.

I brought my hands up to my eyes and gently covered them. My throat was clogged, full of all these emotions I wanted to run from.

"I don't understand," Tess looked back and forth between us. "How are you young again, Melanie? And Ryan…" She smiled big. "Are we going to finally be together again?"

That was more than I could take. I broke with a smile. "Didn't think you'd see me again?" I asked through unleashed tears.

Tess stepped away from Melanie and came to me. She brought her hands up to my cheeks. "No, on the contrary, I've been waiting to see my twin since the moment I lost him," she said with a smile. She dropped her hands. I sucked in a shaky breath as she looked to her husband. "This is very sad, isn't it?" She looked back at me and Melanie. "Saying goodbye to people you don't want to leave behind." This Tess I didn't know. Her gaze was conflicted with sadness and worry, so aged and understanding. "I'm not sure I was ready to leave them just yet… I'm happy to see you, Ryan, truly. I've waited so long to see you again, but—" Her voice clogged up and I stood stiffly. "He's hurting. And my babies, they're gonna miss me."

I brought my hands up to her shoulders and gripped her ghostly body tight. "You'll see them again one day," I told her, hoping it were true. I had no real clue what Heaven was like or how it worked.

She nodded. "You're right." She glanced back over to Melanie. "Will I revert back to my younger self like you, Melanie?" she asked softly.

Melanie had the same look I must have. She was torn. Grim took over at that moment, placing his hand against her forehead. He fed her memories. "I remember," she gasped. A tear slid down her ghostly cheek. "We're not going to be together again, are we?" she asked sadly.

Melanie nodded. "We belong somewhere else, but don't worry." She smiled at Tess. "I'll watch over him." Melanie turned toward me. "As much as he'll let me."

"Good luck." Tess chuckled. Soon her arms were around me, and I hugged her back. "I didn't realize it until now." She pulled away from me as she inspected me. Her ghost fingers hovered in and out of my skin as she traced the tattoos on my arms then she met my eyes again with another bright smile. "Just how much you've changed."

"I should have come to see you," I started out then shook my head. "But a lot has happened, and I've changed."

She shook her head. "I don't care, I don't care," she chanted. "And you shouldn't either. You know I believe everything happens for a reason… if you can't change something, accept it."

It was hard to believe this old woman was Tess. Nothing she said sounded like something my sister would say, but she grew up and grew old…

"You've change too," I added with a hint of sadness in my voice.

"Yeah," she said deeply. "It's kinda what we do in life." She looked back at her husband. "I don't suppose I can touch him like I can you?" I shook my head sadly. "Did you say goodbye to Mom and Dad when they passed away?"

I hadn't expected her to ask that question. Grim had come to me and asked if I had wanted to say goodbye when both of their deaths had come, and I chose not to. "I didn't." I looked away, and it was like Tess was reading into everything I did.

"It's okay," she told me like she understood. "I don't know what happened to you, but don't tell me. I spent a lifetime thinking you were in a good place—"

"I get it," I said quickly.

"Don't be mad at me for choosing not to know." She sucked in a breath. "I love you, and I want you to live comfortably without any burdens."

I couldn't blink or look away from her. I understood all too well. I was positive she did know what I've become, and that was exactly the reason she wanted to pretend she didn't know. For her own sake or mine, I didn't know. I would never know because I'd respect her choice. Because I loved her and still did, even as a monster.

"I hope Heaven is everything you want it to be and more," I murmured.

Grim opened the passage behind her—the light was bright. Fear squirmed inside me. She glanced around the room like she was willing herself to accept what's happened. "I hope the place that keeps you both is a good place," she said quickly. I didn't miss what she meant. She worried for us. Melanie met my eyes and I could see it in her eyes, she knew it too.

"We're not in Heaven, but we're happy," Melanie couldn't help but say. "Don't worry." She smiled and Tess seemed to relax some.

Tess glanced back at me, something in her eyes alarmed me. She quickly looked away like she wanted to forget what she had seen. I glanced down at my hands then back at her but she was already moving into the passage. My insides screamed at me—why did she look at me that way?

"Tess," Melanie said quickly.

Tess cocked her head to the side. "I love you both," was all she said before she slipped into the light and was gone to us forever.

I staggered backward. Melanie studied me, panic and sadness pouring off her. I lifted my head and gripped it. "What was it? Why did she look at me like that?" I tried to recall what her emotions had been but for some reason, I hadn't been paying attention. No, I had been too afraid to breathe them in.

My insides were tearing me to pieces. The red was consuming me. Then I thought back to the moment Grim fed her memories. My anger was hot and bitter against my tongue as I glared at him. "What did you show her?" I screamed. "What memories did he feed her?" Did he feed her a memory of what I was?

"He didn't show her what—"

Of course, Melanie would defend him. She would always defend him. "Stop!" Uncertainty flashed in her eyes, and it pissed me off even more. "Then why did she act that way—why did she suddenly—"

"Ryan," Melanie whispered. "It's your eyes." She closed her eyes like she didn't even want to tell me. "They turned red right before she left, and they still are now."

I grabbed my face and smirked. It was my fault. Of course, it was my fault. "Do you think she knows I'm the same monster that attacked our town?" I gritted the words out.

"No, Ryan, I don't think that," she lied. "She knows you're different, she just doesn't know how exactly."

"Don't you remember, Melanie?" I whispered mockingly.

"What?"

"That I fucking know everyone's emotions—I feed on them, remember?" Her face was sullen. "I smell the lie before you even say it!"

"Ryan!"

Grim stepped forward, placing himself between Melanie and me like I'd hurt her. It made me sick. But then again, I didn't even trust myself when my temper was hot. I wouldn't trust me not to hurt her either.

"You're letting Fear's emotions control yours," Grim told me. "I think you should go take the edge off before he forces himself out."

That was it, this wasn't Fear. It was all me. They just weren't accepting the fact that being Fear has changed me. "You know what." I laughed. "That's a good idea."

Grim nodded, but his essence pooled darkly. "Use your portal chip and head back."

What's your fucking problem? You're being pathetic. Fear growled. *To let him speak to you like that!*

I was already pissed about it, but with Fear's added anger I was livid. "What's wrong?" I smirked. "What do you think I'm going to do?"

"It's not you I'm worried about," Grim said.

See, there it was again.

I was tired, exhausted suddenly. I couldn't remember why I kept fighting for the good in me when there was barely any left. I had nothing. No one. Molly's tall, thin body and face flooded my memory out of nowhere, and I wondered if it was Fear's doing. It didn't matter though because I was about to give it all up. I wanted to escape into the darkness instead of fighting Fear all the damn time.

I'd let him do what he wanted. I just wanted to rest.

"I don't care what he does." I placed the biggest grin on my face as I said it. "It's time you see how much I don't give a shit."

And for the first time ever, I gave up my control.

The very control I've been fighting to keep for a thousand years.

CHAPTER NINETEEN

Fear

Ryan continued to surprise me.

This surprise wasn't one I was thrilled about, though. I was fucking furious. Never once had he run away before, and I've put him through shit. A lot more than this—whatever this was. Not that I gave a shit what Grim or his woman thought, but *he* did. And the fact that he brought me out of his own free will...

Grim watched me with a cool, calm atmosphere. "Let's go take the edge off," he offered, and he meant it, not knowing Ryan hid away.

They cared for Ryan, and yet he only ever saw what he wanted. Their anger and nervousness wasn't because they didn't trust him, it was me that made them that way. That flowery shit that they feel about it each other, well, they exude similar feelings off for Ryan.

Fucking *love.*

It made my skin crawl just being around all this goody-goody stuff. Grim was Death! Why did an entity such as him go around spreading that shit? It was a disgrace. Death, pain, violence, and fucking… now those were things to live for. Was it because he had a different creator? What made him want different things than me?

I didn't care—I shouldn't care… but I wondered why I had to be all about fear. I wondered why Ryan didn't want to be me so fucking bad. I wondered why he fought me so hard only to give up within days… it was a fast change. I didn't know what happened. Did I finally get to him after all this time?

It made me wonder what it was like to *care.*

And that made me wonder why I wondered about all these things I never did before.

Ryan's sister's husband voice drifted into the phone, bringing me back to the surface. He was crying, a blubbering mess as he spoke of his wife's death. I grabbed my chest and winced. It felt… funny. Uncomfortable. I didn't like it. It was strange.

Ryan had been right about that. Everything was *strange* anymore.

As he talked to one his kids on the phone, the tightness in my chest grew… I had to get away. I had a feeling it had something to do with this room, his sister, and her husband.

I glanced at Melanie. She nodded. "We should go," she told me. "I don't think either of us wants to see anymore." She had tears in her eyes.

I couldn't take it anymore. Them not knowing that I wasn't Ryan. "He's gone." Those two words were all I had to say, and Melanie and Grim became guarded and hostile.

"Fear?" Grim growled my name.

I smirked. "Afraid so."

"How could you—" Melanie started then stopped. "How could you ruin that with Tess?"

I laughed. "I ruined nothing. That was all him." She didn't believe me. Not that I cared. "He ran away from, well, I don't even know."

"You're killing him!" she hissed at me.

"Don't worry." I placed my hands in my pockets, letting my finger trace over the portal chip. "I plan to bring the baby out and ask him where his balls went."

"Fear—" Melanie lunged as her husband stood behind her doing nothing. I wasn't stupid. He was waiting on what I'd do.

I pressed the portal chip and entered the City of the Dead. Neither of them followed… yet. I glanced around the quiet streets. "Now. What innocent creature do I kill first, Ryan… to force you out?"

I waited for some sort of response inside me. Nothing. Empty as it always was when I was out. He couldn't sink inside my mind like I could his. I even stood there in the street trying to let him have control. Only I came up blank. It was like he wasn't there.

That weird feeling was there in my chest again. I ignored it and focused my energy—anger—on how many I'd have to kill to get something from him. Anything. It was dead, quiet on the inside. And every second that deadness only seemed to grow, I didn't want it there.

I wasn't about to deal with what he refused to.

I walked into a bar, entering with the depravity that meant countless lives were in danger. The air in the place changed with my presence, not in a good way. Fear pooled from most of their bodies, including arrogance for some. My name wasn't as feared as it used to be, with Ryan, my killings were toward bad demons. He never took innocence. Marcus, on the other hand, had no qualms about killing anything. He'd kill anyone that stepped in his path. Before my merge with Marcus, I hadn't been much different than him about killing anything. I just hadn't been obsessed with power like he had been. The only thing I had felt when I watched him die was relief that I wasn't trapped anymore.

I was doing the same thing to Ryan. I didn't like being left with no control. Why did I expect him to? I was bitter, full of anger when I merged with Ryan… now, I didn't know what this ugliness I was feeling was all about. I had a feeling this was his fault, though. This weirdness going on between us.

Ryan was unusually dark and chaotic while I was…

My skin rippled as I changed into the creature I really was. I did it in front of everyone in the bar and smiled when it was over. I scanned the crowd. Nobody was completely innocent down here in the Underworld, but Ryan seemed to be choosy about who he killed. A sword materialized in my hand—the first time I've called a weapon to me in a long time—and the bloodbath began. Screams erupted as my sword went through the first demon—male. I took his banshee babe out right after him.

"Fear!" someone screamed.

"Why is he—" She didn't get to finish. My blade cut into the bottom of her mouth, ripping out the top of her head. The panic fed what I needed. Sadly, the taste wasn't appealing. It was almost nasty. But I kept going through what was left of the demons that hadn't yet made it out of the door. A skinny vampire sprouted his fangs and hissed at me. He eyed the door, contemplating if he was quick enough to get by me. Vampires were quick. He took his chance. My tail snaked out and pierced his chest. Not quick enough. I sighed as his body dissolved to nothing.

I wiggled the blood off my tail, and it darted out to another one trying to escape. Grim faded in front of him to block my tail. The demon took off running, and I slid my tail back behind me and placed my hands in my pockets. "Can I help you?" I asked, bored-like.

"You're going too far," Melanie said as she faded next to Grim. A scowl was planted on her face. She was beautiful according to Ryan and her husband. *Ah, Molly's better*, I thought. All evil and fucked up, and now I knew that she was also quite needy and clingy. Perfect.

Yep, my kind of obsession.

"Not yet, obviously." I raked my claws across my chin.

"If you're going to kill something," Grim said. "Kill something that deserves it."

I rolled my eyes. "That defeats the purpose. I want him to come out, doing what he does isn't going to do that."

"Why?" Melanie asked, arching a brow.

"Why what?"

"Why do you want him to come out?"

I laughed. What a stupid question. "Because he doesn't get to run away." I dipped my hand into my jeans and tapped a claw against the portal chip. "Blame it on him for everything that I have to do. He'll come out eventually."

I ported to a whorehouse. Ryan frequented this place every now and then, and I still remembered the feisty wolf he came to see occasionally. Although he saw a lot of women, I was sure he wouldn't want something bad to happen to one of them. It hadn't changed anything when I killed those at the bar because he didn't know any of them. He had no emotional tie. I was sure hurting the wolf would be different. I'd take her by force if I had to.

She was busy with a client when I busted the door down. She jumped up, and the fat demon's dick popped out of her cunt. "What," he yelled, then scattered back on his ass when he saw who I was. I wasted no time and killed the ugly ass with my tail. I might be a scary fucking creature, but I wasn't ugly. Not with Ryan anyway.

A surprised gasp fell from her lips before it turned to a dreamy smile. I wrapped my tail around her neck and dropped on my knees. "I'm taking you by force." In my head, it sounded menacing and evil.

Only instead of a terrified shriek I was hoping for, she purred, "Yes."

"No, I'm going to fucking hurt you," I said differently this time.

She nodded worshipfully. "Please, Fear, make me hurt."

See what I mean about my reputation? I was threatening to rape her, and she responded with nothing but lust and excitement. Fucking Ryan. I wasn't taken seriously anymore unless I was killing something. He had every woman drooling over him, not that I was complaining. I normally was into it.

I gripped my tail tighter around her neck and she smiled, bringing her hand to my soft cock. I jerked back so quick she retracted her hand hurriedly. That was new. I wasn't into any of this. Her response relieved me because I didn't want to rape her. I didn't even want her. For some reason, the twinge in my chest grew. It almost felt like I felt bad for doing this.

No, not only that. *Guilty*. I felt guilty. I didn't have any interest in any creature except a raven-haired little monster. She didn't care about me, but I knew she cared about Ryan. If I did this with another woman, she wouldn't like it. The thought of hurting her feelings sent a bad pain in my heart I didn't like.

I released the werewolf's neck slowly and stood. "Fear?" she sounded disappointed.

I ignored her and turned for the door quickly to get out of the whorehouse. The thought of Molly even knowing what I was about to with that woman sent me in a state of panic. I rubbed my face over and over.

But then I stopped myself *only* because I wasn't into it. Not for any other reason. Ryan wasn't going to react anyway. I didn't stop because of Molly. I didn't—

Why was I denying the truth? The same way Ryan was denying everything right now.

"None of this is going to bring him out." Grim was propped against the wall the moment I stepped out on the streets. "You heard him." His essence flowed out of his eyeless gaze as he turned to me. "He said he didn't care, and he doesn't."

"He does," I added bitterly. "Or he wouldn't push me out to do the dirty work."

"I'm not so sure," Grim murmured. "But why are you so upset about it? Isn't this what you enjoy? Making him hurt?"

I shrugged my shoulders like I didn't care.

I didn't fucking care. I gripped my chest.

"Don't act like you know what's going on here," I said. Good to know that I still didn't like Grim interfering with all this change happening inside me.

He couldn't possibly understand what it was like to suddenly experience all these new emotions when all I've known is the bad things. Not this… heaviness of feeling bad after doing something I've always done before. It was completely new, and somehow, I had to deal with what Ryan gave me.

Only I shouldn't have to. He was a part of me. He was good at dealing with this—

That was it!

I frowned, and Grim moved from the wall like he was trying to understand me. He could keep trying, but he'd never understand a monster.

"I'll bring him out," was all I had left to say.

I was looking at this all wrong. The reason all this started, the reason we've began to change, the reason I had wanted to be Ryan—yes, *wanted* to be him. The change started the moment I brought her in the picture.

Molly was the answer to our undoing.

CHAPTER TWENTY

Molly

I slept too long if the pounding of my head was any indication when I first woke. Ryan had already left to go say goodbye to his sister, and I was stuck for hours alone in the house. I made myself a sandwich—the only thing I could make—and sat on the counter with my feet dangling as I ate. Then I somehow ended up with my head hanging off the table as I skimmed through a book. After that, I took a bag of chips with me to the couch and watched a horror movie.

It was lonely waiting on him, and I knew I could go anywhere I wanted with a portal chip, but the thought of missing him when he came home stopped me from going anywhere.

I sighed, splashing water over my face in the bathroom. I studied myself in the mirror. I looked no different, really, but maybe there was a slight color to my cheeks that hadn't been there before. I was eating, I was living, and I was smiling back at myself.

It was time to tell Ryan. He would be mad, and he might not ever forgive me but he deserved the truth when he made me happy, if only for a short amount of time. It was more than I ever remember being.

The moment I stepped out of the bathroom, I knew someone was in the house with me. Only it wasn't Ryan or Fear. I whipped my head around to the bedroom doors.

"Marybeth?" I asked, surprised to see the old witch here. She didn't look like someone that could move very far from her chair. The bigger question was, why was she here? My guard came up and I stiffened. "What are you doing here?"

"You haven't given him the potion yet," she said before lifting the vial up in her hands to show me.

"Why is that any of your business?" I walked over to her, and snatched it from her hand, sliding it into my pocket.

Something in her eyes changed. "So, you don't plan to use it on him or yourself?" she asked with a slightly altered tone.

I studied her. “Not that it’s any of your business.” Her being here only made my choice easier, the one I’ve been pondering on. “I don’t plan to use it.”

She huffed, shaking her head in disappointment. “I should have known this would happen.” What was she going on about? “You think a monster can love, Molly?” she asked with a voice that made my skin shrivel.

“Leave,” I said, turning away from her. “That isn’t any of your business.” I turned back and scowled. “If I want to fuck a monster, that’s my choice.”

Her eyes hardened. “Foolish,” she muttered.

“What?” I bit out.

That cold, bitter smile of hers washed over me with unease. “You can’t be happy, Molly.”

“Bye, Marybeth,” I said through gritted teeth.

The moment she ported, I turned back around and headed for the kitchen. I pulled the vial out of my pocket and went to the sink. I was seconds from emptying the liquid down the drain when Ryan ported into the living room. I jerked my hand back and slid the vial back into my jeans as he scanned the room until his eyes landed on me. He was in Fear’s form, and suddenly I was worried.

Blood coated his tail and his entire body was taut. For some reason, I feared his goodbye didn’t go too well.

I pushed off the counter and went to him. “Ryan?” I asked softly.

Then his tail was around my waist, and I was being slung against the wall. His weight pressed into me next as blood-red eyes bore into mine. I grabbed the tail and tugged at it. “Fear?” I waited for some sort of clue as to who I was dealing with.

Heat spread through me when I felt his erection hot against my stomach. He grinded into me with purpose, and I reached for his shoulders, pulling him in. His eyes widened, almost if he was surprised by my reaction. *This is Fear*, I figured out.

Even I was a bit wary of the way my body reacted to him in this form, but it was what it was. And I wasn’t going to fight it. I had questions that needed answers anyway. About him and Ryan.

He laughed manically, releasing me and turning around, then coming right back a second later and forcing himself back against me. "I'm Fear," he hissed like it pained him to admit it.

"Is something wrong?" I asked immediately. "Why are you so…" I couldn't think of the right word.

"He's gone."

I blinked, heart stopping. "What?"

"He ran," he said, letting go of me again. He brought his hands up to his face and paced back and forth. "He fucking gave in."

I squinted, brows dipping in the middle with worry. "Did something happen when he met his sister?"

"Not really," he answered. "But in his mind, it was. He completely overlooked the fact that his sister loved him, she did." He bobbed his head up and down almost like he was determined to believe it. "She just got startled when she saw the red eyes… she didn't want to see them. That was it."

My heart broke for Ryan. I told him to go see her. I hadn't imagined it would end this way.

"It's not just that," he said, moving toward me again.

I was still leaning against the wall. I swallowed slowly. "Spit it out, Fear," I growled, knowing he had something to pin on me.

"It's you," he replied, smacking his palms against the wall beside each of my ears. "The unraveling began the moment I brought you here."

I raked my teeth over my bottom lip. "The blame game," I muttered.

"What?"

"It's our thing," I whispered. "We blame everyone but ourselves for our problems… You and me."

"I don't know what you're fucking talking about," he lied. The monster lied.

"Yeah, you do." He flinched when I brought my hand to his chest. Fear's heart hammered furiously underneath my fingertips. "We're selfish, too." He watched me with knowing eyes. "We're villains, Fear."

"I never said I wasn't."

"A monster and a dead girl turned immortal." I sighed. "How unlucky for Ryan to cross our paths." I paused and slid my hand down his shirt. "Can't you make him come out?"

He dropped his head. "No. This has never happened before. It's almost like… he's out of my control."

"We should bring him out." I tugged at Fear's shirt.

His eyes reddened even more. "How do we do that?"

"We've played a lot of games in the past—"

"It was Marcus," he interrupted.

I nodded. "I know, but you were there through it all?" He nodded and I went on, "We're good at being selfish, good at playing the blame game. Let's play a new one." He cocked a brow. "Let this one be the truth."

"Truth?" he asked warily.

"Why did you choose to merge with Ryan?"

He snorted. "He was easy prey."

I clucked my tongue. "Lie." He averted his eyes, and I gripped his face so hard it surprised him. "Are you obsessed with me, Fear?" I asked another. I stared into his eyes for the longest time. "Answer them both. Honestly."

"I think I finally succeeded in breaking him." He avoided the questions, but his words alone were enough admittance to what I suspected.

"You haven't," I promised. "You wanted to know what it was like, didn't you?" His eyes widened. He hadn't even realized himself what I already figured out. "You became him for his goodness because you wanted to taste it." He shook his head, and I continued to unravel him the way he accused me of doing. "And when you had a taste of his goodness, it was too much so you blocked it out, kept him separated from your own emotions because you were afraid of what would become of you."

"That's not true," he mumbled. He sounded of defeat and denial to my ears.

"But, it's finally blurring, those lines you put between you and him. But now, you're scared again, only this time it's not because of his good. No... what you're afraid of this time is not being him anymore."

He tried to push away from me, but I held on to him, firmly and *endlessly.*

"It's okay," I said quickly. "I'll tell you a truth that's both yours and mine." He waited patiently for me to go on. "I'm greedy for that goodness, too. In fact, I want to keep him by my side so that I can bathe in it, taste it, devour it. I don't want anyone else to have it." I let go of his face and dropped my hands to his shoulders. "We're not good, Fear. We are very, very bad." His tail wound itself around my right leg. I trailed my fingers down his arms, heat igniting through me. "He deserves better, but he got stuck with you, and now me."

"What do we do now?"

I grabbed a hold of one of his hands and placed it over one of my small breasts, the ones he teased me for, but now I knew he was ravenous for every part of me. "First, you let him in."

"Not gonna work," he growled, bruising his hand against my breast.

I laughed. "Shame on him," I whispered, "for making me love him."

He stilled. "You love him," he gasped.

"You never answered my two questions," I changed the subject. "I already know the truth, so don't dare lie to me. Not if you want to keep your claws on me."

He hung his head between us. "You're right, it's always been about being more than what I am," he acknowledged. "And, you, Molly, you were the very reason I was controlled by someone as weak as Marcus."

I frowned. "How is that?"

"Because keeping you around kept me obedient. All he had to do was threaten to destroy your soul, and I'd listen," he admitted, and my whole body responded with a slow burn that erupted from my core. "You have been my obsession for the longest time." He lifted his head and stared at me with such intensity that it hurt. "Not that you'd want the attention of a murderous entity like me, but you don't have a choice, and neither did I when it came to wanting you."

I pushed myself off of the wall, easing myself closer to him. He stood rigid mere inches away, my breast still in his claws. I swore I could hear his heart pounding. I dragged my hand down to his erection and gripped it firmly. He sucked in a breath, but I wanted him weak in the knees. Ryan would soon realize the fun he was missing out on, and come back to us.

"Who knew you'd be the easiest one to control," I said with a smile, and he had a passion-driven expression as his tail shot up and gripped my neck. My gaze fell on the dried blood.

A moment of panic crossed his face as his tail retreated. I snatched it before it could. His expression hardened then fell again. "I should wash up, then…" he trailed off.

Ryan truly weaved a part of himself into Fear. He might not have realized it quite yet, but this monster wasn't just a monster anymore.

"Why do you want to wash up? Shouldn't you want it filthy?" I studied him. "Have you forgotten how many times I've seen just exactly what it is you enjoy doing to women?" I squeezed my legs together, rubbing them against one another to increase the pleasure building. I gripped his erection through his jeans again.

His nostrils flared. "You don't want me being gentle, Molly?" I was even more turned on with the change in his tone. "You want me to fuck you like the monster I am? You're dirty," he told me. I felt a shift between us and knew I was no longer in control. "Thank fuck. I can do dirty, I can do pain, too. Let me take your lust and drown you in it."

Oh, damn. I should be ashamed how my body was reacting to him.

He grabbed my arm and turned us. "Come on, you can wash my tail before I shove it in your pussy."

I released his tail in my grip when I remembered the vial in my pocket. I dropped it into the trashcan as we walked by it, feeling better now that it was out of my hands.

He led me into the bathroom where he shoved me in front of the tub. He didn't ask anything, he just started yanking off my clothes. First my shirt, then he destroyed the zipper on my pants before forcing them down my legs, taking my black panties with them. He pressed his nose into my clit and inhaled. I grabbed his horns just to feel them then stopped immediately after. My need for him was already dripping down my leg.

He stood, leaned over the tub, and turned on the faucet. He reached for my hand, placing me on my knees as his tail slipped underneath me and into the tub. He gave me a nudge, wanting me to lean over the tub. "Go ahead and soap it up," he ordered me.

I took a shaky breath, not out of fear, I was just so into this. I gripped his tail and moved it underneath the running water. I slid my hand up and down it at first before grabbing the soap and drizzling it all over. I sensed him moving closer behind me. I tilted my head back and saw that he was on his knees behind me. He pressed a part of his tail against my clit, and it caught me by surprise. I gasped, my head dropping into the tub. I stroked his tail harder, and it was a soapy mess. Between my legs, his tail rubbed across me torturously. Soon I was squirming and wiggling myself into it to ease the ache.

His hands fell on my ass, and he spread me open. It only fueled my desire when I felt his breath against my opening. The dirty monster pressed his nose into me and breathed me in. "So dirty… pressing your nose into my ass and smelling," I admitted with a moan. "And it's turning me on so much."

"Oh, believe me, I know. Your desire is filling up the entire house." I shoved my ass into his face and his mouth opened and started greedily sucking at my arousal. I moaned and stroked his tail faster as the back of his tail and mouth worked magic on me.

"I'm going to take your ass with my tail," he promised with hot breaths that made me whimper. "But that will wait until Ryan's inside you too." My orgasm came hard and fast, sending white beneath my eyelids as I cried out. His words sent me over the edge far too quickly.

He jerked his tail out of my lazy grip and ran it under the water to wash the soap off before turning me around. He got off his knees and stood over me. My eyes landed on his erection trapped in his jeans. I smiled and helped myself to him. His eyes were on me hungrily, but there was something else. Something that was more than obsession. He gave an appreciative moan once his erection sprang free, bobbing for my attention and lips.

I ran my hand underneath him and met his eyes. "I've decided," I told him.

He arched a brow with a pleased smirk. "What have you decided, Molly?"

"That I'm going to keep Ryan." He was silent, and I quickly added, "And I'm going to keep you too."

Dropping my gaze, I leaned forward and took him into my mouth. He moaned. "Molly." Never had my name sounded so cherished coming from someone's lips until that moment. I knew it wasn't because of the pleasure I was giving him. It was for the words. The acceptance of wanting to be with him like I have been with Ryan. Living day after day doing whatever the hell we wanted.

I popped him out of my mouth and said, "Let him in."

I took him back into my mouth as far as I could until I was gagging then I pulled back and did it all over again. I cupped his balls and his tail slid down my body and slipped inside, stretching me in one painfully, exquisite thrust. My moan was muffled as I sucked him hard. His tail was brutal as it ravished me until I had no choice but to accept the hard orgasm as it tore through me. He grabbed the back of my head and forced himself to the back of my throat. That alone sent another orgasm crashing through me. I felt him swell on my lips, and against my aching jaw. "Look at me, Blue."

I did. Ryan was back. Tears slid down my cheeks, I was so relieved and drunk off pleasure and Fear and him. "Fuck, I'm coming," he groaned, succumbing to the pleasure I was giving as he kept himself lodged in my mouth and shot the back of my throat. I could hardly breathe or swallow until he pulled out. I sucked in a breath and he lifted my chin. "Swallow." I was swallowing, but he left me with no other choice to begin with. Not that I minded.

I closed my aching mouth and gave a smile free of everything but what I felt for them. "Do you want to talk about why you gave up your control after all this time fighting Fear for it?"

Rubbing his finger across my chin, he shifted out of Fear's form. His smile, like mine, was free. Or maybe it was just what I wanted to believe. Because something about the way he was smiling at me had my heart beating beautifully.

He shook his head slowly. "Momentarily insanity. I'm back to normal now," he told me, and I was relieved. "All I wanna do right now is make love to you."

Make love?

He bent over. "Come here." He scooped me up in my arms, and I fell silent, not use to the nervous feeling in my stomach. No one's made love to me before. And all I was hoping for was for him to forgive me when I told him and for him let me stay by his side.

He only had to say those words and now I was wishing for my love to be returned.

Foolishly, I now wanted his heart too.

CHAPTER TWENTY-ONE

Ryan

That flowery shit Fear and I normally detested rolled off Molly in waves like a smooth caress, calling to me in a way that had me answering. It smelled of all the sweets things in this world and tasted like cotton candy, sugary and too sweet, but I wanted all of hers.

I didn't even care what it meant that she felt. If I was honest, I was all too eager to accept hers. I drank her in as I carried her to my bedroom, pressing my nose into her neck and loving the way she never refused me and the way she showed affection in the strangest ways.

A little lost and a lot of confusion, pain, and hurt messed with me. I let my own darkened thoughts finally get to me. I hadn't expected Fear and Molly dragging me back out of that darkness, tempting me with carnal passions. Like I could stay put when she was giving Fear her body to take. What was even crazier was how easily he had given up this moment alone with her and slipped into the recesses of my mind to experience it through me.

I wasn't a good guy but I wasn't bad all the time either. I could accept that if someone like Molly could still want a guy that was also a monster. She seemed to want both and that was how I knew this could work. Whatever this was, it didn't have to end.

I laid her down on the bed gently, and she was a mess of nerves and love. I raised up to take off my shirt and jeans then found my way back to her. She had her legs propped up, knees bent together with her hands beside her head. She waited for me to do something. The moment I said, "making love" the nervousness in her crawled out. This was new to her, and it might as well have been for me too. The last time I made love to a girl was in high school, and I wouldn't really consider it that. It was just a shared first experience for me and the girl.

I lifted her leg and lightly kissed her ankle before settling between her thighs. Her dark eyes met mine intensely even with her uncertainty. My mouth had yet to get acquainted with her, and now more than anything, I wanted to taste her arousal. I spread her legs further and lowered my face to her pussy. I adjusted my hard-on as it strained against the covers. The view of her was tearing at me, and her scent was thick with lust and need.

Fear hummed inside, and I covered her with my mouth having my first taste of Blue. She bucked. "Oh, God," she cried.

I slipped my hands underneath her and gripped her butt, lifting her up to my face. I ate her like I was starved and fucked her with my tongue. She would lift her eyes to watch me then she'd drop her head back onto the pillow with a moan. Her hands clawed at the covers before they finally found their way into my hair, exactly where I wanted them. I groaned. Her reactions were perfect and the only thing I cared about. I'd keep her sated just to watch her writhe for me.

I fed off her approaching orgasm and increased the pressure of my tongue as she got closer. "Ryan," she panted, equal parts frustrated and tender. I moved one of my hands from her underneath her and added a finger. That was all it took for her to quiver and spasm on my finger and tongue. I drank in her passion greedily before traveling on up her body. I placed light kisses across her belly, mouth still covered with her. Her belly sucked in every time I touched her, and she suppressed a squeal until I kissed her again. She finally shuddered with the next kiss and giggled. "That tickles," she admitted softly.

"I never thought you'd be a ticklish person."

"I never thought I was either." She smiled, raking her hand through my hair. I enjoyed it when she did that. I enjoyed her touch, period. "But I'm learning a lot of new things about myself with you around."

I didn't have to ask if that was a compliment. Her voice alone was full of affection, as was her emotions. So many spilled from her. All of them the sickly, gooey kind. I've never been so grateful for anything in my life. I never wanted her to give it to anyone else but me.

I found my way to her nipples and covered them one at a time with my mouth. She squeezed her arms over my head like she couldn't ever press me into her enough. I understood that feeling all too well. I didn't think I'd ever be satisfied unless I could bury myself into her soul instead of just her body.

I could tease her nipples all day, but I wanted my lips on hers. I scooted on up until my body was covering hers while keeping the majority of my weight off of her. She was thin, and I didn't want to crush her or make her uncomfortable with my weight.

With her hands still in my hair, she forced my head down until her mouth met mine. She took my lips softly, yet I could feel the possessiveness in it. I recognized hers because it was a mirror to mine. Each time she took me in her body, my mind was trembling with the word '*mine*'. She was covered in marks that showed everyone she belonged to me but that wasn't enough until she wanted to be mine… like now.

That's why this moment was everything with her. She had been giving herself to me completely every single time. I had been too afraid to look too deep into what I felt between us. I wasn't terrified of wanting to give into this with her anymore.

I took control of the kiss, still taking it slowly but I slipped my tongue into her mouth and she moaned in response. This alone was amazing. Molly wasn't a person that looked like she did kisses, and neither did I, but together, it was perfect. We made out for a long time like two teenagers who had yet to sleep together. There was no rush. Her hands traveled between my hair and back, and I traced her neck and sides with my fingers until the kiss became more. It was the moment she decided to lift her legs up, wrapping them around my waist. All I had to do was lean up just a bit… and her moan met mine against my lips as my cock slid into her. I sank into complete and utter perfection.

I broke our kiss just so that I could see the look in her eyes. It was everything I knew she'd give and more.

She brought my head back down and continued our kiss. My movements were slow and without a destination to reach that high with her. This wasn't about the pleasure, this was all about the experience this moment was with her. Still, my body shook and responded to the way she wrapped around me, and the urgent way her tongue dipped into my mouth told me she was riding the storm with me. I was determined to take things slow with her, in no rush to succumb to the pleasure. It felt amazing enough just being inside her.

I need to be inside her, Fear words vibrated inside me before his tail materialized behind me.

I broke the kiss and glimpsed back and wiggled the tail. My blood ran hot at the thought of taking her in another way, but only if she'd allow it. I lifted the tail up in the air. "Molly," I whispered, tipping my head where she'd know to look over my shoulder. Her eyes were glazed over with lust, but she did as I wanted and looked. Her eyes widened. I inhaled quickly, searching for fear or worry. Instead, I was greeted with burning passion. She wanted it. No reluctance at all and she had to know where I planned to put it. "Fear wants it in your ass, Blue." I didn't have to tell her that I did too. I wanted to be sure this was okay before I went ahead.

She nodded. "God, yes," she whimpered. "Even with pain, I'll always get pleasure with you."

She had no idea what her words were doing to me. I bit into her collarbone before reaching back to grab her legs and pinning them against her chest with my shoulders. This position folded her up but she never complained as I held her down with my chest. I groaned as I slid into her deeper and she hissed and whimpered as she was forced to take me deeper.

"So deep," she breathed out, and I nodded.

This position gave my tail better access to her ass. I slid my tail underneath me, all the while shrinking it in size. Stretching her with pain was something I wanted to do but not when I wanted to keep this moment gentle for her. It would still fill her up but not painfully. Hopefully, it was nothing but pleasure. She squirmed beneath me the moment my tail slid across her arousal, coating her before entering. I had stopped moving inside her as I slid the tail against her flesh.

She wrapped her arms around my neck then dropped them back down and groaned. "I don't know how to handle what I'm feeling," she admitted while meeting my eyes. She bit her fingers then released them and moved them into my hair. She was a chaotic mess. *My* mess. The one I knew I could withstand and keep. Because she could do the same when it came to me.

Her flowery shit was spilling out of her again, and my heart responded immediately. I didn't try to fight the feeling. I just accepted it for what it was.

I pressed into her ass gently. Her hands slipped onto my shoulders where she gripped. Her mouth fell open as she took in the sensation of being filled by me two ways. I shook slightly, unable to help myself. There was something sensitive with my tail, and it had my cock hardening even more inside her. I wiggled the tail a bit just to test her reaction and she didn't disappoint. "Oh," she screamed. "It feels so good, strangely."

That was what I wanted to hear. I released a breath and claimed her mouth again as I started moving my tail and cock in and out of her. My stomach was consumed with heat, and the pleasure—nothing came close to what was rolling through my entire body as I moved inside her slowly. We were burning, engulfing ourselves in our passion despite the deliberately slow pace I put us in. My movements became jerkier, and Molly's became more urgent and desperate. Our kiss was wild and sloppy but that was what made it fucking better.

She tore her mouth apart from mine only for a second just to say, "You can't hate me. You can't."

Like I'd ever hate her. But soon I'd know why she said those words.

"I'm about to," she whimpered into my mouth. I felt her entire body tensing underneath me, and she pulsed around me with her oncoming orgasm. I knew I was gone the moment she came. "I'm coming," she screamed, pressing her head back into the pillow. Her legs tried to straighten as she scattered into a million pieces but my body kept them from going anywhere. She was forced to ride it out as I swelled inside her. And when I released a guttural groan, I emptied myself inside her. Goose bumps broke out all over my skin, the pleasure was so consuming my legs and stomach—hell, my entire body had a twitch to it. A pleasant one that left me with no strength to do anything, but drop down beside her.

Her legs dropped slowly, and she was already sliding into my arms when I grabbed for her.

CHAPTER TWENTY-TWO

Molly

I stirred from my peaceful sleep, reaching out to an empty bed. I peeled my eyes open slowly and saw that Ryan was missing. My mind replayed last night, and I pressed a smile into the pillow before rising slowly. My hair covered my bare breasts completely as I stared toward the window. The sky hardly changed from day to night here, but there was enough difference between them to make out that it was daytime.

Where did Ryan go?

My stomach did its cue to growl as it did every time I awoke from sleep. "Like clockwork," Ryan said as he entered the room with a plate of food and cup of orange juice. The peaceful smile on his face had me responding with one in return. He placed the juice on the stand next to his bed and climbed into the bed beside me.

"What did you make?" I asked.

"BLT sandwiches."

He handed me one and I took it. "Is there anything you can't make?" I asked, and he laughed.

"If there is something then I can easily learn to make it," he answered while taking a bite of his sandwich.

I tugged a part of the sheet we were sitting on and pulled it onto my lap and covered my chest. He arched a brow. "I was enjoying the view," he told me, and I shook my head before taking a bite.

Pleasant butterflies were in my stomach as I ate while enjoying his presence next to me. Nothing could get better than this, but I knew it could get bad. My butterflies turned to a stampede of elephants. It was time to tell him. Just get it out there so that he could decide what happened between us. It was terrifying to think I was about to give up the one thing that placed what happened to us in his hands. I didn't like to give up control, but I loved him a whole lot more than everything else. It was crazy that I fell for him so quickly but I didn't care that it didn't make sense. I didn't want to stay next to him with this eating away at me every second of the day.

I took a drink of the orange juice then handed it to him. He finished it off, and I turned to face him and scooted close. Then I moved closer because I wasn't satisfied with only this amount of closeness. At this rate, I was going to end up in his lap. He chuckled and placed his hands on my sides. "If you want me to hold you, turn around and I'll place you between my legs," he told me with an easy grin. My mind scrambled in its wake. "We can cuddle." My heart soared. How could I not be afraid of telling him who I was when I could lose this with him?

I smiled and shook my head. "No, I want to face you when I talk to you." He nodded. My knees were touching his legs and he slid his hands up and down my sides.

"You're gorgeous, you know that?" he asked, and I tucked my hair behind my ears and covered myself with the sheet.

"Have you ever done anything truly horrible to someone?" I asked abruptly.

He laughed. "I'm Fear, of course I've done a lot of horrible shit."

"No, I mean… to a good person that didn't deserve it?"

He simply looked at me for several seconds. "No one's truly innocent, Blue. Even the ones that go to Heaven." I didn't know if I could believe the same thing. His hand tangled into my hair and twisted. "Tell me what's wrong?"

"I want to tell you, but I'm scared," I admitted.

He smiled. "Believe me, I know," he said. "But why?"

"Do you think becoming Fear was your fate?" I asked hurriedly.

"No, my fate was supposed to be very different," he told me like he was in the past stuck there for a moment. Just like I was for very different reasons.

"How do you know?"

"Because an angel told me my real fate."

My eyes widened. "Really?" That was surprising. I've never seen one but I would have if I had stuck around with Fear the night they closed the portal in the human world. I'd probably be dead too. "What was your fate?... If it's okay for me to ask."

"I don't mind, and I was meant to be human. Wife and kids and a long life. Vastly different than what it's become down here." His tone took a darker tone toward the end, and I shivered.

"Maybe you got a new fate down here," I barely whispered.

He studied me with his dark, searching eyes. "Yeah?"

I nodded quickly. "I mean, you know how Grim and his wife were destined," I rambled, grabbing my fingers and circling them around each other. "Everyone talked about their love and how they were destined down here even though no one even knew who she was or if she even existed…"

"Yeah?" He wanted me to go on. I knew I was a rambling mess right now. I kept prolonging the hardest part.

I took a deep breath. I wanted to sound confident about this because I was. Ryan and I were good together. I honestly believed that. I lifted my gaze to his and leaned into him. "Maybe everything that's happened—all the bad that we've done and been through was all meant to happen so that we could get to this point."

He lifted a brow slowly and tilted his lip partially. "What are you saying, Blue?" His tone sent a sweet ache to my core.

"I think you are my fate," I told him. "And if you aren't, then I'll make you mine regardless."

He smiled and leaned into kiss me, but I brought my finger to his lips. "There's something I have to tell you," I told him.

"Get away from him!" I jerked backward to Melanie's voice, and a second later she had me thrown against the door.

"What the fuck, Melanie?" Ryan bellowed.

I searched Melanie's face. I didn't understand. "Melanie," I whizzed. "I thought—" She didn't let me finish. She punched me in the face. The impact jerked the side of my head into the wall.

"How long has she been here?" Melanie screamed at Ryan. He looked furious. My stomach churned because right now, he was mad for me. But Melanie was about to ruin all my chances… She had told me she'd let me tell him. "You don't recognize her? Who she is?" she asked him, and his eyes squinted before turning to me.

I shook my head violently and looked to Melanie. "Melanie, shut up! You said you'd let me tell him. I was about to. Please!" I didn't care that I was begging and pleading, I'd do it over and over if it would have made a difference in what happened next.

Her hand went to my neck and squeezed. Her strength was amazing given her size. "Remember how you died in the hospital?" No. No. No. No. "Remember the figure standing in the road the day you wrecked your truck?" Melanie asked him.

"Stop!" I screamed. I was too terrified to even look over at Ryan.

"Remember the ghost-girl that was always next to Fear? *'Good boy, good boy'*," she chanted the words I used to say to him when I was bitter and resentful toward everything so I wanted to hurt the good boy. My face had caught fire, and my throat and eyes burned I was so ashamed, embarrassed, and furious all at once.

I dared to look over at Ryan. His eyes were stony and blank until they locked on mine, and then I knew it all clicked because stone-like eyes became murderous ones. His eyes blazed red as he pierced me with them. Guilty, guilty, I bet I looked and smelled.

"Ryan," I called to him. "I was just about to tell you—"

"Molly," he tested my name. "Molly." This time it was darker, more disgusted and fueled with realization.

Melanie lifted my hand and showed him. "These hands drove a knife into your heart while you were unconscious in the hospital."

I couldn't believe Melanie was doing this. I knew I did her wrong, but this was the kind of thing Marcus would do to someone.

He covered his face with his hands and roared. "You're fucking dead!" he told me, and I broke down and cried, knowing I had lost him. "How could you crawl underneath me and not say a word about who you were?" he asked and I flinched. He grabbed his head again. "Shut up, Fear!" he hissed and shook his head. He looked madder and madder each passing second. Then his eyes widened once again. "That's why you even brought her here!" He grabbed the mattress and flung it across the room. "You knew who she was and brought her here. What was this, some sick game for the both of you?" He was arguing with Fear. My stomach lurched. The food I just ate was about to come up.

Melanie watched Ryan with a smile. Something was unsettling about it. She released my neck slowly and turned around with a killer grin. Leaning in, she whispered, "You didn't think I'd let you be happy, did you, Molly?" I shuddered. This wasn't Melanie. "I wanted you to be eternally miserable, not happy."

The Devil.

He tipped Melanie's face into a devious grin before pulling something from his pocket. "I found this in her room." Ryan raised his head as she spoke. She tossed the vial I threw away and he caught it. "It's probably poison."

"Ryan, this isn't Melanie!" I screamed. "It's the Devil." The Devil didn't even try and stop me from opening my mouth. He knew anything I said, Ryan wouldn't believe now. It was over.

"You'll say anything," he replied, gripping the vial in his hands. He stepped toward me, and fake-Melanie stepped aside with a triumphant smile. Ryan's chin tipped down as he glowered at me. "And fuck if I didn't believe every lie you fed me."

"Ryan," I whispered quickly, searching his eyes for the man that had just been smiling at me. He was gone, replaced with hurt and anger. My untold truth stole him from me. "I was telling you when he walked in!"

He grabbed my bare shoulder and jerked me forward. I stumbled on my feet, clutching the white sheet around me as he pushed and shoved me out of the room. "Go," he ordered me.

I turned my body trying to look back at him as he continued to push me through the house. "Ryan, please, talk to me!" Another shove. I stumbled to my knees but he jerked me back up to my feet, forcing me to walk. "Nothing's been a lie!"

"EVERYTHING's been a lie," he said, eyes darkening into red.

I smacked into the front door, and he gripped my shoulder and pulled me into him so that he could open the door. Despite the turmoil, I wanted to cling to him even now when I had one last chance. Then he was throwing me out, and my chest caved. I grabbed it and sucked in air as I tumbled off the porch steps. I stood and met his eyes. "Just listen," I tried again.

He turned to his right and grabbed the rifle. My eyes widened. "You know what I'm doing," he said to me. "So why are you still standing there?"

"Ryan." He aimed and fired. I screamed and held my hand over my shoulder. There wasn't much left. He almost blew off my entire arm.

"You're mad," I spoke through pain and tears. "But you're gonna regret this when you've calmed down."

He smirked and lowered the rifle. "I don't think I will. You fucking made me… for you." His face was clouded with betrayal and hurt. "But do tell me, why would I regret this?"

"Because." I wobbled. I was going to die soon. I was bleeding out. I could feel my strength waning. "I love you, Ryan, and you care for me too."

He laughed. "I didn't even know who you were," he spat. "Was everything a lie? You being tortured and imprisoned all these centuries?" This was what I was afraid of. He was twisting all my truths and our memories into lies because of my identity.

"Of course, it's the truth," I yelled, vision blurring. "The Devil wanted me to suffer when he made me immortal and now he's doing this because he doesn't want me to be happy, and only you can do that!"

"Wow," he blew out a frustrated growl.

Gravity left me as I lost all my strength. I slumped forward onto the ground. When I rose from the dead, I was somewhere in the woods wherever Ryan must have carried me. He stood above me. "Back from the dead, are we?" he asked and I raised up, reaching out for the sheet he tossed off my body. I knew it had to be on purpose because it was several feet away. "I don't think so." He prevented me from moving any further. I tilted my chin up to look at him. "Mind telling me what this was for?" he said, tossing the vial down in front of me.

"I was going to use it on you to trap Fear," I told him.

He tossed his head up and laughed. "Here that, Fear? Still wanna protect her?"

"I couldn't use it unless I was one hundred percent sure you were you during the time I gave it to you. If you weren't, I could have risked you being the one trapped instead."

He cocked a brow. "Oh?"

"I'm telling the truth!" I hissed, lunging for the sheet and covering myself back up. "It's not poison, but I had thrown it away last night. I didn't want to use it on either of you."

He looked pissed again. He lifted his rifle and aimed it at my head. "Playing kiss ass to Fear now too?" He glared. "Like I'd let him save you."

"I'm immortal," I told him. "Kill me over and over if that's what makes you feel better, but you won't get rid of me."

He snorted. "You're crazy stupid if you think I'll let this go." He pressed the barrel onto my forehead. "You killed me. Because of that, my entire life was stolen."

I stood slowly to see if he would even let me. He did. The rifle was still pointed at me, though. "This is exactly why I didn't want to tell you and the reason why I wanted to get away from you both. Then Marybeth gave me the vial and told me what it could do, and I switched tactics. I figured if I could trap Fear, you'd let me go since it was never you that brought me here, to begin with. Then my priorities shifted after being around you more, and I wanted to save you from Fear."

He laughed and laughed some more. I glared. "Don't. Fucking. Laugh." I punctuated each word. "My wants kept changing because I didn't want to just save you. I wanted you. In the process, I decided I wanted to keep Fear too. So there." I took a deep breath. "That's the truth, and the night I gave you my name. I had given you a chance to remember and you didn't."

"So, it's my fault?" he asked.

"If you don't believe her, make her take what's in the vial instead," the Devil said still as Melanie.

"That's not Melanie!" I glared.

"Take what's in the vial," he told me.

"Ryan," I whispered.

"Don't," he hissed.

"If I take it, I'll become mortal again. That's what it will do to me."

"You can kill her," the Devil baited him using Melanie's sweet voice.

How could he not see that wasn't Melanie?

He gripped his head with one of his hands and lowered the rifle. He kept jerking his head, and I thought maybe Fear was doing something. "Take it," Ryan told me then he twitched. "You aren't getting out." He had to be talking to Fear again.

I glanced over at the Devil who was grinning from ear to ear. My stomach was in knots. Who knew what he planned to do to me after this. Maybe this was my fate to be destroyed by the boy I killed and later fell in love with. I couldn't change anything, though. I didn't want to. I loved him, and he was hurting because of me.

"Fine, I'll take it." I bent down and grabbed the vial, popping it open. "All you'll have to do is kill me once and it's over for me." I waited for a flicker of something in his eyes. Some sort of sign that he still cared despite everything. He just watched me expressionlessly, and I couldn't tell what he was feeling or thinking. "You won't care if I'm not here anymore?" I couldn't help but ask.

I wiped the tears away and brought the vial up to my lips.

"Fucking wait!" Ryan hissed, cupping his face then holding one hand out to stop me. He met my eyes and it was enough for hope to spread through me. "There's no fun in killing you once. I want to make you suffer."

I didn't care what he said at that point. All he gave me was hope.

I smiled, but it was short lived when the Devil ported behind me and forced the vial up and the liquid filled my mouth. "Melanie, stop!" Ryan roared. I tried to spit it out, but he clamped my mouth shut and held my nose until it trickled down my throat, and I was forced to swallow.

Ryan pulled me away from him but it was too late.

"That's not Melanie," I told him again.

"Like he's going to believe his killer over his best friend," the Devil said as Melanie.

He gazed back and forth between us. Some of his rage was directed at fake-Melanie. "Where's Killian?" he asked.

He forced Melanie's lips into a pout. "Do you believe her over me?"

Ryan was silent for several seconds before shifting into Fear, and his tail was shooting out for... Me? I froze and closed my eyes. Something happened but it wasn't my death. I reopened my eyes and saw that Ryan's target hadn't been me. Some sort of powerful explosion changed the entire air around us. I fell forward and stood back up as soon as it was over.

"You want to go against the one that made you, Fear?"

The Devil was no longer Melanie. My back tingled and my skin crawled. It took a few seconds before I was brave enough to turn around and see his true form. He liked parading around in other people's skin instead of his own.

Ryan laughed. "He has no problems going against you." He met my eyes for a split second. "His mind is one-tracked so he only ever focuses on what he wants."

"I know exactly how I made him," the Devil responded. "That's why you and Molly have to go."

I finally turned around. What I saw shocked me. It was scary how similar he was to Fear. Instead of pale skin though, his was black. Same red eyes. Same horns. Just different facial features. His eyes snapped toward me. He ported. I took a step back and quickly glanced around. Pain shot through my chest and stole my breath. "No!" I heard Ryan behind me.

I looked down at my chest. Nothing was there, but that was because he attacked from behind. My eyes widened when I felt him move his hand around in my chest. The pain was fading fast.

Then I died for real.

I stumbled out of my body as a ghost and twirled around to see the Devil behind my lifeless body. He still held me up. His hand shot out of my chest. He held my heart in it. He crushed it before he pulled his hand out. My body fell forward.

"Now," the Devil muttered. "That's better."

"What's going on?" The real Melanie faded between us all. Her eyes took in everything, and her eyes hardened.

Ryan was in motion. He lifted the rifle and fired. His tail darted out at the same time. The Devil stopped the bullet in motion and it dropped to the ground. He ported but Ryan moved, dropping the rifle like he knew exactly where he'd port to next.

Ryan ran in my direction and his tail snaked out and grabbed me. I gasped as he pulled me through the air. "Behind her, Ryan!" Melanie told him.

I glanced back to see the Devil in the air behind me. He reached out for me but Grim faded behind him. Grim swung his scythe and the Devil ported again. When he reappeared, Ryan met him head-on. He dropped me down onto the ground next to Melanie and his tail joined the fight. Grim stepped in, then Melanie, and how the hell did I become the weakest link in the group? I knew that answer. The Devil.

I snarled and dived for the rifle on the ground. I went to pick it up but my hands went through it. I was a ghost again. I couldn't touch anything at all. I was completely useless! I focused on the four of them fighting, bouncing around in the woods like a game of ping-pong.

Everyone stopped at once. Ryan, Melanie, and Grim landed on the ground together.

"Where'd he go?" Melanie asked warily.

"He's still here," Grim tightened his grip around his scythe.

Ryan glanced my way. "It's Molly," he yelled, running. "He's after her."

I looked around anxiously. A passage opened next to me. My eyes widened. "I'll visit you when I'm done here," the Devil whispered in my ear before tossing me in it.

CHAPTER TWENTY-THREE

Ryan

I attacked the Devil with my tail as the passage closed after taking Molly. He caught my tail with his hand and held it there as he grinned. Some inhuman guttural scream burned out of my lungs as Fear fought to climb out.

My thoughts were all over the place. Molly was my *killer.* She kept who she was a secret from me and so did Fear. Not that I expected any less from him. I was so disgusted and furious with myself. I was deceived, fucking tricked by her. I actually fell for—my killer!

I'm going to go get her back! Fear boomed in my head. I shook my head furiously.

"She's gone," I told him happily. *She's gone*. No matter how hard I tried not to, some of that happiness left me. "She's gone," I said furiously this time. How dare he take her when I hadn't made her pay!

"Problems on the inside, Fear?" the Devil asked, and I lifted my head up. "You should have known this merge would have never worked out."

Fear was seeping all through me. He wasn't even blocking himself from me. Soon, it wasn't just his feelings I was getting but his thoughts as well. *I'm gonna fucking shut him up. Like I care what he thinks about my choices. I'll get her back.* Did he not realize I could hear him?

Then he told me, *I'm coming out. I have to get her back.*

"No," I gritted my teeth. It felt like my body was about to burst. I never tried so hard to force him to stay inside before. "You can't have her," I told him.

Get over it already. We don't have fucking time for this.

My nostrils flared. Get over it? How could I get over this? I hated the way I felt right now! It wasn't just about what she did—it's that I felt so fucking betrayed right now. My chest was all kinds of messed up, and it hurt so bad because I've never wanted anything as much as I wanted her, since… Melanie. Even more… so much more that I couldn't get over this!

"What are you still doing here?" Grim asked the Devil, his voice seemed distant while I fought to stay in control.

"Just waiting on the other thing I came to get," the Devil replied nonchalantly. "Why aren't you attacking?"

"Just leave," Grim told him.

"Ryan." Melanie touched my shoulder and I flinched. "What do you want to do?"

What was she asking me?

She's asking if you want to go after Molly, you little—

"No!" I pushed her away. How could we get her back? What if I really never saw her again? Damn, my chest was killing me. Was I having a heart attack?

Ryan, Fear sounded different. *Stop, if you don't, you're going break our merge. You're doing something—*

Like I cared. I was so tired of this battle with Fear all the time. I wanted it to end once and for all.

Not this shit again, Fear muttered. *Ryan, stop—*

"How are you…" I heard Grim mumble. "He's breaking the merge."

"Wait, Ryan." Someone tugged on my arm and I slung them away. "Don't! It's what he's waiting for." It was Melanie.

My adrenaline kept spiking. My body was pulsing and shifting, and when I finally slid out of Fear, I smiled and laughed. I turned around and gazed at the monster I used to be. Something felt wrong about it, but I was too angry to let it bother me.

"Don't touch him!" Fear hissed.

I glanced back just as the Devil opened the passage again.

Oh, fuck. I was a ghost again.

"Like taking candy from a baby." The Devil laughed right before knocking me into the passage.

CHAPTER TWENTY-FOUR

Melanie

"Ryan!" I yelled after he was already gone.

"What do you want with them?" Grim asked, and I glared waiting to hear his response. How the heck did this happen? I should have known something like this would happen when Molly reappeared. Still… Why hadn't I prevented this from happening? Because, not as Ryan's best friend but as a woman that saw another woman in love, I could tell Molly had been sincere about her feelings. I knew it wouldn't be easy for her or Ryan but for some reason, I let her go.

"Don't even go there, Grim." The Devil blocked an attack from Fear who went after him. "I always get all the bad guys, you know this."

"Ryan's not—" I started to say but stopped.

"Oh, yes he is," the Devil said while blocking attacks from Fear. "Everything he's done since he became Fear was still him."

"Where did you take them?" Fear asked, his tail wrapping around the Devil's legs.

The Devil was completely at ease with Fear's tail wrapping around him but his eyes sent a chill up my spine as he looked at Fear. "I took them from you. You're losing who you are to them."

"I can't ever change what I am," Fear snarled. It was crazy how similar the two of them looked side by side. Obviously, there were differences, but still.

"Don't pretend," the Devil replied with a threatening voice. "Why are you so desperate to change? I've sat back and watched as one of my darkest creations slowly turned weak and foolish because he chose to merge with a human ghost!"

"I'm not weak," Fear sounded amazingly calm. "Why did you take Molly?"

"Molly's always been quite the little monster, hasn't she?" He smiled and waited for Fear to react. "Someone like that can control you too easily but… someone like me, she can't control. She'd be good by my side, and that's where she'll stay until I grow tired of her."

Fear lost it. He jumped for the Devil but he vanished and appeared behind him. "And Grim." The Devil turned his head toward us. "Melanie." He looked at me. "Don't try to come after the boy, he's mine now. As for what you guys have been searching for… give it up." He had to be talking about the lost demon souls we've been searching for. Like I could give up searching for all the souls that deserved an afterlife instead of being stuck God knows wherever he had them. "Out of anger that you might end up finding them, I destroyed every single last one. You have no one to blame but yourself. Not that it would have done much good. They all eventually give into the darkness, and then they're mine to take."

"You killed them?" I threw my scythe the same time Grim did. We knew the Devil would leave again before it even hit but sometimes you just had to respond to your anger.

Speaking of anger, I was positive that was the reason Ryan was separated from Fear.

The Devil didn't come back this time. His goal was Molly and Ryan, and my guess was riling Ryan up using Molly and Fear was his goal from the very beginning so he could break the merge. I held my hand out and waited for my scythe to return. Grim stepped beside me and placed his hand on my back. His touch gave me comfort.

His eyeless gaze met my eyes, and we were so in sync with each other anymore that all we had to do was look at each other and we'd just know. We both turned our attention to Fear at the same time. Only he was gone.

"Do you think he's…" I let my words drift away.

"Yeah, I think he's going to get Molly back," Grim answered. "Come on." We faded into Ryan's house where Fear gripped a portal chip in his hands. It hadn't taken him long to destroy the living room and kitchen. He was upset, that was easy to see.

He didn't even bother paying attention to us. "Fear," Grim called to him.

"What?" he snapped back.

"Are you actually going to try taking her back from him?" I asked quickly. "He's the *Devil.* He created you. As entities, we can do so much but even we can't do anything against him."

"Get to the point Melanie," he hissed. "Tell me something I don't already fucking know."

I sighed. "I'm saying, we should work together."

"Work together?" I thought I might have seen his lips twitch into a smile. Almost.

I nodded.

"But first," Grim added. "We need to know where you stand."

We waited for him to respond. He looked down at the ground and around him before saying, "Well, I'm standing right here."

I rolled my eyes. My God, why did that sound like something Ryan would say? "He means are you wanting to save Molly or Ryan?" We had to know where his loyalties lie.

"Fuck," Fear muttered, turning his head away. "Do you think Molly's going to stay with me if I'm not him?" he asked. "She's got it bad for him, and he'll get over this shit with her once he realizes how easily he played into the Devil's hands. Believe me, he's fucking obsessed with her. He'll get over it. Of course, he'll get over it. It's Molly," he went on rambling.

What in the world? Who was this creature? This wasn't the same monster that ruined my life. Or was it Ryan that had this effect on him? I met Grim's eyeless gaze and his essence changed colors.

"So, that means…?" I asked again.

Fear growled. "It means why are we still here when we should be getting them back?"

I never thought I'd see a day where we'd work alongside with Fear.

I never thought I'd see a day where I'd want Ryan to return to the monster he had been trying so hard not to become.

For better or worse, the two of them have embedded themselves into one another. I thought Ryan had been given the worst fate when he became

Fear. Now I realize why I was wrong. He survived the monster, became him, and changed him.

I smiled at Grim. Funny how fate could be sometimes.

CHAPTER TWENTY-FIVE

Ryan

I was thrown in a cell. Even when I landed on the ground, the impact didn't make a sound. In fact, I couldn't even feel it. Being a ghost sucked just as I remembered.

"Ryan?" But I could feel every bit of what her voice did to me.

I raised slowly and looked through the bars of my prison. Across from me in a different cell, was Molly. She was completely naked, hunkered down with her hands gripping the bars as she looked at me like she hated to see me. If her knees weren't covering her chest, I would have been able to see the giant hole in her chest where the Devil had ripped her heart out. My anger fizzled all over again just thinking about it. Then I remembered she wasn't who I wanted her to be; she wasn't Blue. She was Molly, the ghost-girl that killed me and now I was angry toward her again.

I looked around. These prison cells—this entire place was made for ghosts like us.

"You're not real," she said finally, scooting away from the bars. "This is my suffering."

"I assure you, I'm very real," I told her, getting to my feet and walking toward the bars.

Her eyes looked coal-black as she peered up at me. She squeezed her knees. "Ryan?" she asked again. "No, you can't be." She shook her head and dropped her face to her knees as she cradled them.

"This isn't some sort of punishment." I sighed. "I don't think your eternal suffering has started yet, I'm really fucking here, and I'd kill you if you weren't already dead." I wanted to hurt her like she did me, but how ironic that I was, in fact, dead too.

She lifted her head and squinted her eyes. "Okay… if I am to believe that, which I don't, then please explain to me why the hell he'd place one of his entities in a cell?"

She didn't believe me. I wrapped my hands around the bar and looked at her. "I'm not Fear anymore," I said hotly. "If I had known I could have broken the merge all on my own if angry enough, I would have done it sooner."

Her eyes hardened and within a second, she was standing up and glaring at me. "Are you stupid?" she yelled. That wasn't the reaction I expected. "You walked right into his trap. You were safe, powerful, and protected as Fear. You do realize your situation is no different than the one I'm in now?"

"You have no right to get mad!" I yelled back. "This is all because of you. I trusted you—"

"I did not want to be anywhere near you at first either! Fear brought me there and marked me, and you played games with me just like he did!" I didn't want her to keep talking. I wanted to stay angry. If she spilled any more words, I'd be forced to listen and I was so weak when it came to her.

"Don't!"

"No, you shut up and listen," she snapped back. "All I wanted was to get away but I couldn't because Fear would come for me and you would have too—I know now that it's because you didn't want him to crawl out and force you inside. I get it, I do. I get why you hate Fear. He's been nothing but awful to you but haven't you realized yet?" She searched my eyes and I glared. "It's because he's afraid of you."

I laughed. "Afraid. He fucking fed on my hatred, disgust, and self-loathing all these years."

"Yes, because he's been trying to deny what he wanted."

"And, what did he want?" I asked bitterly, playing along with her.

"Ryan. He wants to be you because you're good," she whispered with eyes so compassionate that I had to look down instead of at her. "Jesus, Ryan, you're so good it hurts." I really tried not to look back up at her. I really did. "Why do you think we cling to you so desperately? You feel so good. You make us better."

I sucked in a breath and closed my eyes. *Don't fall into her hands again, don't fall ever again,* I chanted to myself then reopened my eyes. "Why are you defending him?" I asked. "I thought you wanted to get away from him?"

"You happened," she replied immediately. "And yeah, I wanted to get away from him. I hated him and blamed him for what I've become, but he was never to blame. I've always been bad all on my own… that day I stabbed you in the neck was the only chance I had to get away from you both. Marybeth owed me so I went to her for a spell that could prevent you from finding me using the mark," she made a sound in her throat in anger, "but I don't think I was ever dealing with Marybeth. I think it was the Devil all along. He gave me what was in the vial and told me that I could trap Fear if I gave it to you when you were in complete control. That had been my next plan since I couldn't get away from you. If I could trap him, I'd be free of him but…" I waited. "The longer I was around you, the more I was reminded of my guilt and what I did to you. I wanted to free you from him then I wanted more from you, so much more."

"Stop," I said, turning around and walking away so that I couldn't see her. My body had no sense of touch or feeling but my chest was aching, and I never wanted to acknowledge who it was hurting for. "I don't care. I don't want to know anything else."

"I love you, Ryan," she said anyway, making my heart stutter in its beats. "Unlike you, you are the only person I've ever cared about before! It's always been about me and what I want. That's why you have to merge with Fear again. That is who you are now. It's okay to want to be bad. It's okay to like being Fear. It's not okay for you to be here right now with me! You don't belong here!"

I didn't say anything. Instead, I leaned against the back wall and squatted. I hated her for not telling me who she was beforehand. But I hated myself for letting that anger control me so much that I got played by the Devil. Now more than anything, I felt lost. I was already in Hell so things couldn't get any worse but all I could think was, *who is Ryan Jones anymore?* "I wasn't meant for this life," I whispered but why did the words feel wrong coming out of my mouth? "Dying was what led me to where I am now. What led me to become Fear. You are one of the reasons I've lived miserably for so long."

"Do you want to know the truth?" I lifted my gaze to her as she spoke. "The truth is, I hate that I ruined your life. I hate all the hard things you've been through because of Fear, but I didn't know you like I do now. And no matter how much I want to feel sorry, I can't be! Yes, I'm sorry that you suffered all these centuries, but I'm not sorry that I took your human life and gave you a new one. Because I'm selfish, and I'd do it all over again if it meant I could spend those days with you again. I'd go through all the pain I've been through again and again. I'd kill you over and over to get those pathetic days with you because that's how much I want to stay by your side."

"Do you even realize how crazy you sound?" I asked her. "You crazy—"

"Don't call me any names," she interrupted, sounding pissed. "If I could do it all over, the only thing I'd do differently was to take you somewhere far away from everyone else and never tell you who I was!" I glared at her. "How's that?" she asked. "This is how selfish I truly am."

I shook my head and just looked at her. "Un-fucking-believable, you are," I muttered but the words didn't sound as harsh I had meant for them to sound.

"No, you are," she shot back. "Would you have really wanted things to be different? I know how much you loved Melanie—it's pissing me off just thinking about it, but would you have really been satisfied as second best?" This woman, she was pressing all my damn buttons over and over again. "Because with her, that's all you would have ever been, second best. If you could forgive me, I'd make you happy. I'm not sunshine or glitter or anything remotely close to perfect. I'm so damn messed up, so dark and prickly, and selfish and cruel but for the first time, I want to be better for someone."

I didn't want Melanie as anything other than a friend. I haven't in a long time. Sometimes I'd think about her while I was with another woman but more than anything she was just a part the past I never got to have. I couldn't get over the past because I still felt wronged. Not because of her. It was just one of those things where I constantly wondered how different things would have been if I had gotten to live. How much simpler life would have been.

I tilted my head as I gazed at Molly. Even with a hole in her chest and the fire in her dark eyes, she stirred something inside me. Was she getting upset all on her own because she was thinking about my feelings for Melanie? I couldn't help but smirk despite our situation. "It was never about Melanie. It was about losing who I am along the way," I said when she was quiet for so long. "Melanie has nothing to do with this so stop trying to use the past to make me forgive you."

She looked so guilty as she looked down that I kept watching her to make her worse. "Besides, why are you trying so hard to make me understand? We're in the Devil's hands now, who knows what kind of suffering we have to look forward to."

She lifted her gaze and smiled. "Because Fear's gonna come for us."

I lifted an eyebrow like I didn't believe her but I didn't doubt that he would be coming for her. I knew just how much he worshiped her. I felt a little irritated and sad when I thought about the two of them being anywhere without me. And just how messed up was that? I was supposed to hate them, and I did. I wanted to hate them, more like.

"Good luck with that," I muttered. "Like he could take you from the Devil."

"He won't be the only one coming, ya know." She was right. Grim and Melanie were probably trying to find me the moment he took me. As always, Grim was coming to get me every time I got myself into trouble.

"Oh, I'm sure all three of them will be coming," the Devil's voice drifted down the hall. His footsteps echoed off the empty walls as he approached. "They might find us, they might not."

"When does the eternal suffering start?" I asked him nonchalantly. "Getting a little rusty, are we?"

"Ryan!" Molly hissed.

The Devil just smiled before turning toward Molly. "Still trying to make him understand your feelings?" His voice was patronizing. "Little too late. He obviously doesn't care, right?" He looked at me. I bit back any remark because I didn't want to play into his games anymore. He smiled at Molly. "Don't worry, you're mine now and I'll take good care of you."

I was up on my feet and against the bars before I knew it, seething. "What do you think you're doing?" I asked him.

He turned his head slightly and cocked a brow. "Pardon? She's mine, what's not to get?" He glanced back at her. "Or better yet, what's actually happening is this: I need little miss chaotic over here to play along and convince Fear that she wants to be with me now."

She snorted. "There's no way he'd believe that."

I had a bad feeling…

"Yes, he will because you have no choice but to convince him." He leaned against her cell so that he was staring down at her. He was too close to her. I didn't like him near her. I didn't like anyone near her. "Fear's gone soft because of the merge. I need my monster back and you and Ryan don't help my cause."

"I won't help you," she promised with a smile. I wanted to smile with her but all I could think about was what he was going to do to her if she didn't listen. "I like my monster the way he is, and most when he's merged with Ryan again."

She met my eyes. My pulse quickened. There were too many moments like this, where she steals what I didn't want to let her have.

The Devil laughed. "I'll kill Ryan's soul if you don't convince Fear. I want you to throw pebbles at the monster who only knows how to love you. That way, he'll be through with the silly emotion when you've broken his dark heart."

The fire dimmed in her eyes so easily by his words. His words worked. I was her weakness, like she had somehow become mine. I already knew she'd listen to him now, the same way I had let her hidden identity consume me.

"Listen, you are not going to do anything he says," I told her plainly. "I'll gladly die instead of letting him mess with my head!"

She ignored me. "Let him leave. You can't send him to the Flames. That's the only way I'll do it." Her eyes were void of anything.

"I'll let him go once you've done what I've asked," he told her with a grin.

"You can't actually believe him?" I yelled. She continued to ignore me. "Molly, don't you even think about it!"

She finally let her dark eyes meet mine again. "Why do you even care? I thought you hated Fear?"

I couldn't respond. I was too stunned. Why was I getting upset? Why was I angry that he wanted to use Molly to hurt Fear? Why was I losing my mind trying to sort out my feelings because of those two?

He slid open her cell door and she stepped beside him. She looked like stone. Empty. A doll. She wouldn't look my way. "Molly," I said. "Molly!" She wouldn't respond. When the Devil grinned, I lost it. "Molly, look at me dammit!" And she did. "You can't do this to Fear. I *was* him, you are the only thing that he knows how to care for. Don't take that from him. Don't give the Devil what he wants." How strange that I had almost said, *I am Fear*. But if that were the case then… I really fucked up.

A tear slid down her cheek before she looked away. "Molly?"

The Devil rolled his neck around and groaned. "Will you stop calling her name? I don't have the tolerance for it." He placed his hand on her back. My nostrils flared and I gripped the bars and started shaking them, then I punched and kicked them.

"You get your hands off her!" I raged.

He started leading her down the hall, further away from me. I never felt so murderous and pissed. I was unable to do a damn thing as Molly fell into the Devil's grasp all because of me.

"Do a good job, Molly, and I'll take very good care of you in return." I heard him tell her. His laughter trailed down the empty cells and I screamed everything I wanted to do to him if only he weren't untouchable. More than anything, I wanted to kill him for staring at Molly the way he had.

CHAPTER TWENTY-SIX

Molly

Of course, I wasn't going to do what the Devil wanted.

But I had to play along until the cavalry got here and got Ryan out of there. If I was good at anything, it was playing docile to please someone's ego. The Devil was eerily similar to Fear during his time with Marcus. He liked obedience and getting his way—the thing about the Devil was we couldn't ever get rid of him. How would Grim and Melanie handle this one? And it was sad that I was relying on those two to step in and save the day like they always managed to do. It used to annoy the shit out of me, but now all I could think about was how much I wished they'd hurry up. My skin wouldn't stop crawling until I knew Ryan was safe, and the fact that he was screaming and cursing at the Devil as we walked away didn't help.

Ryan might have himself convinced, but I knew he belonged as Fear and the fact that he seemed worried for Fear only made me more confident about it.

"I've watched you all this time, Molly," the Devil startled me from my thoughts as we walked up the stairway. "For such a frail body…" His gaze traveled over my body. "You can't be broken, can you?"

I kept hearing some distant sound now that I could no longer hear Ryan. But then again, maybe I wasn't hearing anything but the pounding of my heart.

"Probably not," I said without emotion. That was a lie. If Ryan didn't forgive me, I would be broken beyond repair.

"I need you to convince Fear, but as for staying by my side… I was serious." Ew, I'd rather suffer in his flames. "I can give you back a body." My heart sunk. I had forgotten about that. I looked down at the huge hole in my chest where he ripped out my heart. I didn't even have anything to cover myself up with. Suddenly, I was extremely uncomfortable in his presence. I placed my arms over my chest.

I tilted my head. There was the sound again... it almost sounded like voices. I glared. "Are you messing with me?" I asked him.

He gazed down at my body again with a lustful grin. "Not yet."

There's no way I could ever handle someone else touching me after Ryan… I shuddered. I sighed and shook my head. "I hear something," I grumbled.

He studied me curiously and pulled me into him. I stiffened. The voices were louder now though, and my eyes traveled over him and widened when I noticed the necklace. A green three-dimensional diamond rested against his chest. It shimmered with a very powerful spell.

Hmm, what was so important that he kept it around his neck…

"Like what you see?" he asked, and I suppressed a snort. "Easy, Molly, just because I'm being nice now doesn't mean it won't change. Who do you think I created Fear from? I can sense your moods. I see everything, and I know everything that goes on in the Underworld and human world." Was he bragging about being Satan? I didn't say anything in hopes that he would just shut up. I stepped further away from him once we were out of the stairway.

This was the very place I delivered Melanie to him all those years ago, only one could never be too sure as to what the room really looked like. It constantly shifted and changed with the Devil's mood. Right now, it was empty and soulless.

"What? No throne?" I couldn't help but say.

"I'm not Marcus." His eyes flickered with mayhem. "I don't need something to prove my power," he claimed. He grabbed my arm suddenly and I jumped. "Everyone knows I'm in charge down here."

"Then why can't you just let Fear and Ryan be?"

He lifted his hand and rubbed one of his horns casually. "Because he's making Fear weak."

"He's not weak." I glared.

"Am I going to have a problem with you convincing Fear?" he asked. I gripped my fists and blinked a few times until I was calmer. Just put up with him for now… "I may have disliked Marcus but at least with him, Fear had been a true monster. The things he'd do were downright wicked. If only Marcus hadn't been consumed by his need for more power… anyway, my entities were created to cause problems and disrupt the human world. The more it's tainted, the quicker I rise."

"Wow," I whistled. "That's something to look forward to."

"Play along and I might keep you around to see the day I crawl out of Hell and destroy what Heaven tries so hard to protect." The smile on his face was disturbing.

"I don't see what the point is," I said, shrugging my shoulders.

His eyebrows pinched together. "You might not understand but I do." He laughed then stopped abruptly. "It's show time." He pulled me into him. "Our guests are here already."

I tensed from his words and looked around the room anxiously.

"You got here sooner than I expected," the Devil said. "Most can't even find my place."

Melanie and Grim faded across the room from us, followed by Fear who ported. Melanie was the first to speak, "Have you forgotten that I've been here before?" She smiled.

The Devil pulled me close, piercing my side with his claws. I knew it was a warning to play my part. I placed my hand on his chest. "I don't see how you were able to find it just because you've been here before," he told her.

"There's a lot of things you don't know I can do," said Melanie.

"And that's the very reason I tried to get rid of you." The Devil groaned. "I knew you'd be a pain in my ass."

"Let her go," Fear growled.

His tail shot forward but stopped inches in front of us when the Devil said, "She belongs with me now, right Molly?" He looked at me.

"For now," I mumbled and his claws pressed further into my flesh. I winced. "Until someone better comes along," I added. He smiled, pleased with my response and looked back to Fear.

Fear's tail backed away. Fear ate on emotions to survive. He read my lies. Without a doubt, he at least had an idea of what was going on. I was confident I could outplay the Devil as long as he wasn't thinking about Fear's ability like I was.

Fear straightened his back and stepped toward us. "I know what she wants," he said, eyeing the Devil with mockery. "And you are not it."

"Neither are you," the Devil retorted then proceeded to smile afterward. I felt him shift and change next to me. I looked up and tried to back away from him. "But I can be whoever she wants me to be." The Devil wore Ryan's handsome face. "Ryan will never forgive you but I can look like him while I bury myself inside you."

Fear's tail was around my body the next second, jerking me from the Devil's grasp. A sword materialized in Fear's hand right as he attacked the Devil who blocked it with his hand alone. He tilted his head at Fear and said, "You keep forgetting who created you and the reason why you were created."

"Things change." Fear pressed his weight into the sword trying to get it to move. "Even monsters like me can change but don't worry, I'll never stop killing… it just won't ever be the way you want it to be."

The Devil's—Ryan's face darkened with anger. "I know. I made you, Jackal, and Harvest so that you'd always need a certain something to survive in this world, trying to deny yourself that would only turn you into a bigger monster." I was slung in the air by Fear's tail as the Devil threw him backward. "I won't allow you to merge with Ryan again," the Devil hissed shifting back into his true form. Fear safely planted me back on my feet and released me from his tail before it slid back behind him. He walked toward the Devil again.

"Where's Ryan?" Grim asked, and for a second I had forgotten they were here too.

"The stairway," I yelled, and that got the Devil's attention. His piercing red eyes, so similar to Fear's, turned toward me.

"You really don't care what happens to Ryan, do you?" he asked right before he disappeared.

I looked around desperately, the panic was hitting me like waves. "Fear," I screamed but he was already next to me, taking my hands in the oddest, yet sweetest gesture that made the panic hit me harder. "He's going after Ryan."

"I'm right here," Ryan called out, and I turned to the sound of his voice. I smiled in relief as my feet moved but Fear's hand shot out to stop me.

"That's not Ryan," he told me as his eyes fixated on Ryan. It was the Devil? Of course, it was. My hope deflated. Ryan was still locked in a cell.

"It's really me," he promised, stepping closer. "Melanie just helped me out of the cell."

"Stop the games," Fear hissed.

"Come here, Molly," this overly sweet Ryan whispered. I lifted my hands to Fear's arm and gripped it tight. "We don't need Fear." The real Ryan still hadn't forgiven me.

"Like hell, she'd believe that," that had to be the real Ryan that yelled as he moved out of the stairway with Melanie. She must have released him while the Devil had been distracted. I smiled.

The Devil sighed before switching back to his true face again. He rubbed his horn. "You guys aren't very entertaining." He looked around at all of us. "Neither of them are leaving this place, no matter what you try."

Fear shoved me back as he moved for the Devil but when the Devil vanished, Fear turned back around and grabbed a hold of me. Grim faded and reappeared next to Melanie and Ryan. My eyes met Ryan's for a passing moment then the Devil was in front of Fear and me. "I'm trying to help you," the Devil told Fear then they were attacking each other. Fear's tail wrapped around the Devil just as he vanished and reappeared behind him, kicking him down to the ground. Fear was only down for a second before going back at him.

"Enough!" Melanie screamed, and they stopped and looked at her.

"This is between us, you and Grim may go but you aren't taking Ryan with you." The Devil smirked. "Why don't you try?"

"They don't belong to you," she told him.

He chuckled and looked at her like she was foolish. "Every tainted soul belongs to me," was the Devil's answer.

Melanie's face hardened. "So, you are willing to break the very rule you created for the Underworld?"

He studied her before turning in her direction. "Is there something you're trying to get at?" he asked.

"The mark," the only two words she had to say, and I understood what she was saying. So did the Devil because he looked pissed. "Fear owns both of them, not you."

"She's right," Grim stepped in. "It's the law, and you are the one that created it, not us."

"The rules don't apply to me," the Devil sang.

"I wonder how your demons would react to hearing that what's theirs can be yours anytime you want it?" Fear asked, stepping into the Devil's face. "You made the rule to keep the demons from tearing each other apart." Fear smiled. "Hmm… I wonder what they'd start doing if they thought they could get away with taking each other's marks?"

The Devil stiffened, and I thought he would blow but instead, he smiled and nodded. "You're right," he agreed, stepping away from Fear. "I can't have any of that." Then his face morphed into fury. "Guess I'll just have to obliterate their souls instead."

The Devil's hands were reaching out to me—Fear cut in and the Devil's hand buried itself into his chest. I gasped and slipped my hand across Fear's back.

"Don't get close," Ryan hissed as he jerked me backward into him. I realized it was to protect me, the Devil was still coming after us.

Melanie and Grim stepped in front of us as the Devil jerked his hand out of Fear. Fear roared as the Devil tried to step by him. Fear grabbed his shoulder and prevented him from going any further. The Devil tilted his head and smiled at Fear. "You don't get a say in when they die," Fear growled, "even their deaths belong to me."

"Very well," was the Devil's reply. "You'll grow tired of them eventually, but I wonder…" His eyes locked on Ryan. "If things will go as you want." I turned my head so I could see Ryan. He looked furious but also torn.

"Let's go," Ryan said, choosing to ignore the Devil. My heart fluttered the moment he took my hand. *Let's go…* I heard his words over again in my head… he had meant me too?

Someone snatched my other hand, I looked back to see that it was the Devil. Fear grabbed his hand, the one that snatched mine, and said, "Stop with the games."

The Devil didn't listen, instead, he pulled me into him and smirked down at me. "Tell me, do you want to stay? You can never go back to what you had with him before, now that he knows the truth." His words hit a nerve but I knew an opportunity when I saw one. I smiled and leaned into him. I let my hands slide up his chest as he placed his arms around me, then my hands were around his neck as I smiled up at him. "I knew you were bad," he whispered.

Before I could give my response, I was jerked out of his arms and came face-to-face with an angry Ryan. "You crazy—you drive me fucking insane, you know that?" he yelled at me. "You're in love with me, remember?" I blinked a few times unable to respond then he shoved me away.

"Ryan," I started but stopped when I felt Fear's hand press into my back. I watched as Ryan walked away from me and Fear.

"Let's go," Fear told me. "He'll be going to the same place we are."

"Let's not have another family reunion too soon, okay Fear?" The Devil chuckled behind us. "And, Grim?" Grim turned. "You will regret pissing me off time and time again."

How ominous…

I glanced toward Ryan again as he grabbed Grim's shoulder and Grim faded with him, Melanie followed behind them. I wrapped my arms around Fear as he ported us far, far away from the Devil and his Hellhole.

I was greeted in Grim's woods by Ryan's scowl. I frowned the moment I saw him stalking toward us. "I still don't get why the hell you hugged him back," he said. Was he, perhaps, jealous?

I cocked my head and smiled. "Because." I looked back over his shoulder at Grim and Melanie then met his eyes again. "I knew Grim and Melanie were trying to find all those good demon souls—your friends," it almost sounded like I was stammering. Jesus, was it that hard to do something good? "To send to a better afterlife now that Melanie was here…"

Melanie's eyes widened and she hurried to Ryan's side. "Why does that have anything to do with what you did?" she asked quickly. "He told us he destroyed them."

I raised my eyebrows and lifted my hand out, letting the necklace dangle from my middle finger. "I can't be sure… but I think they are in here," I said nervously. I placed the necklace in Melanie's hand and retreated my hand hastily. "Luckily, it was spelled with powerful magic, otherwise, I wouldn't have been able to carry it out of his place without it dropping through my ghost hands," I added quickly. "Might need to hurry up and see if they're in there so you can send them away before he realizes that I've taken it," I couldn't help my rambling.

Melanie studied the necklace then met my eyes—something was in them I've never seen before, and I was too uneasy with myself to try to figure it out just yet. She turned and her scythe materialized in her hand as she did. She tossed it on the ground and Killian stood by and watched, crossing his arms. Their powers were so much alike. What must it be like to get to be with someone you loved and were meant to be with?

I glanced at Ryan but he looked away from me the moment I caught him staring. I turned back to Melanie just as she swung her blade down over the emerald. A green light flashed around it and within seconds, souls began to appear all around us. The souls of demons that never became ghosts the way humans did. They mostly appeared as a sort of fog or smoke. The eviler they were, the darker their color was, but all these demons… they were white. Good.

Melanie lifted her gaze and the first person she saw was me, and she was smiling. She couldn't be smiling at me, I was just standing in her line of sight first. But she kept smiling toward me, and it was making me feel odd… She finally turned toward Killian and I felt like I could stop being a statue when she did.

I jumped when someone tapped my shoulder. I looked to my right to see Fear holding his shirt out to me. "Here," he told me.

"I'm a ghost," I mumbled, just realizing that I'd have to walk around naked all the time now.

"You're a ghost with my mark," he replied, pushing my arms up. I raised them up as he slipped the shirt over my body. And it worked. My body seemed more like flesh around Fear. "See," he brought his hand out to touch my cheek. "I can still touch you, still cover you with clothes and whatever else I want because of the mark."

"It's them," Melanie said to Killian, and I looked back toward her just as she laughed while covering her mouth with both hands. Killian stepped in front of her and wrapped his arms around her and smiled with her. "We can send them where they belong now," she mumbled into his chest.

Every time I saw them, I wanted Ryan. Not just Ryan… I wanted Ryan as Fear. I wanted him to forgive me so that we could go back to the way we were.

Could we ever go back to what we were when he thought of me of as only Blue?

While I had been staring toward Killian and Melanie, Ryan had been looking at me the whole time. I knew because the moment I looked over at him, it took him a second to realize I was staring back. He met my eyes once more and my heart twisted when I saw how much I hurt him—was still hurting him.

"Shouldn't they be more than this?" Melanie wondered, and Ryan turned to her voice. I shook away my thoughts and looked too.

"These are probably the only ones that held on this long," Killian told her, and her smile faded. "It's not your fault, you weren't here yet but you are now and will be always to give demons something to look forward to, even in death." He smirked. "The ones that deserve it, of course." She smiled and nodded slowly.

"Do you think Lincoln and the others are among them?" Melanie asked.

"Penny?" Ryan croaked as one of the white souls floated in front of his face. Everyone gasped, including me when the soul took form. Not just that, one by one all of them began to take the forms of the demons they once were. The woman in front of Ryan was an older demon, but she was still beautiful. I could imagine she was even more so in her youthful years.

She smiled at him. "Well, I had hoped to disappear as the hot babe I was, but… it was worth revealing myself one last time to see you again," she told him and he gave her a genuine smile. I hated the way it made me feel even though this was one of the reasons why I took the necklace.

"You know, the showing of your age wouldn't have made a difference to me, right?" he asked her. "I would have still fucked you." There was a murderous twitch in my eye as I listened to them.

"Relax," Fear muttered next to me. "It isn't what you're assuming."

"Does he love her?" I choked.

Fear turned me around to face him. "I've been inside his head, and there have only been two people he's ever loved." My stomach bottomed out. I didn't want to hear this. "And she's not one of them." My eyes widened. "But he cared an awful a lot of about her… looking at her now I realize that maybe I did too because I'm still him. Even now." Somehow, I didn't feel better. Now I was irritated that Fear cared somewhat about her too, and he wasn't supposed to like anybody but me. "I was trying to make you feel better, why is your mood ten times worse now?" Fear asked, and like a little brat, I ignored him.

Penny chuckled softly and shook her head, gaining my attention again. "I know," she told him then she turned her head and spotted Fear next to me. "I see you're still causing trouble."

"It's a long story," he told her with a sigh.

She nodded. "Things are changing, I can tell." Ryan stiffened. "And that's okay, ya know? About damn time, actually."

"I'm sorry," he told her quickly. "You don't realize how much it helped that you were around when—"

"—Ryan, I know," she told him.

"Lincoln!" Killian yelled with a smile. It was a centaur he was talking to and they looked happy to see him.

"Did we—am I really here?" Lincoln asked, looking around.

Killian nodded. "You are."

"Does that mean…" Lincoln broke down in tears.

"You made it out." Melanie touched his shoulder. "I'm sending you all some place better."

Melanie opened a passage, and one by one they all slipped inside the portal. Lincoln looked elated as he walked in. All that was left was Penny, and I had chosen not to listen in on anything else they were saying in fear that I might do something bad when trying to be good.

Standing next to Fear, I realized we were the outsiders here. Everyone was happy and hopeful as they crossed over. It had felt good to do something to help them but now that feeling was gone again, replaced with something bitter… something that reminded me that I didn't belong here. Possibly, not even with Ryan but I adored him too much. I was miserable but I couldn't help it or change it. All I wanted was for him to forgive me.

When Penny stepped into the passage, it disappeared. My feet were moving on their own accord. Ryan turned and saw me approaching him. "Ryan," I started. His eyes felt like daggers as he waited for me to continue, "Doesn't it mean anything at all that I was telling you right when the Devil walked in and ruined my chance?" I asked, pathetically.

He didn't say a word. He just stood there staring. "Be mad. Be as mean as you want," I whispered. "I know it will take time for you to forgive, but don't give up on me!"

"There was never a you to have," was his bitter response.

"What does that mean?" I asked sadly.

"It means… I'm not doing this with you." He turned away and walked off, slipping further into the woods.

"Ryan! Ryan," I screamed and cried. Then my tears brought out my fury. "You will forgive me!" I yelled at his back but he continued walking. I'd make him mine, no matter what.

Fear was walking away with him. I wiped my eyes and said, "Fear? Not you too?" Even my monster didn't want me? My heart caved.

At least he turned around and came back to me to say, "You're mine." He lifted my chin. "Let me piece myself back together… and then, you can yell all you want."

Then he took off after Ryan. I found my feet moving, wanting to go with them until someone touched my shoulder. I looked over my shoulder and saw that it was Melanie. "Give him time."

That made sense. He needed time. I got that. But how did I stop my heart from running after him? I've been alone for so long, I've been through so much. All I cared about was getting to the human world so that I could live out my life without the troubles of everyone I've pissed off in the past but now, I was a ghost again, and more than anything I just wanted to be with Ryan. How did I survive before meeting him? I couldn't figure it out now.

I didn't have a place to go to. Never have. That's something that's never bothered me until now… "You can stay with us until you figure out where to go from here," she surprised me by saying.

I couldn't believe she'd offer her home up for someone like me. "Why would you do that for me?" I blurted.

She sighed. "It's not only for you but for Ryan. Besides, I would have never found what was left of them if not for you."

This was awkward. I wasn't good with this kind of *stuff*. The gooey stuff that warmed the heart, you know what I was talking about, the kind of warmth you felt from doing something good. "It doesn't make up for everything that I've done to you and Ryan," I told her quickly.

"No, it doesn't," she agreed. "I can fix the ghost problem… if you let me," she offered.

My forehead creased while confused. "Huh?"

"Do you want me to?"

I shrugged. "Sure," I mumbled.

She placed her hands on me and her golden-colored power wrapped around me immediately. It felt warm, soft, and kind. I knew something was working because I could feel my chest wound closing. When it was over, Melanie smiled and pressed her hands together. "Now, you work for us."

Maybe I heard her wrong… "I'm sorry?" I squeaked. "Work?" I had a bad feeling.

"I bestowed you with Reaper power," she said it like it wasn't a big deal. She tossed her hand in the air. "You didn't ask how I was going to give you flesh, so I figured it didn't matter."

"Me?" I stuttered. "I can't be a Reaper." I looked down at myself. "I'm me."

"It's kind of too late to say that now." She smiled. "Done deal." My mouth fell open and Killian laughed behind her. "You might want to start asking questions before you give people permission to do whatever they want to your body." I knew she was referring to the deal I made with the Devil, and how easily I had just been tricked the same way.

I was a lost cause.

"You might have flesh now, but you're still a ghost mostly," Killian said.

"So, that means if you die, you're gone for good." Melanie nodded.

Greattt. Considering my life and enemies, I'd give myself a week.

Melanie twirled around in her boots and bounced to Killian. "Come on," she called to me. "We will fill you in on your new responsibilities."

I sighed. How the hell did it come to this?

So weird…

Story of my life.

CHAPTER TWENTY-SEVEN

Ryan

It had been two weeks since I left Molly standing in the woods, screaming my name with her dark doe-like eyes and bluish-black hair whipping around her shoulders like the storm she was.

And I wasn't bothered about it. In fact, I didn't care at all. I didn't mope around the house miserably because I couldn't visit Grim or Melanie since they decided to take in the she-devil. I didn't think about how much I missed her body or her infuriating attitude.

There was nothing to miss. She was my killer. And now that it was out in the open, it made everything about her so much clearer. She was snarky, bossy, and so damn selfish. She couldn't cook—she could hardly do a damn thing on her own, obviously, except killing people. How did she survive so long? Not that I cared. She was a mess—a vexingly beautiful, disturbing mess… that I couldn't get out of my damn head.

Something must be wrong with me. Why couldn't I stop myself from feeling anything after knowing who she was?

When I got out of the shower, I came out to Fear munching down on a bowl of popcorn on the couch. He turned off the movie when I stepped out. This has been a common occurrence in the last two weeks. I couldn't get rid of him. Not that I really tried. I mostly said, "Why are you still here?" or "This is my home."

We weren't merged anymore but his response was always, "Waiting," or, "eating," or some other stupid excuse.

I just stared at him for several seconds, sitting there casually eating popcorn like he wasn't a damn monster that ate on emotions and killed. I didn't know what was happening but we only continued to get weirder and weirder…

I dropped down next to him on the couch. "Where have you been?" I asked, stealing some popcorn.

"The usual," he muttered. "Took care of a few people that might still hold a grudge on me from my past with Marcus."

I arched my brow. "Why?"

"Because," he sighed, placing the popcorn in my lap. "As you already know, Molly's no longer immortal. I can't have her wandering around doing Reaper work if all these demons hold grudges. So, I killed them and will kill anything that poses a threat to her soul." That was another thing... Molly was obviously working for Grim and Melanie now as a Reaper.

I tilted my head and snorted. "You do realize Molly doesn't need her past to piss someone off, right?" Shit, now I was worried too. I stopped smiling. "With an attitude like hers, she's liable to piss off the whole damn Underworld."

Fear's eyes widened. "You're right." He got up quickly. "We can't do this any longer."

"Can't do what?"

"I can't leave her alone any longer," he told me, and I tensed, knowing where this was going. "I've kept my distance from her for you, and I've also given you time to sort out your feelings." I met his eyes as he spoke. "She means everything to me and I can't waste another day when you just reminded me how dangerous she can make things for herself."

"Why are you telling me?"

"You know why," he growled and I stood up to face him. "I know how you feel about her—before when we were still one and even these past two weeks, your feelings haven't changed." I tightened my jaw and he frowned. "You might lie to yourself but you know I can taste everyone's emotions and I know exactly what yours are for her."

"How do I feel about her then?" I asked, feeling my chest cave. I knew the answer. I've been covering it up… my unwillingness to let go of the past and just let myself go get her like I wanted…Shit, that was all I wanted to do was go get her and bring her back but my pride had kept me from doing what I wanted. Pride was also the very thing that has kept me from admitting the other truth: I wanted to be Fear. No, I still felt like him for some reason.

"The same way I feel about her." I nodded, accepting the truth for what it was.

He extended his hand out between us. A little of my uncertainty came back. I didn't want to keep fighting for power with Fear. "It won't be like last time," his words mirrored the doubts I was having. "It will be real this time."

I took a deep breath. "Will I… even exist after?"

"You'll be me—my memories, everything, you'll know them, and you'll still be you with your memories and feelings—only this time, we'll just be one."

It didn't matter what happened afterward because I already knew I wanted it. I took his hand.

I discovered a lot about Fear I hadn't known before. With Fear's memories, I now knew that he—I had been trapped in the merge with him while Marcus held complete control with some sort of spell. It didn't mean that I wasn't bad, I was. It just helped me understand the reason why we couldn't have merged the first time properly. Not when Fear had been trapped in his first one for so long…

I ported into Grim's castle where he and Melanie were in a deep discussion in the ballroom. Whatever they were chatting about didn't look too good considering the worried exchange they gave each other before glancing at me. Melanie took one long look at me head-to-toe and smiled. "About time," she told me and I smirked.

"I know," I admitted, scratching my chin and looking around. They were grinning at me while I did. "What?" I asked sheepishly. I continued to look around. "I thought you guys had a guest?"

"About that…" Melanie drifted off.

I turned my attention back to her. Not already. She couldn't have gotten in trouble so soon. "What did she do?" I asked immediately, wondering what my little ghost could have done now.

Melanie smiled. "Nothing, at least, we don't know if it's her."

Which meant it most likely was.

"Just tell me." I sighed.

"We just got word that we have a new Reaper going around asking witches and warlocks for a memory spell," Killian informed me.

That sounded fishy… and entirely like something Molly would go looking for since I haven't forgiven her… or at least, that's what she thought.

"Has there been any new Reapers besides Molly that you've created lately?" I asked.

Melanie dropped her eyes. "No." She blew a frustrated breath. "But she's been so mopey lately all because of you, no wonder she'd—"

"Are you taking her side?" Killian interrupted her by asking.

"No," Melanie whined, "but who wouldn't want to erase their memories if the person they loved couldn't forgive them." She was totally taking Molly's side. "What?" She straightened her spine. "I've forgiven her already," she told me with a smile. "You love her, Ryan, or you wouldn't have gotten so freaking crazy on her when you found out."

"Yeah, but," Killian butted in, "with someone like Molly… What's to say she isn't wanting to get the memory spell to use it on Ryan?"

I nodded. That made more sense to me. Molly was wicked like that. My dick responded to my thoughts and I had to dial it down. Guess we made a good pair.

"Don't worry, I'm going to go get her," I told them.

"And kiss and make up?" Melanie smirked. *Oh, we are going to do a lot more than that*, I thought.

I grinned. "I'll take her back now. I know how she gets." So needy and whiny. "Only I can put up with her shit."

Killian couldn't help but say, "Are you sure you want to go down this road with Molly? Just think… every time you piss her off, she'd be the type that might put a curse on you or who knows what."

Melanie slapped his arm and laughed. "Killian."

I chuckled. "And who do you think she's dealing with?" Killian shook his head and smiled, and I added, "She's not perfect. She's selfish, evil, and an all-around mess of emotions but for a monster like me, that makes her perfect." And I also knew that Molly wanted to be good sometimes.

I walked away from their smiles to go get Molly.

She was still the Blue I wanted.

But it wasn't until she told me her name was Molly that I fell in love with her completely.

Chapter Twenty-Eight

Molly

I twirled the dagger through my fingers before stabbing the table with it. The witch didn't even jump, instead, she glared up at me. "So you're saying you can't make me the potion?" I asked her again with a syrupy voice.

She leaned over the table, placing her elbows against the dirty wood as she gazed at me. "I can't make a memory spell that only erases one little piece of information of something." I sighed and she went on, "I can, however, make a person forget about someone permanently."

I plucked my dagger out of the wood and placed it back in my belt. I was decked out in a black getup. I didn't understand why Reapers had to wear black, but whatever. It was nice having weapons again, and now that I was a Reaper, I felt a little more comfortable walking around the Underworld. Maybe because I figured I'd get left alone now that I was one, but since I haven't had any bad encounters yet… I could be right.

I lifted my hand to my face. "I don't want him to forget me completely… I just want him to forget one little piece of information," I mumbled to her as I circled around and paced in front of the table.

I knew the memory spell wasn't the right way to go, but I never claimed to be good or patient enough to wait for Ryan to forgive me. What if he never did? The thought nearly drove me mad. Or maybe it already did, or else I wouldn't be here doing something I didn't really want to do to him.

He made me crazy.

But I missed him so bad.

"It doesn't work that way," she told me firmly. "However, if you don't want this person to forget you, you could always take it yourself and forget him."

I lifted my head. "Fine. Give it to me." I extended my hand over the table.

"What I asked for first."

I sighed and plucked the bottle of vampire teeth out of my pocket. "Here ya go," I said in a humming beat.

"I want more than this," she stated.

"The deal was this many," I reminded her. "Now give me the spell—potion, whatever it's called." I brought my hand out again.

"I don't like your attitude," she replied, rising from her chair. My hand moved to the sword lying against my back on instinct.

"A deal's a deal," I informed her.

"And I said I want more now." The witch smiled. Ew, she was messing with the wrong dead Reaper… that sounded so weird, even in my head. "Does Grim know what an insolent Reaper you are?" I glared. She did not want to go there and threaten me. As crazy as it was, I didn't want him or Melanie to hate me any more than they already did. Great, thanks to her, I felt even more guilty about going out and looking for this memory potion.

I'd just take it myself and forget Ryan. That was the only way. At least that way, if he decided to forgive me, he'd just have to make me fall for him all over again. Not like it would be hard. I couldn't explain how much I was drawn to him.

"Just give it to me," I said again.

Surprisingly, she turned and moved to the shelf behind her full of creepy voodoos and what-not. Then she came back and handed me the black tube of liquid. "What's the name of whom you wish to forget?" she asked.

"Ryan," I stuttered.

She twirled her hands around the tube, casting some sort of spell before she handed it to me. "There ya go."

I stared at her warily. "That's all it took?" Seemed kind of too easy.

"That's all." She pointed toward the door. "Now leave."

There was a knock on the door, I turned around just as it opened. My heart did that thing it always did in his presence. "Ryan?" I whispered as he walked into the room. Wait, something was… Did he merge—

"Wait," the witch sounded worried. "It was Fear you wish to forget?"

Ryan's eyes darkened at her words and moved over me. I shivered with both fear and exhilaration. He held out his hand to me. When I moved to place my hand in his, he shook his head. "The spell, Molly, give it to me."

The disappointment buried itself into my heart. I hesitated a moment before stepping back and saying, “No.”

His smile was absolutely terrifying. “No?” That one word invoked so many emotions inside me.

I nodded. “Either you are going to take it and forget about me, or I’m going to take it and forget about you.”

He smirked. “You actually think you can weasel your way back into my life if I forget about you?”

I felt the truth splash over my cheeks. I bit the inside of my cheek. “Don’t act like that,” I hissed. “You’re not the only one that’s hurting right now!”

“Jesus, I’m going to have to teach you how to be somewhat normal,” he muttered then he grabbed me. I wrestled him, trying to keep the spell but it was a pointless struggle. He blew out a frustrated breath and it hit my ear. That alone sent a wave of heat through me. “Will you stop?” he told me. I ignored him, though. “You crazy, selfish creature—stop! Nobody’s getting their memories wiped tonight.”

He had the spell now. I looked down when I felt my eyes water. I didn’t want to cry. I wasn’t going to cry.

When I looked back up, he had the tube open as he brought it to his nose to smell. I gave him a funny look but then his eyes did that sexy thing I got off on when he was pissed. The witch started running for the back door. Ryan shifted into Fear. He grabbed her by the tail to prevent her from going anywhere as he stalked to where she was.

“What are you doing?” I asked him quickly.

He ignored me. The witch tried casting some sort of spell on his tail then she was panting frantically and screaming. Her eyes widened as he grew near. “I want to know,” he said, gripping her shoulder. “What you were trying to poison her with?” So, it hadn’t been a memory spell?

The witch started begging, “I wouldn’t have if I had known she was someone you knew.”

“So, it really is poison?” He looked frightening. Why did I love it so much?

"Don't kill me," she said, shaking her head. "She didn't take it! She didn't take it!"

Fear smiled. "You really shouldn't have messed with what's mine," he told her. "Didn't you see the mark on her neck?" he asked, and her eyes roamed over me until they landed on his mark.

"No, I hadn't noticed."

Fear looked back at me. "Lift up your shirt and show her some of the others," he told me, and I scowled. "Do it, she needs to know," he said again. I wasn't even wearing a bra, but I did as he asked and lifted my shirt. He looked pleased as he glanced back to the witch. "See," he said. "She's covered in my marks. That means she's mine and you just tried to kill her."

"I'm sorry."

"Open your mouth," he ordered her but when she didn't, he forced her mouth open.

"Stop, please—" she begged as Fear forced the poison she had given me down her throat. She started convulsing immediately and within seconds, she was dead. He dropped her body down on the ground and turned his attention to me.

I was nervous and excited as he stalked toward me, and all I could think about was having his hands on me again. But if he wouldn't forgive me…

He shifted back to normal. "So, you wanted to forget about me?" he asked.

"Ryan," I whispered. "The more I think about it, the easier it seems to just forget about you."

"Did I say you could?"

"You're never going to get past me killing you, and even before knowing, what was I to you then?" I met him halfway, never taking my eyes off his. "Was I just someone you were sleeping with? Just something Fear brought home and left you to deal with?" My stare turned to gloom. He dared to smile. "See, you're driving me crazy—"

"Don't even blame your crazy on me," he cut in. "You were crazy way before I met you."

I glared. "Do you love me or not?" I huffed. "Are we going to get past this or not?" I didn't give him a chance to reply when I said, "Forget it, I'll just find another witch to make the memory spell and one of us will take it." I tried to walk away from him but he stopped me.

He laughed then abruptly stopped. "You know how sexy you look in those tight black jeans right now?" he asked me suddenly, and my heart leaped.

"What?" I looked up and mumbled. Then one of his hands were in my hair and the other against my back. The flush of heat that spread through me was immediate. "Ryan?"

He pressed his lips against my neck. I gasped then wound my arms around his neck. "Missed this," I thought I heard him mutter. Before he snapped out of whatever this was, I lifted his face up and brought our lips together. I could have cried when he kissed me back. I whimpered when he invaded my mouth with his tongue, biting and nipping my lips and tongue with his teeth. This was too perfect with him. Now I was even more positive that I couldn't live without him. He made an addict out of me.

I pulled away from him just enough so that I could say, "Please, let me be with you." I ran my hand through his hair as I looked at him. "I know I can make you happy. Let me erase my past with you… Let me be Blue again." My eyes were wet. "Please let me be Blue. I liked being her, and I liked how you looked at me when I was her."

"No." I swear I could hear my heart shattering. "It's Molly that I fell in love with, Blue just happens to be the name I call her sometimes."

I became a mess of tears when he smiled at me—the smile I've been aching to see him give me again. The one I wanted nobody else to have but me. "Ryan," I cried, pulling him down into my arms and squeezing him with all the strength I had. I've never felt this much relief and happiness in all my years of being dead or alive, or dead again.

He hugged me back. "Remember the night you told me your name was Molly?" he asked with his mouth at my ear.

"Yeah?"

"When I heard your name, I thought of the ghost-girl from the past, but of course, I couldn't imagine my Blue ever being her. My mind was tricking itself because how could I have not known you were her?" He tilted his head back and just looked at me. "Especially with Fear marking and bringing you home…"

"Ryan—"

"I wasn't bringing it up for you to apologize," he told me with a smile. "I just meant, it crossed my mind that night and I ignored it because I didn't want to ruin what I had with you… I'm saying, I'll shoulder the mistakes you and I've made together, because I want to be with you."

I knew he was too good for me, but I'd make up for that by loving him with everything in me.

"Just me and you?" I asked.

"Just me and you." He nodded.

"Just so you know, I'm not ever—ever, ever, ever, letting you go or sharing you with someone else. I know you have needs as Fear, but I can give them to you."

"Glad that's out in the open because you're mine and only mine. And I'll need a list of all those that's held you captive or hurt you in any way."

I lifted my brows. "That's going to be a long damn list."

"Good, you know how I get off on killing demons." He waggled his eyebrows.

I smiled. "Can I help you?"

"Only if you let me fuck you while we force them to watch or maybe standing over their dead corpses?" he contemplated.

"Deal."

"You're my kind of girl," he told me and I laughed. "I fucking love your crazy ass."

"I fucking love you too," I told him.

Then we kissed, and he took me home where he bent me over the couch cushion until I was a hot mess.

It was amazing, and just my kind of wonderful.

EPILOGUE

Ryan

Several years later…

I followed behind Grim as we walked through the piles of dead demon bodies, most of them were killed by me. "We were too late," Grim muttered as he glanced around the small village in the Underworld that was in ruins by the demons we were too late in killing.

"What were they after?" I wondered aloud.

He brought me along a lot just so I had something to kill. If I wasn't killing for him or Melanie, I was doing it in cage fights. Don't ask me how she did it, but Molly was now the owner of The Den. She won it by betting on herself in a fight with Darrian for it. I nearly killed her when I found out, I was so pissed. Darrian had been too after losing his pride and joy to her. I felt a little more relaxed now that I knew she was the owner instead of one of the fighters. I could rest a little easier but not much since she was a handful after all. One that I loved and worshiped more and more with each passing day. No matter how much I tried to tell myself to play it cool with her, there was just no way. She drove me up the wall.

Nobody might understand us and that was okay. She fit the monster I was so well that I practically purred around her.

"I don't know," Grim said then sighed. "The entire village was massacred before it was any of their time to part from this world. We will have to bring Melanie back here to ascend the ones deserving." He rubbed his skull before shaking his head. "And I didn't want her to have to see this."

Killian and Melanie were parents to a three and one-year-old, who were both boys so Melanie was busy with them more than anything. I've never seen them happier. Killian was so proud of everything the boys did. Sebastian Reaper, the oldest, had blond hair like his mom and he was desperate to learn and be just like his dad. Barron, on the other hand, was dark-headed like his dad, and I was convinced the boy was destined to be an even bigger devil than the Devil himself, and he was only one! He had the attitude of a giant. Or maybe it was because of all the things I told him to do. Shh, don't tell his parents.

"Let's go get Melanie," Grim said.

Then we heard it. "Do you hear that?" I asked him, looking around for where it could be coming from. Most of the houses were burned down except a few.

It was a soft cry that only grew louder. "I think it's coming from that house." Grim pointed to the small cottage to our left. We followed the crying inside. It was surprising that we could even hear it since the sound seemed to be muffled by something.

I looked down at the wooden floor as it creaked. The crying was coming from below. "I think it's right here," I said as I noticed the give in the floor where I was standing. I bent down and pulled back the loose piece of wood. There it was, wrapped in a brown blanket. "It's a baby," I reached down and picked it up. The baby immediately calmed down after being in someone's arms. I peeled the blanket from his body. "It's a boy," I told him, covering him back up since he was naked underneath.

"His parents must have hidden him there right before the vampires attacked," Grim stated but I was too busy staring down at the baby boy in my arms. This baby hadn't been in the world long but it had already been thrown into the ugly side of it… even so, I knew fate worked in mysterious ways. Something in my chest stirred, and I just knew this baby landed in my arms because he was meant to. "I'm sure Melanie will want to keep him," Grim told me.

"No," I said abruptly. "I'm going to be his dad." In my heart, in my mind, I knew it felt right. It sounded right. I hated that he lost his parents, but I was going to take care of him now alongside Molly… as soon as I broke the news to her.

"Ryan, are you sure?"

"More than anything," I whispered, smiling down at the baby in my arms. He watched me with his giant baby eyes. "I've always wanted to be a dad. I mean… me and Molly are probably the worst two people to take care of a baby but at least we'd give him something."

"You'd give him a family." Grim wrapped his arms around me as he shifted into Killian and smiled. "Welcome to parenthood."

Molly was already back from her Reaper duties by the time I got home with the baby in my arms. She was in the kitchen and turned, smiled, then her eyes fell on the bundle in my arms. "What is that?" The scared look she gave me told me she had a good idea what it was.

"Surprise," I told her, shoving the baby in her fearful hands. She held him awkwardly and looked down at him like she had no idea what to do with him. "We're parents now, you're a mom."

Her eyes widened to show her fear. "What?" she mumbled. "Ryan, who's baby is this?"

"He came from the village that was attacked by the vampires," I said, looking down at the baby. "He's the only one that survived."

She looked down at him with sadness this time before looking back up at me. "Ryan, we are the two absolute worst people to choose to raise a kid." Her fear was real. I tasted it all around us.

"He needs us." I placed my hand on her shoulder and kissed her forehead. "We're monsters in our own way but my needs as Fear will never hurt him. We're perfect with each other, let's make a future with him in it with us."

She looked down at him again. Tears slid down her cheeks. "He's so tiny," she murmured, voice full of emotion. "I'm scared," she admitted, "I don't want to hurt him."

"We won't," I promised. "He might get embarrassed of us once he's older, but we'll never hurt him." She snorted and laughed with tears running down her beautiful face.

"What's his name?" she asked softly.

"I don't know who he was before I found him." I wrapped my arms around her and looked down at him. "But we can give him one."

She nodded. "Payne," she had already decided. "If he's to be Fear's son…" She looked up at me and grinned.

"It suits him, I can tell already," I told her.

She looked down at him again. "Hi, Payne," she whispered to him. "I'm going to be your mommy now, I feel so sorry for you."

———

Payne had been a part of our lives for weeks now. I've watched Molly evolve into something beautiful around him. The first week was awkward and bumpy for her, she'd handle him with so much fear and not have a clue what she was doing sometimes. But it was because of all that fear, I knew she'd be a great mom. She didn't want to ruin his life in some way.

She started visiting with Melanie a lot, taking Payne with her. Melanie helped her get the hang of the life I had suddenly thrown at her. Payne stayed with me when Molly went into the human world as a Reaper and most of my time with him was spent staring down at him. And every time he smiled up at me, I turned all sappy. Every night I asked him, "What kind of demon are you?" I knew we'd find out eventually in time.

And every time he smiled around Molly, she'd laugh and say he looked like an old man.

Through the nights, Molly got up with him. She'd go into the living room with him every night thinking I was asleep when truthfully, I lived for the moments she got up with him. I'd sit on the floor of our room and lean my head against the wall as I listened to her ramble on and on to him about crazy stuff—beautiful stuff. Things that made my heart tighten and clamp up. I closed my eyes every night and just listened, never wanting to disturb her moments with him.

And every single night, in her moments, I'd think, *ah, this is my moment, listening to her bond with him.*

———

Those weeks with Payne in our life quickly turned to months. We even brought him to The Den with us every time we went and considering Molly owned it, we were there a lot. It was okay though, the Underworld was a tough world. We couldn't hide it from him, but we could protect him and prepare him for it.

Sometimes we'd be looking at him sitting up between us in the bed at night, and I'd wonder why I loved him so much. I couldn't answer that question. The moment I saw him, I just felt that connection and now he was our son.

He fell asleep on my stomach one night as I laid on the couch. Molly sat on the floor next to us, watching him peacefully when she broke down in tears. She scared me at first until she said, "You're not the only one in my heart anymore." She lifted her hand to his head and rubbed it softly. "I love him so much."

I didn't think I could have loved her any more than I already did. I was wrong. I fell so hard for her that night.

"What if he doesn't love us back?" she surprised me by asking.

I wiped her tears away. "Why wouldn't he?"

"Because he might look at us one day and decide he doesn't want us to be his parents," she whispered. "We aren't exactly good either."

"That's not going to happen," I promised her, ignoring my own fear of the same thing.

I was careful with him as I moved from the couch and took him to his crib then I came back to the living room and made love to Molly. I've been with her years now and she still fell apart in my arms like it was the first time.

I'd take her again, this time as Fear as she muffled her cries to keep from waking Payne. Then once we'd make our way to bed, I'd hold her in my arms and think about how easy it was to be a better guy when you had something to be happy about.

Even though I was Fear, that didn't mean I couldn't still be Ryan.

It just meant I learned to live as both.

And Molly loved when I was better, and she loved me the days I was worse.

I placed a kiss on her forehead.

I'm glad you killed me too, crazy woman.

New Series Coming!

SEVEN DEADLY

Series introduction…

Be careful of the darkness, for what lies in it will drag you in and keep you. In its depths, the Devil reigned. On the outskirts of his domain, a bothersome entity resided who had destroyed his evil time and time again. They called him the Grim Reaper, and though he used to be a man without weakness, he wasn't anymore. His wife delivered him seven beautiful, healthy children. The Devil saw them as his chance for retribution for keeping his evil at bay, for he could never reign over the human world until the day people were more bad than good.

On the day the seventh child was born, the Devil came to them with curses. Each would be cursed with one of the seven deadly sins.

Grim's three sons were playing outside the castle when they looked up and saw the Devil standing next to them. He started with the closest one, uttering the word, "Sloth," as he pressed his finger against the blond-headed boy's forehead. He dropped to the ground in a deep sleep. He turned and proceeded to his dark-headed brother and grinned. "Greed." The boy's eyes lit up with the curse. He smiled and went to the third dark-haired brother. He pressed his finger against the boy's forehead and said, "Wrath."

He chuckled as he slipped inside the house and found three daughters. He moved to the brunette first and did to her as he did to her brothers and whispered, "Pride." Then to the next, "Lust." The third, "Envy." Lastly, he made his way to the seventh child who was tucked away in her room resting. He leaned over the crib and grinned. He brought his hand down to the child and the moment he pointed his finger, the baby reached out and grabbed it. The Devil tried to scare her by revealing his horns and eyes but her only response was laughter. He studied her curiously before placing his finger on her forehead and whispering, "Gluttony." He retreated from her smile rather quickly, rubbing the place her tiny fingers touched as he did so.

By the time they figured out what the Devil had done to their children, it was already too late. They could only sit back and watch as the sins slowly consumed them.

The Devil set into motion that day seven fates that would forever collide with his.

A new generation of Reapers has arrived.

First book in the series will be Sloth. The first book won't be released until 2018 so I can work on a few standalones I've been dying to write, but believe me, you don't want to miss this series!

ACKNOWLEDGEMENTS.

Shout out to those that have helped keep my spirits up while writing *A Grim Awakening* series.

My sister: for faithfully reading everything I write and loving my words from the very beginning.

Nikki: for reading that first book I ever written start to finish despite being someone who doesn't read and loving it and continuing to faithfully read everything I write and giving me helpful feedback. I'm glad I could show you the fun in reading!

Carol: for always helping me with my edits. I couldn't have stumbled upon a better person in the book world to have been so helpful and honest from the very beginning!

Julia: for being that first reader to private message me just to let me know how much you loved the series. You made me so happy! I hope I don't ever disappoint you with future books.

And to every reader that gave a new indie author like me a chance and dived into the series, I can't thank you all enough and always love hearing from you guys, so feel free to at any time.

ABOUT THE AUTHOR

Michelle is from a small town in Eastern Kentucky where opossums try to blend in with the cats on the porch and bears are likely to chase your pets—this is very true, it happened with her sister's dog. Despite the extra needed protection for your pets, she loves the mountains she calls home. She has a man and twin girls who are the light of her life and the reason she's slightly crazy.

As a kid, she was that cousin, that friend, that sister and daughter, *the talker* who could spin a tale and make-believe into any little thing so it was no surprise when she found love in reading and figured all these characters inside her head needed an outlet. They wanted to be heard, so she wrote.

The voices keep growing faster than she gets the time to write.

The stories are never going to end. That's perfectly okay, though. We never want to stop an adventure.

She writes and loves many different genres so sign up to her mailing list to keep updated on her releases!

http://eepurl.com/cRXrUX

Like her Facebook page and connect with her there:

https://www.facebook.com/michellegrossauthor

Instagram: @michellegrossmg

Twitter: @AuthorMichelleG

Made in the USA
Las Vegas, NV
15 August 2023

76159151R00120